"People who think they know everything are a great annoyance to those of us who do."

—Isaac Asimov

View the author's website at www.arsenex.com

Visit the author's Facebook page at www.facebook.com/stephenarseneault10

Follow on Twitter @SteveArseneault

Ask a question or leave a comment at comments@arsenex.com

Cover Art by Kaare Berg at:

bergone.deviantart.com and bitdivision.no

Cover Design by Elizabeth Mackey at:

www.elizabethmackey.com

Novels written by Stephen Arseneault

SODIUM Series (six novels)

A six-book series that takes Man from his first encounter with aliens all the way to a fight for our all-out survival. Do we have what it takes to rule the galaxy?

AMP Series (eight novels)

Cast a thousand years into the future beyond SODIUM. This eight-book series chronicles the struggles of Don Grange, a simple package deliveryman, who is thrust into an unimaginable role in the fight against our enemies. Can we win peace and freedom after a thousand years of war?

OMEGA Series (eight novels)

Cast two thousand years into the future beyond AMP. The Alliance is crumbling. When corruption and politics threaten to throw the allied galaxies into chaos, Knog Beutcher gets caught in the middle. Follow along as our hero is thrust into roles that he never expected nor sought. Espionage, intrigue, political assassinations, rebellions and full-on revolutions, they are all coming to Knog Beutcher's world!

HADRON Series (eight novels)

HADRON is a modern day story unrelated to the SODIUM-AMP-OMEGA trilogy series. After scientists using the Large Hadron Collider discover dark matter, the world is plunged into chaos. Massive waves of electromagnetic interference take out all grid power and forms of communication the world over. Cities go dark, food and water supplies are quickly used up, and marauders rule the highways. Months after the mayhem begins, and after mass starvation has taken its toll, a benevolent alien species arrives from the stars. Only, are they really so benevolent? Find out in HADRON as Man faces his first real challenge to his dominance of Earth!

ARMS Series (eight novels)

ARMS is cast in one possible future, where Earth was nearing an apocalyptic event. Two competing colony ships were built, taking five million inhabitants each through a wormhole to a pair of newly discovered planets. The planets were settled and not long after the colonies looked to the surrounding star systems for ownership and expansion, which led to a centuries-long war between them. A truce was declared after the aggressor side began to lose ground.

Tawnish Freely and Harris Gruberg are genetically engineered Biomarines. Their lives have been dedicated to fighting the war. With a truce declared, they find themselves struggling to find work among a population that fears them. Work is found only by delving into the delivery of illegal arms to the outer colonies. Things go awry when they discover their illicit dealings may just be the catalyst that brings back the Great War. They are determined to prevent that from happening.

FREEDOM Series (eight novels)

After a period of domination over the lesser alien species of the galaxy, humanity finds itself enslaved for nearly five hundred generations. A highly addictive drug called Shackle has made Humans little more than drone workers. They are abused, sold, traded, and hunted, valued only in credits. But a mysterious virus is sweeping through the Human population, altering gut bacteria, making them immune to the drug that subjugates them. Humans are becoming aware of their condition. They will fight for their freedom.

Find them all at www.arsenex.com

ARMS

(Vol. 2)

Harris' Revenge

Chapter 1

Trish and Gandy were given six weeks off, paid, as the *Bangor* was taken away for her upgrades. The two caught shuttles back to Domicile to visit family and flaunt some of their newfound credits.

Tawn and Harris spent several weeks of the downtime with their first DDI contact. The meetings were all about the organization of the supply business, analysis of the truce colony needs, and where they should establish supply routes. The colonies of Eden and an Earther colony on Jebwa would be the highest priorities. Their first order of business was to make contact with a list of suppliers on Domicile.

Harris belched as he emerged from an all-you-can eat diner in Juniper City. A manufacturer of nuts, bolts, washers and other fasteners was eager to do business with the partners.

Tawn asked, "Who's next?"

"Metal fabrication machines. There's a company here that makes a complete shop setup to turn out steel bars that can be formed to whatever shape is needed. They take raw materials through smelting all the way to finished product. If you have the ores, they can produce enough steel in a year to build out a standard fifty thousand settler colony."

"I saw another ad for a colony company this morning," Tawn replied. "They're offering transportation, housing for a year, and a job if you move out to their settlements. No education or experience required."

Harris nodded. "They're following what New Earth is offering settlers. This is a race for having colonies that favor one side or the other."

Tawn sighed. "And what are the chances these colonists will get along with each other and the whole plan backfires?"

Harris laughed. "No way. Will take a couple generations before loyalties are no longer strongly tied to where they came from. This will all come to a head long before that. And that first well on Eden will be complete and functional, probably in a few weeks. By the time we get the *Bangor* back, the New Earth colonists could be streaming in there."

Tawn stopped in front of the next building. "Life sure has its twists and turns. A slug and a stump... first gun runners and now spies. I have to wonder what comes next."

Harris shook his head as he chuckled. "Probably fugitives."

***

The hull of the *Bangor* was chrome in color and texture. A multitude of small protruding additions had been added to her exterior.

Tawn remarked, "For a box, she doesn't look half bad."

Harris frowned. "Gonna draw attention looking like that."

The mechanic handler stood behind them. "The skin is active. It can be changed to whatever color or simulated texture you desire. You can add numbers or company logos or whatever you like, all electronically. You enter a pattern, press a button and the ship is covered with it. You should have several exterior images already entered for you to select from."

The mechanic began to walk the outside as he talked. "Those antennae gather electronic emissions, sending out canceling signals to anything they find when turned on. On planet, the best sensors out there will have to be within a half kilometer to detect you. Out in space that jumps up to fifty kilometers."

He stopped at one of a number of small boxes dotting the hull. "These are your new plasma absorbers. They wrap the ship in an ion field and they'll knock a full power plasma round down by about half. Given your hull thickness, you should be able to handle a dozen rounds without taking major damage. That's not a foolproof system, by the way, just estimates."

The hatch was opened. "The active surface can also be used as camouflage. You have a selection that will mimic your surroundings. Not perfect, but it will make you much harder to see."

The mechanic stepped up into the cabin. "Your bunkroom has been updated to hold the four of you. As requested, mil-grade mattresses were installed. Most of the cabin, except for your benches, was left untouched. In the cockpit you'll find most of the modifications."

The mechanic pointed. "Displays have been upgraded to the latest hi-res units. Your ship's computer as well, including a redundant unit buried back in the bunkroom. There's also a virtual console back there where the entire ship can be controlled from if necessary. You also have copies of the latest nav-maps, and your sensor displays are now state-of-the-art."

The mechanic stopped. "Who's responsible for the auto-feeder on the railgun?"

Harris replied, "That would be my first mate, Trish."

The mechanic smiled. "Nice work. We only changed a few of the mountings. Both rails are now active. I saw a practice firing. You get within a couple kilometers of any ship and you can open her up. We don't have armor thick enough on anything in the fleet to stop even one of those rounds. New Earth will be the same."

Harris chuckled. "Yeah, who wants to be within a few kilometers of one of those warship monsters?"

The mechanic shook his head. "That's in atmosphere. In space it's more like the fifty to a hundred kilometer range. Depends on the reaction time of the ship or her pilot. Anything over that distance and we're getting in the seconds range for reactions."

"When can we take it out?"

The mechanic headed to the hatch. "It's yours. Oh, and I have a bracelet for each of you. Press this button if you're in comm range and the ship will come to you. When it arrives, press it again and the hatch will open. If your second attempt

4

is a press and hold, the cabin will evacuate and the airlock will open instead."

Tawn nodded. "That could come in handy. Could have used that our first time on Eden."

The mechanic replied as he hopped out onto the tarmac where the ship sat. "It's an untested feature, so you'll want to get in a few practice runs to see how well it works... or doesn't. I'd suggest your first move before taking off should be to set the outer skin color. Try out the samples and see what you like."

The mechanic hopped out and began to walk away.

Harris called after him, "Where do we bring it for problems or repairs?"

The man yelled back as he continued to walk: "Don't care! You're on your own from here on out!"

The mechanic disappeared behind another ship on the tarmac.

Tawn moved to the cockpit. "I guess that's it, then. We begin here and now. Hello, fellow spy."

Harris shook his head as he moved to the hatch and hopped out to look at the exterior. "Are you a slug or a nerd? Pick us a color scheme and I'll tell you what works."

Tawn selected *Newly Abandoned*.

Harris frowned. "Looks like too much of a junker. That would draw attention on its own."

Corporate Shuttle was set.

Harris laughed. "Dripping with credits. Too posh looking."

Aid Ship was next in line. "Not for traveling. Could come in useful at some point though. What else?"

Tawn made the next selection.

Harris laughed. "Looks just like the old *Bangor*. What'd they call that one?"

"Slug and Stump Gunrunning Spy Ship," Tawn replied.

4

Harris smiled. "At least they had a sense of humor. Let's go with that for starters."

The skin was set and the updated ship taken to Belmont, the city where Trish and Gandy were waiting.

Gandy hopped into the cabin looking around. "New benches, that it?"

Harris pointed at the control consoles. "Mostly here. New sensors. And we have exterior shielding that should ward off plasma strikes for a bit longer. Railgun two is also operational."

Gandy shook his head. "I still can't believe the government didn't find that and then arrest us after you took down that NE ship."

Harris shrugged. "Who could say. They know it's there now."

Trish asked, "So what's the plan?"

Tawn replied, "We're heading out to Eden. The Earther colony there will be looking to retool and expand. In six months that might be the capital. If we hustle, we could be a major supplier."

Trish scowled. "We're helping the Earthers?"

Tawn sighed. "They are expanding whether we sell them supplies or not. If we take control of that effort, not only will it be profitable for us, but we could cause timely material delays if need be. If we can stall that well coming fully online for a few weeks to a month, it gives us time to come up with a better plan."

"So we haven't given up on Eden?"

Tawn half smiled. "If we're not successful slowing the colony growth, maybe we can slow the opening of the mines, should it come to that. So no, we're not giving up yet. But we'll want to play nice in the meantime. One of our goals is to build trust with the Earthers."

Gandy sat in the cabin. "None of this makes sense. We killed a hundred and fifty of their colonists. We shot down a destroyer. Why would they let us anywhere near that colony?"

Harris crossed his arms as he sat back in his chair. "Maybe they still don't know or believe we shot it down. The latest news reports have been saying it crashed on its own. And that the crash was planned as a way to get leverage in the Eden talks.

"We invaded. They lost a ship while stopping that invasion. As to the hundred and fifty NE soldiers, we'll find out if that's an issue. If so, we focus our efforts elsewhere. One thing we have to remember is Eden is a truce world. Domicile and New Earth are not supposed to interfere."

Tawn said, "We've been busy while you two were vacationing. We've been lining up legitimate suppliers and cutting deals. If they allow us, we're hoping to be the major supplier on that planet. Maybe even delivering the well drilling equipment ourselves."

***

The *Bangor* landed in the intense daytime heat of Eden at the colony of Boxton. A handful of other ships were parked on the newly poured concrete tarmac.

The administrator working in the welcome room greeted the new arrivals. "Welcome to Boxton. Are you settling? I wasn't expecting anyone today."

Harris replied, "No. We're here to do business. I have word you require well drilling equipment?"

The man nodded. "We do. The funding for that is being lined up now. Once that comes through, we'll be putting out for bids. You suppliers?"

Harris smiled. "We are. And I can provide financing for the equipment if needed. We want your business and are willing to take it on at cost to get ourselves established."

"Wow," the man replied. "If you'll excuse me for a moment, I need to fetch my boss. He will be making the actual decision."

As the man left, Tawn turned to face Harris. "I thought we were going to slow this effort down?"

Harris nodded. "We will. But first we have to earn the job."

The boss walked into the room several minutes later. "I'm Garp Huukov. I'm told you can supply water-well equipment?"

Harris held out a powerful hand for a shake. "Harris Gruberg. My associates and I are suppliers. I see this colony as a tremendous opportunity to grow our business. And I was telling your administrator here we'd be willing to finance the drilling equipment as well as supply it at cost. We would consider it an investment in our future for doing business here."

Garp gestured toward the door. "Come to my office where we can sit. Have you eaten?"

Tawn grasped his shoulder, as a reminder to stick to business.

"We have, but I can have an appetite at times. Let's discuss our options first. Afterward we can eat if you like."

Garp nodded as they walked. "Wholly acceptable."

The five turned into the office of Garp Huukov and were seated.

Garp leaned forward on his desk. "This equipment... what size well head are we talking?"

Harris scratched the back of his neck. "We can go from a thousand liters an hour up to about four million. I have the suppliers back home already lined up."

Garp asked. "You're Domers, aren't you?"

Harris nodded. "We are."

"And aren't you against the expansion of New Earth colonies out here? You know there's been violence, right? We lost a bunch of colonists just a short time ago."

Harris sat forward. "We heard. Our government is against any Earther expansion, that's no secret. But the rest of us don't care. We're not at war. And we all have to earn a living."

Garp sat back in his chair. "Technically, we are still at war. That was a truce they signed. An Armistice. A cessation of hostilities. The war never officially ended."

Harris smiled. "Our government is busy with its own problems. I can get that equipment out here in as few as three days. My government will be under the impression it's going to an outer colony, which it will be when the drilling is complete here. And you won't actually be purchasing the drilling equipment. Just leasing it."

"And what about the well head?"

Harris replied, "My government couldn't care less about the sale of a well head. They just don't want the well drilled. Besides, if we don't supply it I'm certain some company from New Earth will."

Garp tapped his fingers on his desktop. "This is interesting. It's the second offer I've had for drilling equipment in two days."

Tawn asked, "Who else has been out here, if you don't mind my asking? We like to keep tabs on our competitors."

Garp opened a desk drawer, pulling out a tablet. "Let's see. Rumford mining supplies. It was a tall, red-headed gal. She offered a competitive package, but nothing like yours."

Tawn nodded. "We know her. We've had a few shady business dealings with her in the past. Our last venture didn't go so well for us."

Harris said, "Look, Mr. Huukov, we want this business. And I'm prepared to offer you a piece of the pie, so to speak. We plan on moving a tremendous amount of material out here in the coming months. We have the ships, we have the personnel to do it, and we may be willing to negotiate in a percentage for parties who assist us in growing this business."

"Is that a bribe?"

Harris leaned forward. "I like to call it a business investment. And for those involved... they may earn a few extra credits, but they'll get the job done out here faster and for less."

Garp rubbed his chin with his hand. "That's quite the interesting proposal, Mr. Gruberg. Getting that well up and running early might actually go a long way toward cementing my position here as the colony buyer. I have the authority, at least initially. That well would certainly increase any support given by my bosses."

Harris held out a hand. "Equipment could be here in three days."

"Are we talking the four million liter equipment?"

Harris smiled. "If that's what you want."

Garp walked out from behind his desk, taking Harris' hand and shaking it vigorously. "And before I give any go-ahead to you to begin this process, what can I be expecting as a cut?"

Harris released his hand as he sat back. "In the past we've paid consultants as much as 2 percent of cost. However, given that I'm feeling generous today, I'll bump that to 3 percent of cost and 2 percent of profits. That extra 2 percent gives you incentive to pay a fair price for our goods on future deals, thus ensuring a fair profit is made by us all."

Harris stood. "Can I see your credit store?"

Garp asked, "Why?"

"I'd like to pay you a consulting fee for today's session. How does a thousand credits sound?"

Garp was silent for several seconds before holding out his store with a big smile. "It sounds fair. Very fair. Does that include the conversion rate to New Earth credits?"

Harris smiled. "Certainly. You mentioned food earlier?"

Garp gestured toward the door. "I did. And I'm feeling generous today, so when we get there order whatever you like. It's on me."

Trish said, "That might be a mistake."

Garp turned. "Why?"

Trish pointed. "I've seen these two eat. They just might eat that thousand credits, or more."

The meal was consumed and the business crew walked back to the *Bangor*.

Trish asked. "How is it they don't seem to know who we are?"

Harris replied, "Bax did say all records and logs were scrubbed. And these are new people at the colony. Maybe that info just wasn't passed down."

"Either way," said Tawn, "we're snaking this from under Bax. She'll be pissed."

Harris nodded. "Couldn't have gone better. I actually want to have the first of that equipment out here tomorrow."

"You told him you'll be taking it to some other colony afterward," Gandy said. "Where would that be?"

Harris though for a moment. "How they set for water at the Retreat?"

Tawn replied, "The colonel was in the process of ordering an additional well if I recall."

"Perfect. Looks like the Retreat will soon be getting a four-million-liter-per-hour well drilled."

Tawn shook her head. "That's way more than they need."

Harris smiled. "Bigger is better. And since it won't be costing them anything, I'm sure the colonel won't refuse it."

They stepped up into the *Bangor*. Coordinates to free space were entered and the craft lifted up through the atmosphere.

Trish looked over the nav display. "We have another ship coming down. Transponder says... it's the *Fargo*."

Chapter 2

Bax came over the comm. "What are you doing out here? Shouldn't you be locked up somewhere?"

Harris replied, "They let us go. The Earthers wouldn't admit we shot the destroyer down, and our own people cut us a break because the news reports were all saying the pacifists had all been killed. We got slapped on the hand for trying to do what we thought was right."

"And what are you doing here?" Bax again asked.

"That would be our business and not yours," Tawn said. "We could ask the same of you. You selling weapons to Boxton?"

Bax shook her head. "I'm out of the weapons business. And I hope you're not dumb enough to still be in it."

Harris leaned in toward the comm camera. "And I hope you *are* dumb enough to be caught out in free space by yourself. Baxter Rumford could suddenly disappear, and again... no one would care."

A scowl was returned before the comm abruptly closed.

Tawn nodded. "Nice touch. Now, let's hope Garp doesn't spill the beans before we get that equipment here."

"I don't think he will. He didn't seem very impressed with her. And we shook on a lucrative deal. He can't know if she's up for offering kickbacks unless she offers those up herself."

Trish said, "Her trajectory is taking her to Dove. Probably heading there to see what deals she can make with them."

Harris looked back at Tawn. "When we get back we should scan for titanium sites. Maybe we've been looking at this all wrong. What if we drilled wells and staked claims to the top three or four titanium deposits? With a wellhead we could open up our own mining colonies."

"Take the ore before the Earthers do? I like it. And I bet we could get funding for the initial buildouts."

Harris nodded. "Worst case we have Domer colonies who control the ore. Even if we were forced to sell ore to NE, we could at least charge a premium. Make it expensive for them to do business out here."

Tawn crossed her arms as she thought. "You know... we might be able to make our fortunes just from opening colonies and controlling claims. As the claim-holders we would lease mining rights back to the colonists, who we supply with all their needs. I could see this getting big really fast."

Gandy added, "We don't have the people to manage something like that. You'd need a small army to handle the logistics of that kind of undertaking."

Trish said, "Those colony companies are starting to pop up everywhere back home. You have the credits, you could just buy one or two and grow from there."

Harris turned back to face his first mate. "Brilliant. And the small army of workers... Tawn, you think you could raise that army at the Retreat?"

"I don't know that we want to be raising any more armies there. We got lucky they were all let go after our assault of Dove."

Harris shook his head. "Not an Army-army. An army of workers to manage setting up colonies. How many of those slugs and stumps are also in need of a job?"

"OK, I see where you're going," Tawn said. "And I'm liking this idea. We turn back, scan for titanium deposits and possible well sites, and then drop in to Dove to see if we can steal any business away from Bax."

Harris chuckled. "We can't go to Dove, remember? We've been banned. We go back and we risk incarceration or a fine."

Tawn winced. "Forgot about that."

Gandy asked, "If we scan, won't we only detect what's near the surface?"

"We have new sensors," replied Harris. "Top of the line. We should be able to pick out any significant deposits going a half kilometer down. That's opposed to a few meters, which is what our old sensors would do."

Trish turned the *Bangor* back toward the planet. "Pick out what you want to scan for and I'll set us into a pattern. Couple hours and we should have a map of what's available."

Gandy said, "You're wanting to identify water sources deep down? If so, we're gonna need a thumper."

"A thumper?"

"Yeah, it bangs the ground, sending a shockwave deep down. Run it long enough and from enough points and you can map out potential well sites before actually drilling. I watched a colonization documentary that talked about it."

Harris nodded. "Then we get a thumper."

Two hours were spent mapping the surface of Eden. Four high potential mine sites were identified. Another dozen showed to be much smaller or to have ore of a far lesser grade. After a trip back to Domicile, the group returned with a thumper and the analysis equipment to make use of its results.

Gandy stepped out of the *Bangor* onto the hot sand. "Man... even with this reflector suit it's insanely hot out here."

Harris set the device on the sand.

Gandy shook his head and pointed toward a rock outcropping twenty meters away. "Put it up there. On the rock. The sand won't give us a good return."

Harris grunted as he picked up the heavy machine. "I could use a hand here you know."

Tawn hopped down from the ship, grabbing one side. "Come on, Junior. Let's get this done and get back inside."

The device was placed in a location approved by Gandy. The team hurried back into the protection of the climate-controlled ship.

"That's just too hot. I can see why the pacifists thought nobody would bother them out here," Gandy said as he removed his reflective wear. "Anyone else thirsty?"

Harris pointed toward the small pantry. "Always hydrate before going out in something like this. How many more of these do we have to do for this location?"

Gandy smiled. "This is it. Four should do it. Let the analysis run and we should have an answer in about five minutes. It will show as a three-dimensional map. If there's water we'll know just where to drill. When do our teams get here?"

Tawn replied, "Any minute. One will put up a makeshift drill house while the other gets started on our first official building. When those are done we can file our claim."

Harris said, "I think we should hold off on the filing. As soon as one claim gets registered the wolves will come out. There are four major plays out here and I want us to register all four of those at once. So when our team arrives, we give them direction and we move on to the next site. We get these all identified and wells started today and we might just be filing those claims tomorrow."

Tawn nodded. "Sounds like a plan."

A comm was opened to the incoming freighter with its all slug and stump crew. "This is Freely. I'll be passing you coordinates for the first drill site. Put the office up as close to it as you can. And keep us informed with status."

A voice replied, "Will do, ma'am."

The *Bangor* lifted and was soon settling at the next-largest deposit. Five readings were taken and the data analyzed. The nearest water source to the second potential mine was twelve kilometers away. Piping would have to be purchased and delivered.

By the time they reached the third site, drilling had begun at the first. The laser head cut quickly through the sand and rock that capped a deep aquifer. The foundation for the office building had been laid.

A comm came back to the *Bangor*: "This is Mirv Davis. We have a minor setback. The concrete foundation we're pouring is drying too quickly. It needs to stay wet for a good twenty to thirty hours to properly cure. As it is it's just gonna crumble."

Gandy asked, "How long before the well is operational?"

"We estimate another sixteen hours of drilling. Adding the wellhead will take another two. We should be operational after that."

Gandy turned. "They can use the well-water to keep it wet."

Tawn frowned. "That will set us back a day, but I don't see that we have a choice."

Mirv added, "We do have a water supply here on the freighter. Might be enough to get us through this."

Harris said, "Will the foundation support the building long enough for us to file our claim?"

Mirv nodded. "It should. Will have settlement problems down the road, but should be OK for a few months."

"Then let's move forward as planned. The offices can be a throwaway once we have our claims filed."

Water sources were identified for the third and fourth sites. Wells were drilled and buildings constructed. The *Bangor* attempted to land at the city of Dove and was denied. An hour later, Gandy Boleman and his sister hopped off the freighter and were soon standing in front of a desk in the claims office.

"Welcome to Dove. What's your business?"

Gandy held out a data device. "We have evidence of four claims we would like to file. Those claims include water rights as well as mineral rights."

The worker returned a disturbed look. "We were unaware there were claims going to be filed. Why weren't we notified?"

Trish replied, "We followed your charter. There is no mention of pre-notification. The instructions for filing a claim have been followed to a tee. Water resources are available and a permanent building, with a staff, has been constructed. The data shows sufficient water supplies to cover the areas as outlined in the claims."

The worker stood. "Well, I have to take this before the council."

Trish placed her hands palm down on the desktop. "Look, is the data there or not? Does this office follow the Charter of Eden or not? These mines are gonna be opened one way or another. If you let us open them, maybe we can slow all this down and keep that titanium ore out of the hands of the Earthers. You don't want them building warships with it, do you?"

The worker returned an indignant look. "Certainly not. I do however reserve the right to conduct business in this office as I see fit. And at the moment I need to place this in front of the council for discussion."

Gandy said, "You do realize that in the coming days or weeks you are going to get flooded with claims as the Earthers ready themselves for mining, right? Help us by pushing this through and we promise to do what we can to keep the ore out of the Earthers' hands."

The worker huffed as he stood and walked out the door. Trish followed.

Gandy ran after, saying, "What are you doing?"

Trish grinned. "The council is open to everyone. If he's gonna have a say, I'll be following it up with a rebuttal."

The claims worker stood on the center stage. His peaceful and yet very biased rant lasted for forty-five minutes. Trish Boleman took the stage as he stepped down.

"OK. So he says the claims should be denied. On what basis? He gave no lawful reason as to why they should be denied, only his personal feelings about what may or may not happen. Are you a people of laws? Does the charter you created have meaning or value, or do you just make things up as you go?

"Approvals have been given to drill a well at Boxton. That colony will soon be flooded with colonists. Are you expecting colonists to follow your laws when your own people are refusing to do so? If your own officials ignore these laws, why would any new colonists follow them? Are we headed to anarchy here on Eden? If so, what chance do you think the residents of Dove will have against the lawless?"

Trish stepped down from the platform. The claims worker climbed the steps in his robe and sandals.

"I would ask for a vote of non-approval. May I see a show of hands?"

Five of the fifteen inhabitants raised their hands. Trish and Gandy followed a dejected government worker back to his office.

The claims were brought up on a display and a digital signature added. "There. Your claims are official. Have a nice day."

Trish replied, "Believe it or not, we're on your side. We want peace not only for Eden, but for all the free worlds. Oh, and just to let you know, we will likely be back in the next few days with more claims. I was going to ask that you keep this quiet. By broadcasting that someone was filing claims you probably just set off a rush. Everyone at Boxton is here for that titanium, and now they'll be digging all over this planet in an attempt to find it."

Trish walked from the room with a smug look on her face.

Gandy followed. "You think it was wise to get in your jab just before leaving? We still have to do business with them. You get us kicked out and they won't let us file any more claims."

Trish looked over her shoulder as she walked. "Not that it would be ideal, but we could have any of the slugs or stumps on our drilling team come in and file a claim. And if not them, I'm sure we could hire someone from Domicile. And as I told them, if it's not us it will be Earthers."

A transport carried the first mates to the tarmac where the freighter was waiting. After a short ride, a transfer was made back to the *Bangor*.

Trish walked into the cabin with a smile. "We have our claims."

"Excellent!" replied Harris.

A quick flight had the team out to the first of the smaller sites. Of the dozen identified, eight had drill-able water sources. The freighter was given an order of priority with the same mission: establish a wellhead and construct an official office. With the drill mission well underway, the *Bangor* made a jump to Chicago Port Station to line up additional supplies.

Harris emerged from a merchant, where kitchen supplies were being purchased to outfit each of the new mining offices.

Clovis Bagman was standing outside, waiting with four of his thugs.

Harris said, "Clovis. What brings you out of your hole?"

Clovis scowled. "I've done some checking around. It appears someone fitting your description was involved in cheating me out of some merchandise."

Harris crossed his arms. "I have no idea what you're talking about."

Clovis stepped in close. "The *Kingfisher*. I want it back."

Harris chuckled. "You can have it. It's been scattered across the desert floor on Eden by a New Earth destroyer. I'd be happy to give you the coordinates."

The four thugs took a step closer.

Tawn called out from behind. "What's the holdup? You need a hand?"

Harris looked up to the sight of Tawn Freely and three of her slug friend. All were sporting a half grin at the thought of a fistfight coming on.

Harris said, "Mr. Bagman was just telling me he'd like to repurchase the *Kingfisher*... at a discount."

Tawn smirked. "I'd be happy to sell it to him for a discount. He'll have to go collect it himself though. Any sale won't include delivery."

The four slugs crowded in close to Clovis Bagman and his henchmen. Several shoves saw the normally hostile loan-shark and his thugs backing away.

Harris said, "You'd be well advised to drop this matter and move on, Bagman. I have another four thousand friends just like these ladies that wouldn't hesitate to come down hard on you and your operation should anything happen to anyone related to this. You got paid more than a fair amount. Take your profit and move on."

Clovis Bagman scowled. "We aren't finished, Gruberg."

Harris half smiled. "We're finished today. And as I said, you mess with me or my associates and you mess with the entire force of Biomarines. We're a tight group. You best just go back into your hole."

As Clovis Bagman and his thugs walked away, Tawn said, "Good thing me and the girls came to your rescue."

Harris shrugged. "I could have taken them, but I do appreciate the help. Last thing we want is to cause issues that bring attention. You ladies able to find what you needed?"

Tawn nodded. "Twenty kilometers of piping. We pick it up from a yard down planetside tomorrow."

"We have the wellhead for Boxton?"

"Freighter is picking that up now. Should have it on the surface in a few hours. The drilling will be finished by the time we get back."

Tawn turned to her friends. "I think we're good here. Marcene, see to it that wellhead is aboard before you head back to Eden."

The slug, Marcene, nodded with a near toothless grin as she turned to head away.

Harris frowned. "What happened to her?"

"She likes to fight. With that mouth you'd think she wasn't very good at it, but that girl can brawl with the best of them. Savage on the battlefield too. Would be one of my first picks for my own private squad."

"What about the other two?"

Tawn half frowned. "I'd put both in the average category. For slugs that is. Both would have mopped up Bagman's boys on their own."

With orders for new materials placed, the *Bangor* exited Chicago Port Station on its way back to Eden. A short ride, followed by a wormhole jump, had the centuries-old warship plummeting through the atmosphere as a fireball, pulling to a stop only meters above the concrete tarmac of Boxton. The group was soon seated in the office of Garp Huukov.

"You've certainly lived up to your word, Mr. Gruberg."

Harris nodded. "Wellhead should be here shortly. Couple hours after and you're ready for a flow test. You have the piping installed for your buildings yet?"

Garp sighed. "We had that deal signed with Rumford before you got here. She has promised we'll have it in another week."

"Sounds like she's slow rolling you," Tawn said. "Pipes are a no-brainer."

Harris leaned in. "Just do your buys through us. You won't be disappointed."

Garp nodded. "Speaking of that, how are you set for delivering concrete and steel?"

"You planning to expand?"

"It's been said that within the year we could expect a thousand miners a day coming through here. This planet is rich in minerals. And from what I'm told, we have more volunteers signing up for contract stints out here than we have work for."

Tawn said, "Work on New Earth slow?"

Garp shook his head. "The opposite. The Empire keeps things running smoothly. We're a patriotic lot, Miss Freely. Even though the government has no part in this expansion here on Eden, they will make allowances for any volunteers who want to come."

Garp gestured toward the lunchroom. "You hungry?"

"These two are always hungry," Gandy replied. "You sure you can afford them?"

Garp nodded. "I get comped, so yes."

Chapter 3

Harris sat with four plates in front of him. "Give us your take on New Earth, Mr. Huukov. What do Earthers do for entertainment? We're taught that your government is an empire, ruled by an individual with a party council to back him or her up."

Garp nodded. "Mostly true. Only it's always a he. The emperor has any number of wives, with children by most. Most of those children end up on the council of laws, which ensures the emperor's rule will continue and that his desired line of succession is followed. We believe it to be a fair and equitable system. As I said before, Earthers are a patriotic lot."

Harris nodded. "Same with us."

"During the war, we had no shortage of volunteers for either war fighting or factory work. We are duty-bound to follow the emperor's wishes. In return he provides for us, giving most an equal status. The ruling family does of course have special privileges... as they should."

Trish asked, "What kind of special privileges?"

Garp shrugged. "What you would expect. Any violations are handled discreetly by the family, not aired in public, if you would. For entertainment I would expect we have the same as you. Sports, music, the Colosseum..."

Gandy raised a hand. "Wait... the Colosseum? What is that?"

Garp gave a confused look. "You know, gladiators? Wild animal fights. You don't have those? My cousin Duade has been on the highest ranked massing squad for seven months straight. Only one broken bone and one stab wound during that run. He swears he is going to retire when he hits a year. If that were to happen he would be well taken care of for the rest of his life. Three months is a long run in the Colosseum."

Gandy asked, "These wouldn't be fights to the death, would they?"

Garp again shrugged. "They can be. Usually the crowd asks for mercy. On the rare occasion, if you've severely maimed a favorite you might get the thumbs down. I tell you what, since the war stopped, the gladiator ranks have been overwhelmed with veterans. Those fights are the one thing I think I'll miss most while being out here. You don't have those kind of games?"

Gandy shook his head. "Sounds barbaric."

Garp laughed. "It's in our blood. It's in your blood. The games came from Earth when the colony ships fled. We were told they once flooded an arena with water and held mock naval battles back on Earth. Every now and then talks spreads of one of those, but the emperor refuses to allow it. We don't have water navies, so he finds it all frivolous and unrelatable."

"Do you not have oceans?"

Garp shook his head. "We have more than a hundred small seas. Lots of swampland. You?"

Gandy replied, "Well, I guess we don't have a navy either. Plenty of ships though. And one big ocean along with one big land mass."

Garp took a generous bite of his food, chewing for several seconds before offering a response. "We have sixteen continents. I've been to four of them."

Trish asked, "I haven't seen any of your women out here. Are they allowed to come?"

Garp nodded. "If escorted by a husband. He can bring as many wives as he likes."

Trish scowled. "We only allow a single spouse."

Garp took a swig from a cup. "What good is that? What if your husband tires of you?"

Trish put her hands on her hips defiantly. "Then I send him packing."

Garp chuckled. "We'll that's just silly. Who would put up with a bossy woman? Now I see why you have women fighting in your military. You have extras that nobody wants."

Harris put his hand on Trish's shoulder, keeping her in her chair. "Our culture is different, that's all. Our laws treat everyone as equals. If women want to join the military they have every right to."

Garp looked at Tawn. "You've been quiet through this conversation. I don't suppose you served, did you? You certainly have the build for it."

Tawn leaned forward. "I did. Did you?"

Garp nodded. "I did my required eight. Was in the Supply Corps, which was how I landed in this job. Never got lucky enough to see combat. You?"

Harris shook his head at the female Biomarine as he saw her stare beginning to turn into a glare. "Tawn and I both served. And we both saw action. Not something we'd care to talk about. Lost a lot of good friends."

Garp smiled. "Well, that must have been something. They stuck me in supply because my wrists were too small. Said I'd get my ass kicked on the front lines. Really... how hard is it to carry a plasma rifle and pull the trigger?"

"Too easy," said Harris. "Tell us about your expansion plans here. What can we expect in the coming months as far as supply orders?"

Garp nibbled on the New Earth equivalent of a chicken leg. "I should have designs for a dozen new buildings in the coming week. A couple warehouses, a fabrication shop, a second fusion reactor building. I'll have to admit to being a bit nervous about relying on a single reactor. I heard rumors it had been threatened with destruction when the pacies raided. You know about that, right?"

Harris shook his head. "What'd you hear?"

Garp leaned forward. "I heard the pacies hired mercs to come in and clean house. We just happened to have a ship in orbit that called in a destroyer. Chased them off."

Gandy said, "I heard a New Earth destroyer got shot down."

Garp laughed. "Yeah. That was put out by the pacies. There's nothing out here in the truce worlds that would take out a destroyer. None of these ships even have armaments. Your own fleet came in to cart the mercs back to your territory for trial. I heard they got hanged. Any truth to that?"

Trish said, "Nope. We gave them a big parade and welcomed them home."

Garp was in the process of eating a spoonful of blue-colored pea-like vegetables, almost spitting them out. "Good one. Sparky sense of humor from that her. Gonna make a good wife someday... with the proper training."

Harris again held Trish in her chair. "Mind if we wonder around the compound a bit once we're done here?"

Garp thought and then nodded his head. "I'll have Mr. Chen from the welcome desk escort you around. Not much to see, but you're welcome to take it in if you want."

The meal was finished and a tour given. The Boxton compound was made up of twenty-four windowless, concrete buildings that were connected together by underground tunnels. As Garp Huukov had alluded to, there wasn't much to see.

A short time later, the wellhead arrived from Domicile. The hookup went smoothly and within two hours the first of the aquifer water flowed out onto the sand. The next few days would be spent plumbing out each and every building.

The crew climbed aboard the *Bangor* and the hatch was closed.

Trish asked, "We checking our claims?"

Harris nodded. "Yes. And any that are ready we'll be taking in to the claims office to be registered. Anyone wants to mine titanium here on Eden will have to go through us."

Tawn leaned back on one of the benches. "I have to say, this all went a lot better than I thought it would."

"It's only temporary," Harris replied. "As soon as the Earthers take control the laws will all be changed and our claims likely thrown out."

Gandy said, "Dove has twenty-thousand residents. Boxton has a few hundred right now. If their plan is to flood the colony with settlers so they can take over the government, why don't we do the same? Maybe work with a colony company back home to bring settlers here. We have a few of the Retreat residents who are willing to come out, but we need tens of thousands to run these mines. And the more we have from home, the fewer will get sent in from New Earth."

Tawn crossed her arms. "That might actually work. At least for the short term. Earthers won't come if there are few jobs. We could end up controlling all of the titanium without having to shoot anyone. Do either of you know anyone who has dealt with one of the colony companies?"

Harris said, "As suggested, we could go back and buy one of those companies. Can't imagine any of them are making so much right now that they wouldn't have an affordable buyout price. Would fit perfectly with our business model as well. We bring the colonists out and we supply them."

Gandy added, "We could also build the housing and transportation of these colonies—basically control everything. They work for us and we house, feed, and clothe them. We could even sell them entertainment."

Trish pushed into the conversation. "You want people to move out here, you need to build a dome. Doesn't need to be transparent, just a large enough open space that people don't feel confined like you do in Dove or Boxton."

Harris chuckled. "Now where would we get the money for that?"

Trish shrugged. "Don't know what it would cost. They did build a domed city on Rega III. The colony went bust due to financing, but there is a design and there's obviously someone who can do the manufacturing."

Gandy said, "Why don't we see if we can buy that city and move it here?"

Trish laughed. "You can't move a whole city."

"Why not? Somebody moved it to there."

The *Bangor* set down beside the largest claim. A twenty meter dash across the hot sand had a door to the single office building opened and closed.

Trish scowled. "It's as hot in here as it is out there."

A voice came over the comm: "Mr. Gruberg, this is the *Troventa*. We should be setting down beside you in the next few minutes. We have the reactor and cooling equipment for the offices. Your location will be the first to be outfitted. Unless you would rather we begin elsewhere?"

Harris shook his head. "No. Here is good. How long before we have a tolerable climate?"

Trish said, "You can keep talking, but I'm dying. I'll be back on the ship."

Harris gestured toward the door. "Let's all move back."

The voice over the comm replied, "For that single build, less than an hour. We really only have the reactor and the thermoelectric cooler. We won't have the humidifiers for a few more days. By the end of the week all these buildings should be livable."

"Fantastic news. Keep us informed."

Harris hopped back into the cabin of the *Bangor*. "They need a bit of time to have that room cooled."

Trish said, "We can jump back to Domicile and check on colony companies if you like."

Tawn nodded. "That might be our best move. We'll want to look at ground transportation and mining gear too. Maybe contract some mining consultants? Basically we'll need everything anyone would need to run a colony."

Harris sat in the pilot's chair. "Take us home. Juniper city is probably a good starting location. Lots of industry there."

Two hours later the *Bangor* was landing on the homeworld surface. Trish and Gandy were given the task of gathering information on colony companies, with a focus on those who had been at least moderately successful. Tawn and Harris made their way to a company that manufactured vehicles which could be ruggedized for harsh climates.

After being dropped by an air-taxi at Hosh-Morgan, a truck manufacturer, they were intercepted by a handler from the DDI.

"Miss Freely, Mr. Harris, I'm here to collect status."

Harris unloaded about their current plans. After a lengthy conversation, the man asked them to wait where they were as he walked around a nearby corner. Fifteen minutes later, he returned.

"You have approval to move ahead with your plans. A revolving credit account has been set up and linked to your accounts. It has a two hundred fifty million credit limit at the moment. We can adjust that as needed. Don't be concerned with overspend. Certainly don't be frivolous, but spend what you need. Buy out a colony company. Enlist any mining consultants or designers or whoever you need to get this operation up and running.

"And I'm told you are to be congratulated on registering claims. Word is getting out about this. Expect other players to be contacting you about leasing or buying those claims. Do not sell or cooperate. String them along, but don't sign or sell anything."

Tawn asked, "When will the credit account be available?"

"Check your stores. And keep in mind now that you have something the Earthers badly want, and they'll stop at nothing to get it. You are now officially valued targets to them for kidnap and extortion. Watch your backs. If they come it will be hard and fast."

Harris asked, "When will you make contact again?"

The man smirked. "You'll never see me again. Just know that you are being watched, and if we feel the need to make contact we'll do so. Take care."

The man turned and headed back toward the corner of the building, quickly vanishing behind it.

Tawn said, "I like that we're being watched, but I don't like that we're being watched. I have to believe the *Bangor* might have a dozen tracking devices hidden on it."

"Maybe we should ask Trish and Gandy to look into it. No one has been seen around the ship, but something must be getting broadcast."

Tawn winced. "And if we find something?"

"Well, we obviously can't remove it, but we could certainly think about how we might modify our behavior, depending on what it records."

Harris pulled open a door, held it and followed Tawn inside.

A man sitting at a reception desk stood. "Welcome to Hosh-Morgan. How can I be of assistance?"

Tawn said, "We need vehicles."

The man smiled. "You'll want to visit one of our dealerships. I'll get you the location for here in Juniper City."

Harris replied, "We're talking an initial buy of maybe a hundred such vehicles, capable of operating in a constant sixty degrees Celsius environment."

The man paused. "I see. The Juniper City sales team will be able to help you with that. I'll get you—"

Tawn cut him off. "We would like to speak with someone higher up the chain of command, if you don't mind."

The man nodded. "My apologies. I'll see who I can find."

A second manager, and then a third, came to the lobby. Each was turned away for someone more important.

The Vice-President of Dealership Relations approached. "Bob Mendez. I'm told you desire to speak with a senior individual about a potential large sale?"

Harris held out his hand. "Harris Gruberg. And this is my partner Tawn Freely. We're looking to make an initial fleet purchase of a hundred or so ruggedized vehicles. And when I say ruggedized, I'm referring to sixty degrees Celsius average daytime temperatures. This is an urgent need. We have the funds to make the purchase, and we'd rather not have to go through a dealer who will only add delay and cost."

Bob replied, "I can assure you that any cost difference or delay would be minimal, Mr. Gruberg. We have a tight relationship with our dealers. I can personally begin a conversation with our local dealer if you'd like."

Harris asked, "Let me ask you this... what's the average cost of one of your best transports that will operate in that environment?"

Bob thought for a minute. "Anywhere from twenty thousand... all the way up to a hundred, depending on options and capabilities."

Harris sighed. "Let's begin with the hundred thousand figure. We're in the market for an initial purchase of a hundred such vehicles. That's a ten million credit sale. Are you certain you want to lose that deal over passing it off to a dealership?"

A commotion could be heard coming from a hallway behind the reception desk. Bob Mendez stood, hurrying off in the direction of the disturbance.

Tawn crossed her arms. "Well, that was rude. Can't say I care much for Bob."

Harris replied, "Sounds like someone is getting an earful. We'll give him a few minutes before we walk. The next closest competitor is all the way down in Miamiville."

Chapter 4

Two minutes later, a stodgy old man walked out to the lobby. "What specifically are you looking for?"

Harris said, "We're spinning up a complete mining operation in a dusty, hot, sixty-degree-C environment. I believe the humidity runs around 7 percent or less. We'll need 'dozers, dumpers, cranes, concrete pumpers, the works. All ruggedized for that environment."

The man held out his hand. "Bannis Morgan."

"This is Tawn Freely, and I'm Harris Gruberg."

Tawn gestured toward a large sign on the wall. "As in that Morgan?"

Bannis smiled. "Yep. Family owned and operated for four hundred seventy-two standard years. And the equipment you're looking for will require modification. We used to make a few military vehicles for that type environment, but nothing of late. I'll need a list of what you'd like converted. How soon are you gonna need them?"

"Immediately if possible."

Bannis Morgan chuckled. "Wish I could snap my fingers and have them ready, but last I checked my snapper wasn't working, at least not like that. We're probably talking three months for the first set."

Tawn frowned. "We're ready to begin colony construction today. How about if we pay for any development costs, including labor?"

Bannis asked, "What colony this for?"

Harris leaned in. "Eden. You've probably heard about it on the news lately. The Earthers are wanting to take control. We want to stop them."

Bannis stood straight. "Eden? It's a desert world. Nothing there. Who cares?"

Tawn replied, "New Earth needs titanium. Eden is rich in it. And please don't spread that around as we don't want the media all up in our business. We're looking to do this quietly if possible, outside of the public eye. There will come a time when we're looking for colonists and miners, but we aren't there yet."

Tawn turned. "Which reminds me, we should order biosuits for our people. Those are at least a six week lead-time."

Bannis Morgan rubbed his chin. "I suppose I could take this project on myself. The grand-babies are all teens now and could care less about grandpa. I tell you what... what if I could have the first units available in that same six week timeframe you mentioned? I could even throw in a couple of the old military units we have sitting in storage. You can have those today if you're willing to provide any feedback to us for producing any others."

Harris said, "We can arrange for a pick-up, probably tomorrow. What kind of vehicles are they?"

"Climate controlled personnel carriers. They're armored, but not armed. I know you don't need the armor, but the other systems will be on whatever we deliver. How's that sound?"

Tawn asked, "And what's the price?"

Bannis asked, "Can I send a couple of my techs out with you? We could use the feedback during the modification process."

Harris nodded. "Absolutely."

"And you're looking to purchase a quantity of at least a hundred such construction vehicles?"

"We are... as a starting point. Could go way bigger."

Bannis replied, "For the cause I'd be willing to do the initial mods for cost, if you're already purchasing the standard vehicles in that quantity."

Harris held out a hand. "Mr. Morgan, I believe we have a deal. You wouldn't happen to have any friends in the mining equipment business, would you?"

Bannis shook Harris' hand. "I would. Peacock and Company. Owner is Beatrice Peacock. She's my cousin. And I'm guessing you'll be needing equipment to operate in that same environment?"

"At least some of it would have to be. Anything for digging and transport of the ore. We could build indoor processing facilities. In fact, we were toying with the idea of constructing domes for the colony. My first mate said she saw some documentary of a domed colony that was under construction on one of the outer colonies. It went bust, but there must be designs and such for it still around."

Bannis leaned back against a counter. "I saw that. Was an interesting piece. Wasn't going on a hot dry world though. Nothing like sixty Celsius. That's serious heat. I can make a few calls if you'd like me to ask around about it."

Tawn nodded. "That would be great. Looks like we came to the right place."

Bannis sighed. "You caught an old man with time on his hands is what you did. And a patriot. News says New Earthers are becoming active in the truce worlds. If true, Domicile needs to be doing something about it."

Harris nodded. "We're trying. Can't be any government involvement though. Both sides have people watching."

"I employ a few of your kind here at Hosh-Morgan. Can't say I was happy to see how you were treated when the truce was declared."

"For what it's worth," Tawn replied, "we did get slightly more compensation than the regulars who were put out, but most of us had no training or experience for living in a civilian world, so those benefits didn't last."

Harris added, "And people are scared of us. Most of us aren't the best at normal conversation. We're crude, blunt, and quick to temper. Add in the distrust from fear of us and most Bios have had a rough go of it."

Bannis replied, "I'll admit to being frustrated at first with the few Biomarines I hired. Took some patience and a good bit of understanding. Now, though, I'd say they are some of my better workers. I've tried to hire as many vets as I could, and Bios."

"Have I said I like this guy?" Tawn held out her hand for a shake. "When all this is over we might send a few worker candidates your way. At the moment though we'll be needing their services for ourselves."

Bannis crossed his arms, leaning forward. "I know a number of industry leaders who are Domers to the core. If you like, I could act as a sort of liaison for you. They are powerful people and would readily enjoy being involved in any effort to keep the Earthers from gaining a foothold on the truce worlds."

Harris scratched the back of his neck. "Ordinarily I would be gushing yeses for that kind of assistance, but I have to warn you, we are being watched closely by the DDI. Any assistance you attempt to give us will be known to them."

"Last I checked we were on the same side. Is there something I should know?"

Harris leaned forward. "If you want to do this, I'm all for it. I just wanted you to be aware of the risk you're taking by doing so. Should you provide assistance beyond what would be considered normal business, and if something were to go bad or wrong, you would be on the hook for answering to the DDI.

"That could be anything from confiscation of your business to imprisonment to an untimely accident. You'll want to be discreet and put confidence in only a trusted few. The fewer the better."

"You make it sound dangerous, Mr. Gruberg."

Tawn said, "You have to look at the bigger picture, Mr. Morgan. We're talking about preventing the Great War from restarting. There are those on either side who want it to return. And they would kill anyone they feel is interfering with their plans. You'll be poking your head into a big tent with a lot of bad people who won't hesitate to chop it off. We'd like your head to stay attached is all."

Bannis nodded. "I understand. I'm old, I've accomplished all I could desire. My life is complete. There would be no higher honor than to give it in the service of protecting my fellow Domers."

Harris shook his head. "It's not just you you're putting at risk. It's everyone you know. As I said, there are very bad people involved in this effort. If you're willing to risk involvement, you need to fully understand what that means."

Bannis smiled. "Are you trying to get me excited about joining your cause?"

"Just letting you know what you might be getting yourself into. People are already dead over this. As things heat up, more deaths will likely follow."

Bannis stood. "How can I get in touch with you, Mr. Gruberg?"

"It's best that you don't. We're being watched. We'll make contact with you next time through this facility. After that we'll have to figure something out."

The meeting ended with a handshake. An effort was coordinated with the crew of the freighter to retrieve the two armored personnel carriers from a Hosh-Morgan warehouse. The *Bangor* next flew to the city of Post London, where meetings with several colony companies were to take place, the first of which was at the Gregor United Settlements Company.

A spokesman from GUSCO was waiting in the lobby. "Mr. Guber?"

Tawn laughed.

Harris shook his head. "It's Gruberg."

The man held out his hand. "Alphonse Duane. My apologies. Our receptionist must have entered the name wrong. Please have a seat."

Alphonse walked to the other side of the table and sat. "How can we here at GUSCO assist you?"

"We're building a mining colony on one of the truce worlds," said Harris. "Eventually we'll want to staff that colony with miners. We're looking for a partner, or perhaps even a buyout if necessary, to make sure we have the personnel we need when the time comes."

Alphonse frowned. "We aren't in the business of purchasing mining companies, Mr. Gruberg. However, I may be able to assist with the partnership."

"We aren't looking to be purchased, Mr... Duane. We would be doing the purchase if we find a company that matches our needs. Can you tell us how many colonists you've placed in the last year?"

Alphonse slowly rocked his head back and forth in thought. "Across all colonies... close to two hundred."

"What about for the truce worlds?"

Alphonse smirked. "We haven't had any clients asking to be placed out there. Nor have we had any colonies from there requesting personnel. We deal strictly with the free colonies, and most specifically with Havron V."

Tawn asked, "Would you know of any of your competitors who deal with the truce worlds?"

"I believe there are only two who are registered to do so, Falston Company and Middleman Enterprises. I want to say each operates a colony on New Mars. Middleman had a colony on Jebwa. You might have heard about the massacre there. It was thought to be because of some killings on Eden. Either way, you'll want to talk to one of those two outfits. Middleman is right here in Post London."

They looked up the business address and an air-taxi took them to the location. In the front of the office a heavy woman, smoking a virtual pipe, had her feet propped up on a desktop as she watched a local video broadcast.

"Got an appointment?" she said with a raspy voice.

Harris shook his head. "No. Just dropping in. We'd like to discuss making arrangements for settling personnel to a new colony if you have someone available."

The woman had a short coughing fit as she set her feet on the floor.

When her throat was clear, she reached out for a button on her desk. "Fritz, you got people out here."

Fritz Romero was an extremely thin and yet tall man. His black hair stood in contrast to a pale complexion. As he came down a hall to the front office, his gate was more of a lumber than a walk.

"Good afternoon." Fritz stood with an impish smile, tapping his fingers together. "What would be your pleasure?"

Harris stared for several seconds. "We're building a colony. We're interested in staffing it in the near future."

"Superb," Fritz replied. "Please come this way."

The group followed the lanky salesman into his office, a small room with a single chair and a short bench. "Please have a seat."

Harris said as he sat, "Before we get started on our needs. Can you tell us about your placements? How many people have you moved and to what colonies?"

Fritz nodded. "Close to ten thousand over the years. Many of those out to Bella III, but that was over half a century ago. Our latest venture was to a new colony on Jebwa. Unfortunately, that colony was the victim of a mass genocide. Retaliation for killings on Eden. It has been quite the setback for our company. I had to lay off my staff, move to this building, and hire the temp you saw out front."

Fritz leaned forward in his chair. "I have a colony with thousands of homes, five dozen sizable farms, and a small mine that is sitting empty. You wouldn't happen to know of anyone who would be willing to move there, would you?"

Harris shook his head. We're in the business of looking for potential colonists. It sounds like your business is about to fold."

Fritz frowned. "Only a few short months ago I employed close to a hundred people. The colony on Jebwa was about to undergo a major expansion. I had a half dozen large businesses lined up to build out there and close to five thousand colonists on my interested list. And then the massacre..."

"What if we gave you a contract to enlist colonists for a new colony?"

Fritz frowned. "Not on Jebwa I hope."

Tawn replied, "Nope. On Eden."

Fritz started with a low laugh that soon turned into a bellow, followed soon after by a coughing fit and a sip of a beverage. "Sorry. Sorry. You aren't serious, are you?"

Harris nodded. "It will be a mining colony. With protection provided by former Biomarines."

Fritz shook his head. "You aren't going to get settlers out to Eden. With the troubles they've had... there won't be any interest."

"I don't think that's true. Look around at the unemployment. We're two years out of the war effort. The vets are all seeking work. And at the same time the defense industry has been winding down contracts and shuttering factories. Eden and the other colonies offer opportunity. If we promise security, food, housing, and decent pay, I believe the colonists will come. We can even guarantee return to Domicile if they don't like it."

Fritz returned a half scowl. "I think it may be a tough sell."

"What assets do you have stuck on Jebwa?" Tawn asked.

"As I said, housing for thousands of families. And enough farming and mining equipment to keep those families working."

"Would you be willing to sell the housing interiors and the mining equipment?"

"Honey, I can't afford the transport to bring it back here."

"What would you estimate its value to be if you had it here?"

Fritz turned to his desk. "My guess would be 20 percent on the credit. I spent... three million credits on it. Would be lucky to get six hundred thousand if I had it sitting right outside here."

Harris crossed his arms. "What if we give you six hundred thousand and we'll transport it from there?"

Fritz laughed. "I'd close up shop and retire like I should have done a year ago."

Harris placed his hands on the front of Fritz' desk. "Would you have any interest in joining our company as a recruiter for Eden?"

Fritz sighed. "You give me a glimmer of hope for getting out and then you suck me back in. I suppose the purchase of the assets is tied to my coming aboard for a recruiting job?"

Harris nodded. "Yes?"

Fritz rubbed his forehead for several seconds. "You buy out my company assets and I'll come work for you... for a year. Then I'm out."

"Sounds reasonable."

Fritz Romero took in a deep breath. "When do I start?"

Harris stood with his hand out. "Welcome aboard. First thing we need to do is get you a better office. Something with a little flash that says we're a crack outfit. We'll be looking for miners and support personnel, probably in the range of a thousand or so to start. We'll need people for the actual mining, for transport, for processing, and possibly shipping."

Fritz nodded. "You'll need bookkeepers, maintenance and service people as well."

Tawn smiled. "I think he understands."

"When will you want to start the staffing process?" asked Fritz.

"Immediately. Start with the coordination people, managers and such."

"I'll put together a list of colony jobs needed to support a mining colony of a thousand. The numbers will be rough, but I should have something for you in a few days. From there we can decide on priority. After that I will work to put together a marketing campaign. And there is the question of compensation."

Harris replied, "How does twenty-five thousand credits a month for you and a staff sound? And give us a budget figure for a low-end, medium, or high-end marketing campaign. I'd like to have our first mining assets breaking ground in two months."

Fritz tapped his fingertips together. "It seems you want the world. I can only promise that I will do my best to meet your needs."

Tawn said, "You bring this together nicely and we might even make you the colony governor. Will eventually be needing one of those."

Fritz stood from his desk and walked into the hall. "Miz Burritz? You're fired. Get out."

Turning back, Fritz Romero smiled. "I've been wanting to do that since they sent her to me. And I believe my old office building is still available. We should go and negotiate a lease. My demise was unexpected. The owners may be willing to bargain to get me back. I was a good tenant."

Chapter 5

The wheels of industry were quick to get rolling. Fritz Romero had the new office open and staffed three days after the initial meeting. A personnel plan was put forth and prioritized. A high-end marketing budget was funded and media outlets contacted. The human recruiter expected fruit from his first seedlings within two weeks.

A return trip to Juniper City and the Hosh-Morgan manufacturing facility saw two climate-modified personnel carriers loaded aboard a freighter and taken to the new colony on Eden. As a joke, the colony received the name Fireburg, which was registered at the government office at Dove.

Bannis Morgan had been a busy man. He'd made contact with the owner of the failed domed city on Rega III and the assets there were fully purchased. The dome construction was modular in nature, requiring a special ship to transport and drop the many pieces in place.

The slugs and stumps on Eden were forwarded the designs for constructing the concrete foundation. Pourings had already begun by the time the *Bangor* arrived.

The group looked over the display as the *Bangor* hovered over the colony site.

Trish said, "That dome must be huge."

"Two kilometers in diameter," Gandy replied. "Just over three square kilometers of floor space. Should fully support our first several thousand people and then some."

"And after that?"

"After that..." Harris said, "Mr. Morgan purchased the designs and the defunct factory where the parts were made. He's branching into the colony-dome manufacturing business with several partners. That gives them a business presence without the appearance of being directly involved in all this."

Trish asked, "Will we be building a dome at each mine claim?"

Tawn nodded. "Eventually."

Harris added, "We plan on building this colony out fully before starting the next. Mr. Morgan advised that we take this first one to full production. Once the yields fall by half we start moving these domes and all the people to the next site. When the major sites are depleted, we split up the domes between the smaller ones."

Gandy said, "Sure wish we could have gotten all those claims. Did we find out who got the last one?"

Tawn scowled. "It was Bax. She bribed the claim processor. He said he was never given the documentation you turned in."

Gandy huffed. "I carried it in there myself. I saw the digital signature. He's lying."

"Doesn't matter," Harris said. "The claim was filed and registered. I looked over what was available from our scan. I would say there's enough ore there to build a dozen warships. That's according to Mr. Morgan. Not enough for them to restart a war.

"Besides, word has gotten out at home that she wants to sell titanium to the Earthers. Nobody is willing to sell her mining equipment. She'll have to get that from New Earth – which she will – but at least it slows her down."

Gandy grinned. "This is all so fantastical and exciting. I can't believe we're building a mining colony on Eden. We fly around wherever we want in our own ship. We're making huge deals with industry leaders. And we shot down a New Earth destroyer! Life just doesn't get any better than this!"

Tawn took in a deep breath. "Starting to remind me about the last time things were going this easy for us. We got roped into nearly starting a war all on our own. I have to wonder what schemes Baxter Rumford and the Earthers are cooking up for us. They aren't just gonna let all this titanium go back to Domicile."

Gandy said, "We can protect any cargo with the *Bangor*. She can handle anything Bax can throw at us. Even a NE destroyer."

Harris laughed. "We aren't going up against any more warships in this. They wouldn't let us get close enough to offer a fight. What we're gonna have to do is keep our eyes peeled for any signs of Earther ships in the area when our freighter takes off. They'll be vulnerable for about forty-five minutes from liftoff to jumping through a wormhole. If they can traverse that safely, they're home free."

Tawn nodded. "No way they are jumping destroyers after them. That would be a treaty violation our military wouldn't stand for."

Gandy asked, "When we get the refined ore back to Domicile, what do we do with it? I thought that market is already fully supplied."

"We'll stockpile if we have to."

Trish winced. "Can we afford that? Don't we have to be making income? Just selling supplies can't possibly pay for all this."

Tawn smiled. "You let us worry about that. For now, let's just keep moving forward."

Several days had passed before the first of the dome beams arrived. Scaffolding stood ready to support the beam as the custom transport lowered it. Before the day had come to an end, a dozen such pieces were in place.

Gandy looked on in awe. "Those have to be two hundred meters each. Hard to believe five of those fastened together will be strong enough to hold up one side."

Harris replied, "They said three weeks to move them in place, a week to check for issues, and we follow with the crown. After that the roof goes on, then we insulate, and finally power and cooling equipment are installed and brought online."

"How long to cool it down?"

"Another three days. A month from now we should be able to comfortably walk the insides."

Gandy shook his head. "That's just crazy. And your people are all out there working in those flimsy reflective suits. I don't know how you can stand it."

Tawn gave an answer. "Not so bad now. They have cooling vests they swap out about once an hour. And plenty of water. It's not ideal, but it is manageable. Next week we should see the first of the biosuits finally coming out of production. They'll be able to work all day after that."

Trish asked, "Any word on Bax and her operation?"

"We've had a couple scouts sneaking out there to evaluate," Tawn said. "She's still working on her first building. I don't think she's getting much support from the Earthers. They must be fuming about how we scooped all the claims."

The construction of the dome framework was completed on schedule. The roofing material was applied and the underside insulated. When the last of the roof panels were fastened into place, the reactor was installed, started, and the cooling equipment powered up. Over the three days that followed the temperature inside dropped from sixty degrees to thirty six.

Trish walked across the concrete floor, looking up. "I can't believe we just built this. Still like a sauna in here though."

"Temp is expected to drop about seven degrees per day," said Harris. "Should be sitting at a tolerable level in another three days. Longer than we thought, but workable. Those box-like structures over by the coolers are humidifiers. I've been told 50 percent is our target."

Colonel Robert Thomas walked up to the foursome. "Harris, Tawn, looks like we might just get this thing built."

Harris replied, "Couldn't have done it without your help, Colonel."

Tawn added, "Everyone is working so hard."

Robert nodded. "You've given them purpose again. Jobs, a future, and friends. They appreciate all that you're doing here. And as the miners arrive, some are eager to transition to full-time security work."

Harris said, "We still need construction workers, Colonel."

Robert smiled. "And you'll have no shortage of them. We're picking up another twenty or so recruits a day from the colonies and Domicile. Seems every Bio has their eye on working here."

Harris looked around at the insides of the giant dome as he rubbed the back of his neck. "I just hope we can keep things running this smoothly. I'd like to get started on the next dome as soon as possible. Mr. Morgan thinks he's only weeks away from producing the first pieces."

"You somehow lit a fire under that man. He has worked tirelessly in support of this project."

Tawn smacked the colonel on the shoulder. "No harder than you, sir."

Harris said, "The first acclimatized mining gear should be here tomorrow. We have all the pipes for the plumbing and wiring for the power. Buildout of the housing should be underway right after those. After that it will be time to start bringing in colonists."

The colonel asked, "How's that effort going?"

Harris replied, "Fritz says he has close to three hundred signed up. His ad campaigns will be going out tomorrow. He expects a flood after that. Says what he's seeing is completely different from what he expected. With the right message, the worker supply might only be limited by whoever wants to stay on Domicile."

A comm came into the colonel from a Biomarine perched on the top of the dome. "Sir, I'm seeing a column of soldiers coming in from the south! They appear to be armed! Will be here in three to four minutes!"

The colonel flipped comm channels. "Major! Assemble the security force as we practiced! Looks like we have company!"

Another switch was made. "Everyone, listen up, we have hostiles incoming. All personnel move to your pre-assigned safe stations and await my commands. Security teams... I will see you at the weapon's locker."

Harris asked, "You need weapons? We have a handful on the ship."

The colonel shook his head as he walked toward his armory. "We brought in several dozen plasma rifles, Mr. Gruberg. Hope you don't mind."

Harris laughed. "Mind? I'm thrilled."

Tawn said, "We should go back and get the *Bangor* in the air. We could take out that whole column with ease."

Harris replied. "We fire anything from that ship and the pacies will ban us... permanently."

Robert Thomas yelled across the open floor. "We'll handle this. You two get back to the safety of your ship."

The lookout passed down a new assessment. "Column is spreading out. I estimate four to five hundred soldiers... all with plasma rifles."

Harris sighed. "Come on, we need to get these two on the ship. Gonna get heated out here."

A quick sprint took the group to a covered docking hangar where the *Bangor* was parked. Tawn and Harris changed into biosuits, collected their arms, and headed to the hatch.

Harris said, "Take her up to a half kilometer and wait. And don't try to get involved no matter what you think you see. This is our fight."

The hardened ship lifted from the deck and shot skyward. Tawn and Harris hustled back into the dome, heading for an exit on the other side.

As she sprinted, Tawn said, "We should coordinate with the colonel."

Harris replied, "He has his people doing what he wants. We'd just get in his way and be a distraction. Besides, he would be putting us at the back of any assault or defense. I'd rather us be on equal ground with everyone else."

The rumble of plasma explosions could be heard as they approached the far exit. The attacking force had spread out to form an assault line composed of three sections. The center section would come straight in while the other two forces worked their way around to each side.

Each plasma round that struck the dome plating ripped a small hole. The colonel's men took position behind a low concrete wall, the attackers behind the numerous rock outcroppings that dotted the sand and dust-covered landscape. Plasma rounds blasted sand and rock into the air.

Tawn said, "They're gonna bust through the east and west entrances. The colonel needs to split his defense."

Harris pointed back toward the north door. "He's already done so."

Two contingents of sixty Biomarines funneled through the north entrance on their way to the east and west positions. Each of the grand doors were blown just before their arrival. Heavy plasma fire was exchanged.

Harris said, "Pick your fight."

Tawn pointed up. "I should be up top."

Harris opened a comm. "Trish, Tawn is coming out the south door. Set down between her and the Earthers. She needs a ride up top."

Trish replied, "Fifteen seconds…"

The *Bangor* dropped in, settling just above the sand and drawing intense fire from the Earther assault force, her ion shielding absorbing all that came her way. The hatch opened and Tawn sprinted out from the dome with a dive and roll. As the *Bangor* lifted toward the crown of the dome, Harris Gruberg joined the colonel behind a concrete wall.

"I'd say we have a standoff at the moment."

The colonel shook his head. "I have five hundred unarmed Marines holed up at the wellhead building. If they make a move toward there it's gonna be a slaughter."

Harris said, "Give me a half dozen fighters and I'll see to it that move doesn't happen."

The colonel gestured to one of his Marines. "Perino, take your squad and follow Mr. Gruberg."

The squad-leading slug snapped back a salute. "Yes, sir!"

Perino pointed at the entrance door. "Lead the way, sir."

A sprint led Harris and his new squad to the north entrance. The Biomarines at the east and west sides had pushed the attackers back outside the dome. Harris and his squad, ran through the north entrance and into the docking bay. As the team moved out into the sand beyond, plasma fire thundered on the ground all around, forcing them back into the cover of the bay.

Harris got on the comm to the *Bangor*. "Can you see the armored carriers from where you are?"

Gandy replied, "They're over by the beginnings of the pit."

"Trish, I need you to drop your brother at the carriers. Gandy, bring one of those to the north docking bay."

Trish pushed the controls over and the *Bangor* darted overhead before settling beside the vehicles. Gandy was out the hatch and quickly inside.

"Haven't driven one of these before."

"Standard controls," Harris replied. "You'll figure it out. And don't worry about plasma rounds from these rifles. The armor on that rig is built to take it. Strap yourself in though, as this will get rough."

Gandy flipped several switches, bringing the electric motors online. The armored carrier lurched forward as he pushed the throttle down with his boot. The six wheeled beast vaulted out of the pit, almost going airborne, before racing across the sand.

"This thing has some power!" Gandy yelled.

The armored carrier shook as it approached the bay, dozens of plasma rounds banging off its hull. As Gandy turned the stick toward the open bay, a missile streaked across the sand, striking the left front wheel and sending the APC over onto its side.

Harris sprinted out into the open, skidding to a stop beside the overturned vehicle. "Gandy! You OK?"

"I'm good. Hit my head, but I'll live."

A dozen Earthers rushed out from their position, throwing out a relentless barrage of plasma rounds as they ran.

Tessika Perino took command. "We're taking that rock formation! Benson, Peck, Herrington... follow the edge of the dome around to that rise. Should give you a good firing angle on their position. Ross, Sanchez, Umbutu, we're taking the hard road, going straight in. You'll be porpoising across those sands. Use what little cover there is. Gruberg, you're gonna have to hold your own!"

Harris peered around the edge of the APC as dozens of rounds popped across the top side of the vehicle. Three squeezes of the trigger on his repeater caught three of the approaching Earthers dead center, cutting their number to nine. A sprint around to the far side of the armored hull saw another two caught in the open, their chests ripping open as the plasma rounds spread out on impact.

Black shards of sand-glass pelted his biosuit as he lay on his belly for the next set of shots. Another Earther fell, his comrades reaching the opposite side of the APC.

Harris thought to himself: "Six on one is not the odds I was looking for."

A handle turned and the back hatch popped open. "Inside! Hurry!"

Harris dove as three plasma rounds impacted the sand at his feet. Gandy pulled the hatch shut, having taken hot shards to his upper chest and left arm. The hull of the APC shook as the attackers outside made every attempt to blow it open.

Gandy collapsed backward. Harris rushed to catch him, setting him down gently.

"How bad you hurt?"

Gandy winced. "Burns. Feels like I'm on fire. Nothing deep though. Do what you need to secure us."

Harris winked. "You're not a warrior until you have battle scars. Just hang tight. I'll see what I can do."

Trish came over the comm. "You OK in there?"

Gandy took a deep breath and replied, "Took some hot sand. I'll make it. Mr. Gruberg is unhurt."

Harris popped the latches on a bottom hatch, flinging it open and shooting another of the Earthers before pulling it slammed shut.

"And then there were five."

A voice came from outside. "Give up and you'll go unharmed!"

Harris laughed. "Not believing it! Earthers don't take captives while the fighting is still going on!"

They heard three quick bursts, a sound Harris Gruberg knew all too well: bodies exploding from the impact of plasma rounds.

Tawn came over the comm. "Can I assume someone is in the APC?"

Harris replied, "Gandy and me. Was that your handiwork out there?"

Tawn growled. "Only got three. The other two are around on the top side. I've got no line."

Harris glanced over at Gandy. "Got your weapon?"

"Right here."

Harris smiled. "If I'm not back in thirty seconds, be prepared to use it."

The back hatch was opened with Harris diving out into a roll. As he came up in a shooting stance, the first of the two Earthers rounded the corner of the APC. Two well placed plasma rounds saw the attacker splitting apart and flying backward. A loud thud could be heard as the last of the group to assault the APC attempted to flee.

Tawn came over the comm. "You're clear all the way around."

"Can you see Perino?"

"Hang on. She's pinned down. But so are the Earthers. I have two stumps who didn't make it. The rest of her squad is trying to work their way back toward you."

"This is Harris. Perino is pinned."

The second APC raced across the sand, skidding to a stop beside Harris. A top hatch popped open and Trish's head came up to eye-level.

"Come on!"

Harris hurried around to the back hatch, helping Gandy out and into the second APC. The armored vehicle lurched forward as Trish depressed the throttle. A short drive had it skidding to a stop beside Tessika Perino. The back hatch was opened and the Biomarine climbed in.

Colonel Thomas came over the general comm. "They're pulling back! Hold your positions and hold your fire. If they want to leave, let them."

Trish glanced back at her brother. "Yikes. That has to hurt."

Gandy replied, "You have no idea."

Harris sat beside him as the APC turned back toward the *Bangor*. "We'll get you patched up and something for the pain."

Gandy winced as he attempted to laugh. "Not in that order I hope."

"Trish, thanks for the pickup, but why didn't you just use the *Bangor*?"

The young first mate shrugged. "You said to not get it involved."

Harris smirked. "Not involved in any shooting. You did good though. That move took some guts. Glad to see you taking the initiative."

Trish smiled. "Can't leave my bro and my captain hanging out there."

The APC pulled to a stop beside the *Bangor*. A flight was made to ensure the Earther force was indeed in full retreat.

Tawn was fetched from the roof before the small ship settled back into the north docking bay.

Chapter 6

Gandy was given a shot for his pain before a med-tech began the chore of picking black-glass shards from his upper chest and upper left arm.

"I've seen this before. Poor guy took it in the face. You'll have some nasty scaring, but it will heal."

Gandy replied, "Just keep that painkiller coming and I'll be fine."

A headcount was performed. Sixteen Biomarines had taken their final tour of duty. Ninety-eight of the Earther force lay dead on the sand surrounding the great dome structure. The bodies were collected, stacked together, and buried in a single mound.

The south, east, and west dome entrance areas had taken extensive plasma round damage. Hundreds of roofing plates would have to be replaced. The climate system worked to maintain the current interior temperature as doors were repeatedly opened and closed for workers moving in and out. Within hours after the assault had ended, the construction work was again getting underway.

Trish shook her head as she watched the slugs and stumps moving about as if nothing had happened. "How do they do it?"

Tawn asked, "Do what?"

"Just go back to work like that. I'm still shaking."

Tawn chuckled. "Hon, we've done this so many times it's like second nature to us. Some will be a little edgy from it for a few hours, but most will move right back to whatever they were doing. It's called a lifetime of training and experience."

"Did you ever want to be somebody else?"

Tawn smiled. "I'm sure we all have at some point in our lives. I wanted to be a farmer once. Got over that notion a few weeks later after going back into battle."

"You never wanted to run?"

Tawn half smiled. "I've had plenty of situations where my brain was screaming to run. But that wouldn't be fair to the others I was fighting beside. So I shoved those notions back to where they had come from and just powered my way through it. Just like you did with that APC."

Trish let out a long breath. "I guess. Does it get any easier?"

Tawn shook her head. "Never easier. You do get used to dealing with it though. I had one fight where we were storming a New Earth destroyer. Just when I thought my team had cleared the last deck, Earthers began popping up everywhere. The ship had dozens of emergency hatches on every level.

"We thought we had them boxed into the lowest deck, but they had been sneaking back above us. What began as a one hour raid ended up taking nine. For a while I thought they were re-spawning after we had them dead. It didn't get any easier, and we forced ourselves to power through it."

Harris sat beside them. "Patching should be finished up in about three hours. The colonel has asked that we fly the fallen back to the Retreat for burial. We'll be flying the freighter back. Afterwards we have a load of supplies to pick up on Domicile."

Trish asked, "The crew can't fly the freighter?"

Harris shook his head. "Nine of the sixteen casualties were the freighter crew. We'll be picking up another dozen Biomarines from Domicile when we get there. Colonel says the new crew will be selected from them. He doesn't want to move any of his other workers from the tasks they are currently doing."

The fallen were collected and a jump made to the Retreat. A makeshift morgue had been set up to house their bodies until internment. A second hop had the freighter landing at Juniper City. Harris and Tawn walked into the Hosh-Morgan offices.

Bannis Morgan came out to greet them. "Miss Freely, Mr. Gruberg, I just heard about the attack. I'm sorry for your losses."

Harris gestured toward the door. "We have one of the armored vehicles out there. They came in handy. This one took a missile to the right front. It's in need of repairs."

Bannis nodded. "I'll have a team take care of it. I would like to talk finances with the two of you while you are here. I've been getting grumblings from my group of patriots who have been assisting. They would like to see that real progress is being made. Perhaps a tour would be in order?"

"We would have no issue with that," Tawn replied. "Your people need to understand this is Eden and it's dangerous out there. As evidenced by yesterday's attack."

"How is the dome coming?"

"The enclosure is complete. Power is in. Base plumbing is being worked. Build-out of the housing section should be starting in a few days. Once the first units of that are complete, we can bring out our first recruits."

Harris added, "If we stay on schedule, mining will begin in two months. How is the equipment coming?"

Bannis smiled. "Excellent. The feedback modifications have been designed in. The first units will be ready for transport in the coming days. It sounds as though the timing will be perfect."

The threesome moved into Bannis Morgan's office.

Harris asked, "Have you noticed the DDI following you around?"

"Yes. And they are persistent. I've had three bugs removed from this office. My security team is on top of it though. They've tapped my car. My home. I have new clients who are forever asking questions but never making a purchase. Too bad our resources aren't being used on those who would subvert us."

Harris frowned. "Just be careful what you say and who you say it to. We both know the DDI agents aren't supposed to have this kind of power without judicial oversight, but they don't seem to have issue with ignoring that."

Bannis leaned forward onto his desk. "Just so you know, our government is split into three factions right now. One, as you know, is the current pacifist party with their 'no war at any cost' mantra. Next is the faction who think we should restart the war, the patriots. They think we should finish off the other side. And then there are the 'don't cares,' who have no position one way or the other.

"The pacifists have control of our military, and have been doing their best to gut it by moving assigned monies to social projects. The patriots have a hold on the intel services, but that hold is slipping. The 'don't cares' are bouncing along with their own priorities. Should the Earthers acquire titanium, and should they be able to build up their fleets, we may no longer have the mechanisms in place to stop them."

Tawn nodded. "We're warriors, Mr. Morgan. There's not one among us that would prefer war over peace. But if war comes, there won't be anyone else standing in line in front of us."

"I realize that, Miss Freely. It's one of the reasons I'm still connected to this project. You're committed to keeping the rest of us safe. Not many out there are looking out for everyone. I've seen to it that my family legacy with the business will continue. I'm now committing my efforts to the same cause as you.

"I've made arrangements to build three ore freighters to be used exclusively for moving that titanium back here to Domicile. They won't be available for at least five months. We'll have to make do with leased vessels until then."

Harris said, "Those were on our list of needs, Mr. Morgan. Thank you for initiating that. Have you thought about what you'll be doing with the refined ore when you get it back here? Can't move that much into the market without crashing prices."

Bannis tapped his fingers on his desktop. "We'll have to store it. Along with the freighters, I have several friends that might be interested in building trade ships. If not for trade with the outer colonies, then for trade with New Earth. Transport prices are at a bit of a premium right now. And the fleet currently consists of mostly surplus military units that weren't designed for civilian cargoes and are otherwise very inefficient."

Tawn asked, "You thinking a low cost titanium source might make that venture worthwhile?"

Bannis nodded. "I am... so long as our consortium has exclusive rights to purchase that ore. I was also attempting to think along bigger lines. What if we expanded the Fireburg colony to also process the titanium into hull plates or other parts? If we grow the population out there to the point we're able to take control of their government, we might just be able to get around the government regs, taxes, and fees that make building ships on Domicile cost prohibitive."

Tawn crossed her arms. "This expedition just gets bigger and bigger. Building a colony is already overwhelming."

Bannis smiled. "That's where industrialists like myself come in. We have the planning staff and designers already in place to bring something like this together. Won't add anything to your burden pile. We'll be handling all personnel needs, resource needs, expenses... basically everything. And with the ships being commercial units, the military shouldn't bother us or feel threatened."

Harris asked, "Won't you have to build an orbital shipyard somewhere?"

Bannis nodded. "We would. It would only be for assembly. And placing that beside Chicago Port Station may be advantageous for garnering support with our politicians. As a group we have the financial capital and expertise to do this. We only need the will."

The meeting with Bannis Morgan was productive. In the two months that followed, the dome was completed, including housing, warehouses, and an entertainment complex to keep miners occupied during off hours. The first three hundred miners had arrived and were settling in.

A wheeled transport pulled up under the overhang at the south entrance to the dome. Four government officials from the colony at Dove emerged and hurried inside. Harris and Tawn met them at the entryway.

Bizzy Mister stood in his robe. "Impressive structure, Mr. Gruberg. How many colonists do you expect it will hold?"

"Up to five thousand when it's fully operational. What is it you are out here for, Mr. Mister. I would think this is cutting into your contemplation time... or whatever it is you do."

Bizzy sighed. "We've had to return to our arts and crafts with the loss of the water income. But everyone is happy to pitch in. We've come here today because of a much graver concern. We've heard rumors of violence. I'm sincerely hoping you have not seen to it to bring any weapons to this planet. Should we have concerns?"

Harris gestured toward the interior of the dome. "Please, have a look around. Go wherever you like. If I were you, I'd be more concerned with the hooligans at Boxton. Have you checked there?"

Bizzy waved to the others to begin looking around. "We have. There were no signs of any weapons and the Earthers residing there were very friendly. They are concerned over your exercising of claim rights for mining. There is a rumor floating around that in addition to the weapons, you are hoarding potential mining sites."

Harris nodded. "We will freely admit to doing that. As I tried to state before, the Earthers want titanium so they can rebuild their war fleets."

"And why is it you want titanium, Mr. Gruberg?"

"To keep it out of the Earthers' hands."

Bizzy crossed his arms. "Is it not being used by the Domers to build up their own fleets?"

"Domicile has a ready supply of titanium, Mr. Mister. You should consider our move here an effort to peacefully keep the status quo. Our methods are non-violent, which I would think is what you desire."

Bizzy frowned. "Non-violent? Really, Mr. Gruberg? After the slaughter of the Boxton colonists and then the attempted raid on Dove? I would hardly classify your methods as non-violent."

Harris shook his head. "Those weren't colonists, those were paid mercenaries who were sent here to annihilate your colony at Dove—at first through intimidation and then through an assault. Those bodies you found in the desert were coming to murder all of you."

Bizzy sighed. "There were no weapons found at the site, Mr. Gruberg, only bodies. The Earthers said they were coming in a peaceful protest to ask for expanded water rights. Are we to believe those who would march a hundred fifty kilometers across the desert to push for ideals or those who would mercilessly butcher them? That incident remains under investigation, by the way. Are you certain you and Miss Freely didn't see anything during your stay at Boxton?"

Harris scowled. "We already gave our statements, Mr. Mister. Now, if you want to continue your check here, I would advise you to be cautious. We have industrial equipment moving around and I wouldn't want to have anyone get run over. And if you want to look in any building or rooms, just ask. We have nothing to hide."

Bizzy nodded as he began to walk away. "Thank you. We will be careful."

"Good thing we got rid of that burial pile," Tawn whispered.

Harris winced. "That would be all we would need. The colonel moved them three hundred kilometers out. Doubtful they'll be found anytime soon. I'm actually surprised by the Earthers."

"How so?"

"They could have asked for their dead. We would have given them over. They could have then dumped those bodies out here just before the pacies checked Boxton. Would have shut down this whole operation."

Tawn smiled. "I guess they aren't as smart as you, then."

Harris shook his head. "They have plenty of smart people. And if this occurred to me it would have occurred to at least one of them. I have to wonder if they have reasons for keeping us going."

Tawn laughed. "What kind of bizarro conspiracy theory you got cooking up there?"

Harris gestured at the dome surrounding them. "You and I built this. That doesn't strike you as extraordinary? We don't have the smarts needed to cover all our bases with this effort. I feel like someone is helping behind the scenes."

"Warmouth?"

Harris half scowled. "Could be. But other than that lame attempt at an attack, why have the Earthers not done more?"

Tawn patted Harris on the back. "Come on. I think I know what you need to put all these conspiracies to rest."

"And what would that be?"

Tawn chuckled. "Lunch. You can't tell me you aren't hungry."

Harris shrugged. "You got me. I can't deny that."

The newly constructed cafeteria was full of workers. Plates were piled high as all food for the colony was provided free. Harris and Tawn stacked their own plates as well. Once finished, and when the lunch shift had ended, the cafeteria cleared out.

Four hours later, Bizzy Mister and the other pacifists returned to their transport and departed. No evidence of weapons of any kind was found. A Biomarine ready-team, with weapons, remained on the freighter hovering a kilometer above the colony, out of sight of the government of Eden's eyes.

Chapter 7

The first of the giant, acclimatized earth movers from Hosh-Morgan were loaded onto the freighter. Crews had been training for days on simulators. The three immense vehicles would bring with them the first ground breaking ceremony for the Fireburg mine. Tawn and Harris waited anxiously for their arrival, joining Trish and Gandy in the cabin of the *Bangor*.

"This is exciting," Gandy said. "How many people does it take to operate one?"

Harris replied, "From what I heard, only one. That operator steers and sets the pace. Everything from there is automated. The grinders loosen the ore, filling up one of four hoppers. The ore in that hopper is then run through an initial refining stage where the output goes into two other hoppers, one for waste product and the other for ore. The fourth hopper can be filled as the contents of the first is being refined.

"When the refined hopper is full, a vehicle pulls alongside and the hopper is picked up and dropped onto its chassis. The full hopper is then brought into the dome for further refining."

Gandy grinned. "I can't wait to see the whole operation in action."

Tawn pulled up a camera view of the mine below. "In six months this whole area will be the beginnings of a giant pit."

"How deep will we go?" Trish asked.

"At the moment," said Harris, "half a kilometer. As we dig, if the depth proves there is more ore down there, we'll go deeper."

An alert came over the nav display.

Trish said, "Two ships just jumped into free space out there."

"Warships? Anything we should be concerned with?"

Trish shrugged. "Don't know what they are. I wouldn't have mentioned it, but they're in the area the freighter usually jumps through."

"Well, let's go check it out," said Tawn. "Won't hurt to know who they are."

The *Bangor* moved up through the atmosphere as a fireball. Twenty minutes later they were approaching the two mysterious ships.

A hail came over the general comm. "Approaching ship, identify yourself."

Harris pressed the connect button. "This is the *Bangor* from the Fireburg colony. With whom are we talking?"

The video connection remained blank.

"We are private citizens. Our business is not your business. Turn away or we will be forced to take defensive action."

Gandy said to Harris, "Defensive action, that doesn't sound all-too friendly."

Harris glanced at Trish. Bring us to a stop and hold this position."

Harris said into the comm, "We only question your presence because this location is a trade route we frequent and we're expecting a cargo delivery anytime now."

The ship's spokesman replied, "We don't care about your business. Back away or we will be forced to drive you away."

Tawn leaned into the comm mic. "Listen, pal, you don't own this space. You think you can drive us out, then bring it on."

Harris looked over his shoulder. "You trying to start trouble?"

Tawn pointed at the nav display. "Those two lame ships can't hurt us. Let 'em try."

Harris shook his head. "We don't need the trouble. The pacifists are looking for any excuse to boot us off the planet."

"Let them try," said Gandy. "I don't know why you're so concerned about what the pacifists think."

Harris said, "Because the truce agreement says they can ask for help from Domicile, New Earth, or both. I'd rather us not get into a pissing match with them, as we would be the ones who would lose."

Harris replied over the comm. "We're backing off. You have our apologies."

Harris nodded at Trish, "Move us back, but keep us within sensor range."

Trish steered the small ship away from confrontation as she gave an uneasy look. "Neither of them are broadcasting a registration."

Harris nodded. "That bothers me too. How do we find out what they're up to without getting into a fight?"

Trish said, "We have a wormhole opening. This should be our people."

The freighter slipped through into Eden space.

Trish yelled, "Those ships are heading for the freighter!"

Harris took control, pushing the throttle to full. "Power up the railguns! You two, you better strap yourselves in. Something tells me those ships are armed!"

Harris opened a comm. "*Davenport*! This is the *Bangor*! Those ships approaching are hostile! Head our way!"

"Thank you, *Bangor*. This is Major Timkins. We're detecting plasma cannons charging. You'd better make haste."

"Be there in eight minutes, Major. Do what you can to avoid fire."

The major said, "Roger that, *Bangor*. We have a team standing by in case they attempt a boarding."

Three minutes passed before the first of the two ships fired its cannons. The slower freighter turned to port, avoiding fire for the first and only time. The rounds that followed found their mark on the newly exposed starboard side, ripping into a support deck, killing all who were in that bulkhead section.

For the next five minutes the *Davenport* swerved, dove, and rose, all with little effect as the gunships continued with a relentless barrage. The outer sections of the freighter took serious damage, but the inner bulkheads were holding. Then twin shots from the second gunship tore the cargo doors of the second bay open, and two further blasts had the first of the three digging machines in shambles, portions of its digging arms spinning away from the freighter out into the dead of space.

The *Bangor* closed fast, firing a stream of tungsten rounds in a spiral pattern, hoping for a hit as the targeted gunship turned hard to starboard. All rounds missed.

Harris turned his effort toward the second ship, again firing off a burst of railgun rounds in an outward spiraling pattern. The fifth round grazed the gunship, heavily damaging an outer layer of armor plating. Two plasma cannon bursts returned, both impacting the hardened hull and shielding of the *Bangor*, causing little more than a rumble and a short vibration.

Harris turned back toward the first gunship as it again fired on the *Davenport*. Explosions rocked the port side as the freighter attempted to turn into the oncoming fire. Internal fires raged as the burning freighter powered toward the planet of Eden.

Harris spun the *Bangor* around for another burst at ship two, now within fifty kilometers. This time the spiral shot found its mark, digging a hole through the gunship, taking its fusion reactors offline, sending the attacking vessel adrift. A quick turn lined the *Bangor* up for a kill as the gunship fired its plasma cannons into the onrushing vessel. Rumbles shuddered down the ship's hull as the weak plasma rounds impacted.

A steady burst from railgun two cut the attacking ship in half, its mate turning to flee after releasing a final barrage from its cannons. A wormhole opened and the remaining gunship slipped through.

The major came over the comm. "Thank you, *Bangor*. We have heavy damage... but we'll make it."

"Roger that, *Davenport*. Should be clear going in. But keep it slow through that atmosphere. Looks like you've lost a third of your exterior plating."

The major nodded. "We'll do our best. See you on the ground."

Harris turned the *Bangor* toward the now defunct gunship.

"What are we doing?" asked Trish.

"We're checking for survivors. I think we have a good idea of who sponsored this. Would like to know for sure though."

The centuries-old Zwicker class shuttle pulled to a stop alongside the larger of the two ship remnants. Trish performed a bioscan.

"Hmm. I show two life-signs. Over in this section of the nose… might even be the bridge."

"Take us in, Miss Boleman. Extend the docking tube to any of those exposed decks."

Harris stood from his chair. "Miss Freely, may I escort you over to the remaining portion of that ship?"

Tawn nodded. "Yes you may."

Gandy nervously checked the charge on the Fox-40 strapped to his hip.

After moving through the airlock, the two Biomarines hopped onto the exposed deck in the middle of the ship.

Harris asked, "Trish, have the two life-signs moved?"

"Still in the same spot. You'll have to get through that bulkhead and then through an inner door."

Tawn looked over the wall in front of her. "This looks solid still. Trish, any way around this? Does the structure of the area they're in show any compromise?"

Trish altered her view of the scan. "It does actually. Go down two decks. You should find a seam split, allowing you through. Beyond that is a set of doors that look intact. One leads up a stairwell that runs to the top deck. You get through that door and the door two decks up should be functional. The life-signs are about ten meters forward from that point, and then three meters to your left."

The duo clutched disjointed metal beams and wiring as they dropped the two levels to the open bulkhead. Harris entered first, checking the hallway beyond.

"Doors are shut and locked."

"Nothing my Fox won't break through," said Tawn.

Harris replied, "We do this and they'll know we're coming."

Tawn smiled. "I'm counting on it."

Harris stepped back. Two blasts from the Fox-40 blew the lock away and the door flung open. The sudden rush of air slammed the slug back into the wall behind her.

Harris laughed. "Saw that coming."

Tawn scowled. "Why didn't you say something?"

"Two years out and you forget all your training already?"

Tawn hesitated. "Yeah, I guess that about sums it up. Wanna go first?"

Harris stepped forward. "Heck yeah."

The two flights of stairs were traversed in seconds.

Trish said, "Still no movement of the bios."

Harris pushed Tawn away. "Step back. I'll handle this one."

The slug took two steps back down the stairs. Harris Gruberg unleashed two rounds from his pistol. The hinges on the right side of the door gave way, sending a fierce gush of air down the stairs, almost relieving Tawn of her footing.

Again Tawn scowled. "You did that on purpose."

Harris smirked. "Not the first time either. Had a squad partner that used to do that to me. Been waiting for years to use it on someone else."

Tawn moved up the steps in front of her partner. "Hope you're proud of yourself."

Harris nodded. "I kind of am, actually."

The Biomarine slug moved slowly down the hall, quickly poking her head around the corner and pulling it back. No weapons fire came her way.

"Looks like they're unconscious."

The partners walked around the corner at the same time.

Tawn shook her head. "This one's a goner. Collect the other and let's get back."

Trish came over the comm. "You might want to hurry. I'm seeing a building heat signature three decks below. If that's a reactor it might be about to melt down."

Harris said, "Move that docking tube down to the deck we came through on. We'll be coming out there."

Harris picked up the unconscious survivor, throwing him over his shoulder.

Trish said, "You might want to hurry! Temp is rising fast!"

Harris followed Tawn through the hall and down the stairs. After squeezing through the open bulkhead seam, the two Biomarines sprinted to the other end of the docking tube.

As the airlock door shut and sealed, Tawn yelled, "Go, go, go!"

The *Bangor* moved hard away as the tube retracted. Seconds later, the bright flash of a fusion reactor exploding rocked the heavily armored ship.

Harris laid the unconscious soldier on the deck. "Trish, take us to Fireburg. We'll have the colonel's team look him over."

On the surface, Harris carried the captive into a medical care facility inside the dome. Several hours later, the man awakened.

Harris and Tawn stood on either side of his bed. Restraints held him securely in place.

"Who do you work for?" Harris asked.

The man remained silent.

Tawn leaned in. "You do realize that things are gonna get very nasty and very painful for you, right? You can either cooperate or suffer. You killed a number of our friends out there with that raid. And your mission failed. That cargo is being unloaded as we speak."

Harris leaned in equally as close. "Look, you may not realize it, but we're on your side. This titanium is meant to go to New Earth. First thing we have to do though is get it out of the ground. And I say it's going to New Earth because there's no market for it on Domicile. They have all they need."

The man replied in a weak voice "You expect me to believe that? You're Biomarines. You're part of the Domicile military."

Tawn shook her head. "*Were* part of the Domicile military. When the truce was declared we were put out on the streets. We're out here just trying to make a living like everyone else. And if we can pull this off we'll end up some of the wealthiest people on Domicile. And wealth has its power and its privileges."

Harris repeated the question: "Who do you work for? We need to talk to them to let our plans be known. Attacks like this only serve to slow us down. You want titanium for New Earth, you need to give us some answers."

The man scowled. "So it's true… the Biomarines are sellouts. I'm not from New Earth. I'm from Post London. Those ships and the men who crewed them are Domers... former military. We're out here to stop you from restarting this war. You sell titanium to the Earthers and they rebuild. Is that what you Bios want? A return to war?"

Tawn rolled her eyes. "We aren't selling anything to the Earthers. That was a ploy to get you to talk to us. We're all on the same side here. No one wants war."

The man smirked. "Just as I thought. Domers out here trying to steal all the titanium. Your poor attempt at a psychological trick backfired. We know who you are and we know what you're doing out here. It won't work. That titanium belongs to us."

Harris gave a confused look. "What? So are you an Earther or a Domer?"

The man spit on the front of Harris' suit. "Earther, you moron. Looks like you slugs and stumps are just as dumb as we were told. Now I know firsthand."

Harris moved out into the hall, waving Tawn to follow. "What just happened in there?"

Tawn frowned. "He made us look like idiots is what happened. He turned our little set of lies against us, getting us to reveal our true intentions. He's an Earther. That raid was meant to destroy our equipment."

Harris growled. "So I guess we are that dumb."

Tawn laughed. "You maybe. For me I'll stick with the notion that I wasn't trained for interrogation—maybe for resisting, but not administering it. Probably should have had a couple of our intel guys running the show in there."

Harris replied, "Well, we did at least learn who he's aligned with. I'd still like to know who he specifically works for. I could see Rumford providing the Earthers with information on our normal trade corridors."

Tawn scratched her right ear. "This means we're gonna have to take on escort duty. This won't be their only attempt at disrupting our progress."

Harris frowned. "The *Bangor* is our only armed ship, and I don't trust letting anyone else pilot her into a fight."

Tawn shrugged. "Not like we're overly busy anyway. The colonel has the personnel issues under his leadership, and we have the efforts and guidance of Bannis Morgan on the other resources. We spend most of our time just observing."

Harris glanced back at the medical room where the captive lay. "We'll have to run out to meet that ship twice a day."

Tawn slapped him on the shoulder. "You worried it might cut into your lunchtime?"

Harris returned an uneasy look. "More worried they'll return with more powerful ships next time. And we can't report any of this to the pacies as they'll question how we were able to fight them off."

Tawn took a step back toward the room.

Harris asked, "Where you going?"

Tawn smiled. "He still hasn't told us who he works for. I'd like to know. And he's gonna tell me."

A heavy press on a cracked rib brought about a shudder of pain. "You know I could do this all day. I kind of like the little noises you keep making. They somehow make me feel happy."

The man held up his other hand in surrender. "OK. I'll tell you what you want."

"First, what's your name? And then, who do you work for?"

"Niles Johavsky. And we're on the same side. I work for the DDI. They want to make sure the titanium never gets mined."

Tawn nodded. "Now we're getting somewhere. Who do you work for in the DDI?"

Niles laughed. "You people are so gullible. I don't work for the DDI. I'm an Earther through and through."

Five minutes later, Tawn Freely had her real answer. A retired new Earth colonel was overseeing an operation aimed at slowing or stopping all Domer development on Eden. His job was to get the titanium resources New Earth required. His budget and resources were coming through a half dozen NE corporations—all government owned, but providing a layer of deniability.

Tawn lifted her hand from the area of the cracked rib in the man's chest. "Tell us what you know about Baxter Rumford."

"Who?"

Tawn applied pressure. The man yelped.

"Baxter Rumford. Tell us what you know."

The man drew in a slow, painful breath. "All I know is she's working to bring that mine online. It's deep, with substantial deposits. We may not need the ore from your mine."

Harris scowled. "We let one slip through and it happens to be a good one. Looks like we'll need to do a little stopping of our own. We can't let her deliver ore to New Earth."

Tawn looked over at Harris. "I'd say we milked him for everything he's gonna tell us. Might be good to pass this all along to the colonel. Let the pros handle it."

Harris nodded. "I have a better idea. We pass this along to the colonel and then we have lunch. I'm starved."

Tawn shook her head. "You, sir, are a bottomless pit."

Harris asked as they walked toward the door. "You saying you aren't hungry?"

Tawn half smiled. "No. Just that you're a bottomless pit."

Chapter 8

Harris feasted on his favorite... barbecue *bogler* ribs. A special flight had been made out to Farmingdale, where packed, dried meat was exchanged for various items required for wilderness living. A special package was sent by Harris and Tawn, containing two Fox-40s and a case of plasma charges for the colony to make use of. The weapons were welcomed.

As they sat to eat, a rumble could be heard and felt coming through the cafeteria.

Harris stood. "That didn't sound good."

One of the colonel's aides ran in. "It's the wellhead! Someone blew it up!"

Tawn said, "Gonna take us a week to get a new one that size. Those are build-to-order back on Domicile. That, or we go pull one from one of the wells at the other sites."

Harris shook his head. "Can't do that. We shut down those wells and the pacies come in and declare the claim void."

"What's to stop them from blowing those up?"

"Don't know. Maybe they think it would leave evidence it was purposefully done? We could contest any attempt to pull the claim from that."

"What's to stop them from stealing a wellhead then?"

"The two Biomarines we have stationed at each one."

Tawn sighed. "I guess we have a trip to make to Domicile. Have to get one ordered. Figures this would happen the day before we were set to break ground."

Harris and Tawn walked to the well house. The colonel was standing just outside. The noontime Eden heat beat down on the threesome.

Harris asked, "Someone got inside?"

The colonel nodded. "Looks that way. I'd say we have a spy or a traitor in our ranks."

"We should have video footage from the dome cameras of who's been in and out of there."

"I have my team looking those recordings over right now."

Harris glanced down at the reddening flesh of his arm. "Don't stay out here too long, Colonel. That sun will cook you alive."

The *Bangor* was called up. Trish and Gandy landed in the docking bay after being on patrol at the normal jump point for the freighter.

Harris stepped up into the cabin. "Take us home. We have to order a new wellhead."

"We heard," said Gandy. "They have any idea who did this?"

Tawn said, "The colonel and his men are looking into it."

"We can't grab a wellhead from one of the other sites?"

Tawn shook her head. "He says the pacies would shut down a claim if we remove the water. We have to get a new one."

"They have one at the Retreat," said Trish. "The one we installed. They can't be using it right now as half the people are out here."

Harris nodded. "Excellent suggestion, Miss Boleman."

Harris opened a comm. "Colonel, can we snag the wellhead from the Retreat as a temporary fix? We can replace it when a new one has been produced."

"Have at it, Mr. Gruberg. The old well remains functional and is all that's currently needed."

Harris turned to Trish. "Take us to the Retreat."

The two-ton item was retrieved, returned to Eden and installed. Eight hours and four minutes after the explosion, water was being pumped again.

Harris grinned as the flow meter showed green. "You know what this means?"

Tawn replied, "The ground breaking can go off tomorrow as planned?"

Harris laughed. "No. It means we can go eat."

Tawn shook her head. "That's getting old."

Harris pulled back. "You enjoy it as much as I do."

Tawn sighed. "I'm not talking about the actual eating. I'm talking about the jokes. You need new material."

Harris returned a fake frown. "Just when I thought I had it nailed."

"Sounds like a malfunction in your programming."

"Speaking of programming, Farker doesn't seem to want to hump your leg anymore. You two have a falling out? He only has eyes for the slug out at the Retreat now?"

Tawn returned a worried look. "Don't know. I mean, I'm glad he stopped, but I don't know why. Hasn't done it since his last visit to the building on Midelon. We should go back and take another look at exploring that place."

Harris gave a half scowl. "That place makes me nervous. When's the last time we did a sweep of the *Bangor* for DDI bugs?"

Tawn shrugged. "Have to ask Gandy about that. Last I knew was a couple weeks ago."

The twins were commed and soon joined the two Biomarines in the cafeteria.

Trish asked, "Any reason we have to join you for your tri-daily feeding at the trough?"

"When was the last time we swept the ship for bugs?" Harris asked.

"Four days ago," replied Gandy. "As far as I can tell we only have the one locator that's running. You said to leave it alone."

"We were thinking of a visit out to Midelon. Before we go we'll have to make sure that ship is clean. If Admiral Warmouth knew we had been out there more than once he would come in and take everything we have. Including Farker."

The dinner was cut short by a visit from the colonel. "We have our guy. Came in with the first crew of recruits from Domicile. He's already confessed to being an Earther spy. My people are working him over right now. We'll know what he knows in the next day or so."

Harris asked, "Can we talk to him?"

The colonel gestured toward the door. "He's awake at the moment. Might not be for long. Come with me."

Tawn stood behind Harris. "You think that's a good idea, given our interrogation record?"

Harris replied as he walked: "I just want to make sure he's asked about Rumford. We know she's here on the planet and she's bad, but we don't know any of her connections here. If we can get a few names, maybe we can piece together her network at some point. Our other prisoner knew who she was. And he gave up a name or two."

Tawn chuckled.

"What's so funny?" Harris asked.

"I was just thinking about how bad our last interrogation went. If it hadn't been for that cracked rib I'm not sure we would have gotten anything. I still don't trust what he told us."

"The colonel's men got the same intel. He told us what he knew."

Tawn again chuckled. "You think the colonel will let me crack a rib?"

Harris shook his head. "You slugs can be ruthless when you want to be."

The attempted interrogation lasted all of fifteen minutes.

Harris pulled Tawn over to the door. "We aren't getting anywhere. Let the colonel's men handle this. I'll let them know to dig up as much as they can about Bax."

Tawn shrugged. "So where to now?"

Harris nodded toward the hall's end. "We go clean up our ship and pay a visit to Midelon. We can let the colonel know we'll be gone for a few hours."

"We ever gonna tell him about that place?"

Harris shook his head. "We aren't telling anyone about that place. The less people who know the better."

Two hours were spent searching the *Bangor* from top to bottom. An additional tracker was found on the outer hull. Gandy had seen a suspicious person lurking near the back of the ship after they had just come into the dome's docking bay three days before.

Harris opened a comm to the colonel as they moved out into the harsh Eden sunlight from the bay. "Colonel, we'll be gone for a few hours. If anyone asks, we're out getting supplies."

"You're covered, Mr. Gruberg. Just remember we have the official groundbreaking in the morning."

Harris nodded. "We'll be there."

The *Bangor* rocketed skyward and was soon into free space. A jump to the Rabid System was followed by a jump to Midelon. Trish piloted the ship through the atmosphere, pulling to a stop half a meter from the ground. An easy set-down followed.

"That was about as good as it could be done," Harris commented.

Trish smiled. "Maybe someday we can actually make use of my new skill. You know I could have piloted her against those gunships—my reactions are good. And I went back through the logs of that fight to study what you did and when you did it. A few of those moves were marginal at best."

Harris patted her on the back as he stood. "The fog of war will make you take actions that don't always turn out to be the best. My flying back there was as good as any."

Trish nodded. "If you say so."

Harris sighed. "OK. You and Tawn are gonna be good friends for the next couple hours. Gandy and I will be looking around with Farker. I would suggest doing a full scan of this planet. Encrypt whatever recording you get. We don't want anyone seeing the data later."

Harris hopped to the ground, with Farker and Gandy just behind. The dog sprinted for the door of the bunker. Harris sprinted after. As the dog approached, the door opened. Harris dove, slipping inside before tumbling to a stop. The hardened door closed before Gandy arrived.

A comm opened. "You made it in! Are you OK?"

Harris replied, "So far as I know."

"What do you see?"

"A door to a hallway going away from me. Farker disappeared down it already. And there's an open table to my right with a single chair in front of it. It's facing a blank wall."

"No computers or anything? Nothing to greet you? Oh, and look for a door handle. Any way to let me in?"

Harris glanced back. "Nothing visible. Think I'll go check that hall."

As he took the first step, the door slid shut, sealing off the hall and enclosing the Biomarine in the outer room.

"Scratch that. Looks like I'm stuck here until Farker returns."

"Anything else in there? I'm not getting any video."

Harris replied, "Four blank concrete walls with a concrete ceiling and a concrete floor. Other than the table and chair we have the two doors and that's it. And a single dome-shaped light in the ceiling. I don't see a switch for it."

The light shut off, leaving Harris Gruberg standing in the dark. "OK. That's not good. They switched the light off on me."

"Who?"

Harris chuckled. "They, the building, whatever AI is running this place. Could just be on a timer, but it's pitch black in here right now. Hang on. I'm feeling my way over to that chair. If I'm gonna be stuck here in the dark, I can at least sit."

Several seconds later, Harris blurted out. "Got it."

The chair was turned around to face the door and the stump-shaped Biomarine took a seat.

Gandy sighed. "Well, we really don't know any more than we did before you went in."

Harris chuckled. "We know not to dive in here after the mutt. Guess I should have followed him down that hall."

"What do we do now?"

Harris rubbed the back of his neck. "You could walk over to the cave and see if you can find anything else. Check all the walls to see if any others are holograms."

"What are you gonna do?"

Harris laughed. "I'm gonna sit here in the dark. Kind of reminds me of the sensory deprivation training I had years ago. Only there wasn't some squeaky-voiced kid badgering me with questions... just peace and quiet."

Gandy huffed. "My voice isn't squeaky."

Harris replied, "I guess that depends on if you are listening to it or me. For me it's squeaky. Don't be alarmed or offended though. Most regulars sound that way to me. Has something to do with our hearing being enhanced in the upper frequencies."

Tawn came over the comm. "If you two ladies are finished chatting... we found something."

"Tell us," said Harris.

"It looks like an underwater structure. It's just below the cliffs on the north side of the island. About a half kilometer under the surface."

"That ship is waterproof, you know. Take it down and have a closer look. Maybe it's a back way into this place. Meanwhile, I'll just sit here and enjoy the dark."

Gandy walked off toward the caves as the girls dropped the *Bangor* into the Midelon waters. At five hundred meters depth, the structure came into view. A large door, they deemed possibly used for launching submarines, covered the center, while a series of what looked to be intake and exhaust pipes surrounded it.

Tawn said, "We have another door. I'm sitting directly in front of it and nothing is happening. Looks like we could easily fit through it."

"You mean you and Trish or the ship?"

Tawn laughed. "The ship. Your neurons stop firing when you're in the dark or what?"

"Could be. What's bothering me at the moment is I keep thinking I'm hearing noises in here. Like some little creature is sniffing around and about to take a chunk out of my ankles."

"You scared of the dark?" Trish asked.

"No. But I may be scared of the little creature sniffing around in the dark."

Tawn asked, "You do have your boots on, right?"

Harris was quiet for several seconds. "I do now. And that helps, thanks."

"Why were they off in the first place?"

Harris sighed. "Thought the cool concrete might feel good. It does, but not so good I'm willing to risk my toes over it."

Harris sat in the dark, intently listening for the sound of whatever it was that was in there with him. Twice he had sworn he felt something brush against his leg. Twice his fast reach down came back with nothing but air.

Gandy broke the silence: "I'm going into the cave. Last time we lost comm while in there. So if you don't hear from me shortly you know where to look."

Trish replied, "We've got you covered. Nothing else to see down here. If you can wait a couple minutes, we'll join you."

"Come on up."

The *Bangor*, dripping with water from the Midelon ocean, came to rest at the bottom of the hill below the cave. A quick hike had Tawn and Trish standing beside Gandy.

He gestured toward the opening. "Ladies first?"

"Way to man-up on this expedition," said Tawn.

Tawn looked at the other cave. "What about that one?"

Gandy shook his head. "Shallow. You can see it all from out front."

Tawn asked, "Did you check the walls in there for false doors like you found in here?"

Gandy shook his head. "No."

Tawn laughed. "Well, go do it. We've got everything covered here."

Gandy took three minutes to work his way around the inside of the cave. No new passages were revealed.

Tawn walked into the other, touching the wall with her hand. "Feels like a cave. Smells like a cave."

Trish piped up: "So good thing we didn't step in it? I haven't heard that one since seventh grade."

Tawn replied, "I have no idea what you're talking about, hon."

Gandy walked around them. "It's up here around the corner."

He entered the room where the false wall had been found.

"Door is right in here. I patted the other walls before, but I'll do it again just in case."

Tawn walked into the previously hidden passage. "We have a door and nothing much of anything else. I assume you knocked, pushed, and pulled on it?"

Gandy walked in beside her. "Yep. Got no response. And for whatever reason, Farker didn't seem to like it in here."

Tawn scratched her ear. "Let's head back and see if Harris is out yet."

Trish said, "Too bad we can't bring a scanner in here."

Gandy replied, "Who says we can't? They're detachable. You just need a power source. The record buffer is with the sensor and easily keeps several minutes of scan data. What do we have with a battery?"

Trish thought for a moment. "Our biosuits have a power source. You think we could rig one up to one of those?"

Gandy shrugged. "We can give it a shot."

Tawn stared at the twins for several seconds. "Well, go. You don't need me to hold your hands, do you?"

A short walk had the twins outside and moving down the hill to the ship. Tawn stopped at the cave entrance.

"Harris, everything still OK in there?"

"If boredom is OK, then yeah."

"The twins are rigging a scanner to a power source. We're gonna take it back into the cave and see what we can find."

Harris sighed. "Tell you what, I'll just hang out here."

Tawn chuckled. "You do that."

Chapter 9

Harris sat with his hands on his knees as he leaned forward in the chair. Several scooches had the chair turned toward the table. As he moved his elbows onto the table in an attempt to prop up his head, a light came on above him.

Seconds later, a hologram image of Alexander Gaerten's face floated just on the other side of the table. "Hello. I am Doctor Alexander Gaerten. I designed the facility you now occupy. Welcome. I hope your journey here was pleasant."

The door behind Harris opened and Farker trotted out. The mechanical pet sat on its haunches beside the chair, staring up at the doctor with his usual grin.

Harris replied, "Hello?"

The hologram continued, "Hello. Welcome."

"What is this place?"

"This is engineering facility number two. An identical facility exists on the planet Paeton. This facility and the other control the boson fields, which allow wormhole travel with starships. The field generators are located in this facility."

"What's behind the door over there?"

The doctor's image replied, "The inner working of this facility will be revealed after the individual seated in that chair properly answers a series of questions."

Harris smirked. "Ask me the questions."

"Do you understand the nature of the boson field?"

"No."

The hologram replied, "I'm afraid that answer is not satisfactory."

Harris huffed. "Yes then. I meant yes."

The doctor slowly shook his head. "I'm afraid my algorithms are quite adept at identifying a dishonest answer. Perhaps you can return when you have an understanding of the boson field."

Harris rubbed the back of his neck. "I know it's a field that permeates all matter. You and your team of scientists discovered it. The generators in our ships allow a portal to be created between any two points within the boson field."

The image smiled. "That is a satisfactory answer. What is your name?"

"Harris Gruberg. You can call me Harris."

"Very well, Mr. Gruberg."

"I said Harris."

"I am sorry, Mr. Gruberg. We are not yet on a first name basis."

Harris chuckled. "What? You're a program. Am I supposed to be your friend first or something?"

"Are you a friend or foe, Mr. Harris?"

"Well, that's a stupid question. Why would anyone say foe?"

"Replying to a question with a question is not an answer, Mr. Gruberg. Please answer the question. Friend or foe?"

Harris threw up his hands. "Friend."

The hologram frowned. "Your expressions and audible tone indicate otherwise."

Harris sighed as he sat his hands on the table. "I apologize. We aren't taught good manners in the Biomarines."

The doctor returned an inquisitive expression. "Biomarine? I am unfamiliar with that term. Please explain."

"I'm a Biomarine. A genetically engineered Human. I was designed and trained specifically for fighting wars."

"I see. So you are hostile?"

Harris shook his head. "No. I'm a defender of my world, Domicile. I fight only to defend Domicile."

"Understood, Mr. Gruberg. Your answer, tone, demeanor and bodily functions, such as heart rate and eye movements, suggest that you are telling the truth. Honesty is seen as a friendly quality."

"So you'll call me Harris?"

The image frowned. "I'm afraid not, Mr. Gruberg. Friendship comes after a minimum level of trust has been established. Continue with the honest answers and we may reach that level in the future."

Harris huffed. "Are we talking ten minutes or ten days?"

"That would depend on your honesty and demeanor, Mr. Gruberg. Shall we continue?"

Harris slowly nodded. "Sure... why not."

"Have you ever taken a life, Mr. Gruberg?"

Harris sighed. "I'm a warrior. Yes. Many lives. But they were all in the name of defense."

"I see. Have you ever stolen property or currency from anyone?"

Harris took a deep breath and let it out slow. "Yes. Weapons. But they were owed to me."

"I see. And how often would you say you lie? Once or more per day? Per week? Per month?"

Harris laughed. "Definitely per day. I'm an agent working for the DDI. I basically have to lie all the time. But it's for the cause. For the defense of my homeworld, Domicile."

I see. "And is it always in the defense of your world?"

Harris thought for a moment. "Hmm. Guess I can't answer yes to that one."

"Explain."

Harris leaned forward on his elbows as he clasped his hands together. "I used to lie about being in the DDI to get meals or drinks comped at restaurants. I know, it's kind of a dirtball thing to do, but I was desperate."

"Desperate?"

Harris sighed as he looked down at the robotic dog. "OK. I was a dirtball then. You know, Farker's recordings led us to believe your AI skills were limited. This is as tough a line of questioning as I've ever had."

The doctor replied, "If you are referring to the AI in Archibald, yes, it is very limited. The computing power in this facility could not be scaled down to fit within Archibald's frame."

Harris scratched the dog on top of its head. "He's a good pup though. Saved my life. I like him."

The hologram asked, "May we continue with the questioning?"

Harris nodded. "By all means. Shoot."

"How did you come to arrive on this planet?"

"That would be because of Farker. Due to an untimely death of a former colleague, he came into our possession. We don't know how the colleague became acquainted with him, but we believe we found evidence that he was once here."

"Are you referring to Joffard Barlow?"

Harris shook his head. "Don't know who that is. Cletus Dodger was the previous owner of Farker."

The AI smiled. "Cletus was my friend. I had many lengthy discussions with him sitting in that very chair."

Harris looked down with a scowl. "Speaking of this chair, you couldn't put something out here with some padding to it? This thing is like sitting on a rock."

"I will take the upgrade of the chair into consideration, Harris. Thank you."

"You called me Harris. Does that mean we are friends?"

"Tentatively, yes. There are many questions to go however. To maintain this level of trust, you will have to answer them fully and honestly."

Harris sat back in the chair. "Exactly as I would do with any friend."

Tawn came over the comm. "We have a scan of the structure around the door. Looks like an empty room with another door. There's some type of shielding blocking any scans beyond."

Harris replied, "Yeah. You'll have to tell me about it later. I'm in the middle of a conversation with the AI of the good Doctor Alexander Gaerten."

"What? When did that happen?"

Harris shook his head. "I just said I'm in the middle of a conversation. Don't be rude."

The comm was closed and turned off.

"Shall we continue, Doctor?"

"Who was on the other end of your brief conversation?"

"That would be my business partner, Tawn Freely."

"Would you consider her a friend?"

Harris returned a nervous glance. "Well, yeah, why?"

"It seemed to be rude behavior on your part and not hers. Is that how you often treat friends?"

Harris pursed his lips. "No. I mean yes. I guess I do treat her that way quite often. But it's not because I mean to be rude or anything. I'm just trying to be a smartass. She knows that and respects it."

"I see. So you consider being a smartass friendly?"

"Well, no, not necessarily. Depends on if I'm joking around or not. Do you understand what I'm talking about?"

"If you are referring to the concept of humor, yes, I have an understanding."

Harris smiled. "Well, good then. You'll recognize that when I give smartass answers I'm just being friendly."

"I see. I believe your definition of friendship may differ from mine. Shall we continue?"

Harris pointed at the hologram. "My friends know when I'm joking. I'd give my life for any of my friends out there. Heck, I'd give my life defending any of the citizens of Domicile. Now, if that doesn't constitute friendly in your book, then your AI programming is flawed. You're defective. Time you had your plug pulled."

"I see. And would portions of that response be considered humorous?"

Harris rolled his eyes. "Yes."

The AI was silent for several seconds. "Perhaps you should learn to work on your delivery, Harris. With my limited understanding of the concept of humor, it would appear your timing is off."

Harris frowned and then began to chuckle. "Was that an attempt at a smartass answer?"

"It was."

Harris laughed. "Well, this is just a sad day for mankind."

"How so?"

"When a two thousand year old machine is funnier than me, it's a sad day in my book. The recording we watched before, the one from your... creator, it said your AI abilities were limited. You seem like you have it together to me. What limits would he be referring to?"

The image replied, "I am a program, Harris. I can only respond with answers that are based on my programming. I take input, and my logic circuits, guided by what Doctor Gaerten programmed into me, governs my response. My weighing of criteria and reasoning are minimal as compared to a Human mind. My decisions are absolute while yours are based on varying degrees of reason.

"As an example, if asked the time it takes to boil an egg, my response would be approximately fifteen minutes. The egg is placed in a pot in cold water, the water heated to a boil and then removed from the heat and allowed to sit for the remaining time. But what if you desire a soft-boiled egg? What if your cooking mechanism brings the water to a boil in an instant?

"The Human mind uses reason to determine what is best or if it is irrelevant, because any reasonable degree of boiling is considered accurate. Given that answer, I return a single answer. Humans may ask a dozen follow-on questions to better define the need, or they may make assumptions based on their own knowledge and experience. My reasoning, when it comes to decisions as such, is limited to what my programming allows.

"What you may reason and deduce in seconds may take me centuries of evaluations before my reasoning on the subject grows to an equivalent level."

Harris half scowled. "So you aren't the answer man. This war we're about to get into, you don't have suggestions as to how to stop it from happening?"

"I do not have the information needed for a response to that, Harris. What war are you referring to?"

Harris crossed his arms. "Back just after your time, the Humans on New Earth decided they wanted control of all the colonies, including Domicile. They built warships and began to attack and take control of the outer colonies. After the first few attacks the good people of Domicile wised up and built their own fleet. When the third such attack happened, it was at the Jebwa colony. Our fleet confronted the Earthers and the Great War started.

"For whatever reason, both sides decided they wouldn't attack the home planet of the other. So we've been fighting over the outer colonies for almost two thousand years. Every time one side has managed an advantage, the other has somehow overcome that advantage. At the moment we are at a truce.

"The Earthers were running out of titanium to build their ships, so they decided to bring the war to a halt. The Domer politicians were all too happy to accept and stop the fighting. Now the Earthers are attempting to get their hands on a huge supply of titanium that sits on the planet Eden. With it they can rebuild their fleets and restart the war. What I need to know is, how do we stop them?"

The image frowned. "I do not have an answer for you, Harris, the information you supplied is very limited in detail."

"I guess you'd need to tap into the historical archives for the data of that."

"My knowledge is based on the information provided up until the end of Doctor Gaerten's input. And what was gained through conversations with Joffard Barlow and Cletus Dodger."

Harris said, "What if we got you connected to the archives? You would have a complete history of the conflict. At least how it is seen by the Domers. Not sure what we'd do to tap into any data the Earthers have, or if they even have it."

"Are you suggesting I should be given access to historical records?"

"If it would help your decision making with regards to our history, then yeah, that's what I'm suggesting."

The image asked, "By what means can I connect and gather this data?"

Harris thought for several seconds. "Could you open a tiny wormhole to Domicile? To the space surrounding it, I mean? Is that something this facility has the ability to do?"

"Wormholes cannot be opened in the vicinity of large amounts of matter, Harris. What is the purpose for your question?"

Harris stood and began to pace. The holo-image and the light above disappeared. He took his seat again and the hologram flashed into existence.

"Got to stay in the chair, huh?"

"Yes."

"OK, what if I brought another ship that we could park in high orbit. If a microwormhole was opened from there to Domicile, can I assume this facility would be able to communicate through it?"

The image replied, "That would be a valid assumption."

What I'm thinking is this: we open a comm to Domicile, we tap into the archives, which are open to everyone, and you educate yourself on our history. There is a huge amount of data there. Is that something you could copy over the comm? Do you have room for a huge data trove?"

"My resources should be adequate, and they are expandable. A connection to this data could be copied over the comm."

Harris half smiled. "Here's what we'll do: I'll get a ship that we can use. You copy the archives through standard comms. After that, you should have enough info to continue your questions with me... and enough to answer a few of my questions."

Harris stood, fumbling his way in the dark toward the outer door. "Farker, can you give us some light?"

The light for the room switched on. Farker moved to his side. The door going out into the grassy fields opened. Harris Gruberg stepped into the daylight and the bunker door closed behind them.

Tawn, Trish, and Gandy came over from the *Bangor*. "Well?"

"Well... I had a good talk with Alexander Gaerten's AI. It's much smarter than Farker, but limited in what it knows about us. We're heading back to Domicile to pick up a ship. We'll park it in free space here. He'll use it to open a microwormhole back to Domicile for a comm connection. When that's established, the AI is going to copy the historical archive and then evaluate our history going from the time it was created until now."

Tawn asked, "And what does that do for us?"

"It lets us ask it questions about what we might do to prevent this war. Given the resources it has available, and the knowledge it will have, maybe we can get an edge on stopping all this. Basically, we keep doing what we're doing and hope this AI can offer guidance."

Gandy asked, "What was the room like? Did you go any further?"

Harris shook his head. "The room had a single chair and a table. That's as far as I went. When I sat in the chair, a hologram of Alexander Gaerten presented itself. We had a discussion. And here I am."

Tawn frowned. "Well, you're just full of details, aren't you?"

Harris nodded. "I do what I can."

The jump was made and a comm ship acquired and brought back. A connection was opened from the AI to the Historical

Archives interface and the AI was allowed to take over. Copying of the data began almost immediately.

The *Bangor* and her crew returned to Eden.

Chapter 10

The newly-commissioned digger sat on the east end of the five square kilometer titanium mine. A speech was given by Fritz Romero as the first of the civilian equipment operators started up the fusion drive. With a wave of his hand, the giant machine's spinning blade-heads dug into the sand and rock. Dust drifted off into a slight breeze as the chewed-up rubble rose on conveyor belts to the first of the massive hoppers.

Harris smiled. "Up and running. Can't believe how far we've come in such a short time."

Tawn frowned. "I won't be happy until we have this all moved back to Domicile. As long as it's here, even in the ground, we're in danger."

Trish said, "We're saving the free world one scoop at a time."

The colonel walked up to Harris and Tawn as they watched the great machine tear into the earth. "Just had word from our scouts. It seems your friend Rumford broke ground this morning as well. They've been flying equipment in there nonstop for the last few days. Our other digger should be up and running this afternoon."

Harris asked, "What's her operation look like?"

"Her machines aren't as big and probably not as efficient, but she has sixteen operating this morning."

Harris sighed. "Sounds like we might have to perform a raid."

The colonel nodded. "We've been planning."

"Tell me what you have."

"Our goal here is to move refined ore back to Domicile, is it not? So long as it's on this planet it can be taken. So we're gonna take it."

"Take it as in steal it?"

The colonel nodded. "She has security around the mine and the equipment itself. The freighter she has parked waiting to be filled... it's wide open. We catch it just when it reaches full, fly it out, problem solved. The ore goes to Domicile instead of New Earth."

Harris grinned. "I like the sound of that. How long before it's ready to steal?"

"We expect it to be nearing full in three weeks. That number could easily move up or down by a week, depending on the level of refining done here on planet."

Tawn asked, "What about our own refining?"

"Our process takes the ore all the way to the final product," the colonel said. "We expect to have our first run of four titanium plates ready for evaluation by the end of this week. If successful, we should be able to ramp our production up to a hundred forty thousand plates per day. A destroyer-size vessel requires fifty thousand such plates. A cruiser class vessel has the equivalent need of double that."

Harris raised an eyebrow. "That's a lot of ship building we could support."

"The Earthers already have shipyards sitting in wait for titanium. And they have the trained personnel to man them. With a new supply, our intel reasons they could be turning out two cruisers and two destroyers a day within three months. This while our own yards sit almost idle. When the truce was signed we had their fleet outnumbered by almost two to one. They could surpass us within a year. All while our politicians sit on their thumbs in denial."

Tawn said, "Just gives credence to what we're doing out here."

Harris asked, "How are we set for guarding our transports? We don't want them stealing titanium plates that are ready for assembly."

"We have a solid force ready to protect our shipments. Our vulnerability is going from here to a jump point. That's at least forty minutes where we're in need of an escort."

"What we need is more ships with railguns," said Gandy.

Harris half scowled. "We could use them. Only they don't make them anymore."

Gandy replied, "Too bad we can't bring some of the old Banshees online. Only they aren't very good against plasma cannons."

"You think you could actually get a couple of those old hulls flying?"

Gandy's eyes grew big. "I bet I could. But how would we protect them?"

Harris pointed back toward the *Bangor*. "What if we covered them with the same boxes we have on our ship?"

Trish stepped forward. "That hull you were looking at is missing the drive."

"Some of the others I've seen aren't. And those hulls were built in the railgun age. If we can shield the electronics they might just be effective weapons. On the Banshees it has essentially the same gun as we have on the *Bangor*."

Harris looked at the others. "We have the freighter leaving in a half hour for a supply pick-up. Who wants to go take a look at a Banshee?"

Tawn turned to an almost giddy Gandy. "You really think you can get one of those flying?"

"I think we can," said Trish. "We'll need to rent space where we can work on it. Actually, if we could get it out to Midelon, our little shop there might be all we need."

Harris shook his head. "We'll rent something on Domicile. You'll want to be there for parts anyway."

The colonel said, "Looks like you have an agenda. You get a few of those up and running and I can staff them with pilots."

"What?" Gandy blurted out. "No! I want to fly one!"

Harris pointed over his shoulder with his thumb. "You already have a ship to fly."

Gandy crossed his arms. "I don't want to sound like a whiner, but she's the one always at the controls."

Tawn nodded. "Might be time we look for something for Gandy and me."

Harris rubbed the back of his neck. "OK. Have a look around when we get back. We have the funds to refurb just about anything. Pick whatever you want."

A jump to Domicile was followed by a visit to the Magnessen boneyard. A fair price was negotiated for the Banshee and two of the three Zwicker hulls. A warehouse was leased and a complete suite of mechanics' tools and shop machines purchased. Two days later the Banshee was ferried to the warehouse and moved inside.

Gandy hopped up onto the port wing. "This is awesome."

Trish looked over the exterior. "We need to replace a lot of this plating on the outside. You said the nav system was gone? What else do we need besides that and the drive?"

Gandy popped the latch on the canopy. Using a manual crank, it was raised up to vertical.

"I'd say the entire cockpit is a rebuild."

Harris asked, "You sure we can fix it?"

Trish cut in. "We can do it. Can you spare us for a couple weeks? We'll need that to get a full assessment of what we're looking at."

Tawn said, "Any of the mechanics school students you know need work? You can't talk of its purpose, or that you plan to enable the gun, but you could say you're looking at restoring it for a wealthy aficionado. That would be me."

Trish grinned. "I know three who are currently working retail to get by. They would jump at the chance for a part-time job working on this."

Harris said, "We should ask Mr. Morgan if he can spare a few mechanics. He'll be building those freighters."

Gandy nodded. "I have a couple friends I can ask."

"Bring in whoever you like," Harris said. "Just keep those two items under wraps. They can't know who or what this is for and they can't know you plan on bringing up the railgun. Are we clear?"

Trish smiled. "Clear. Now who here is hungry?"

Harris pulled his head back. "Well, me."

Tawn added, "I guess I could go for some grub too."

Trish pointed at the door. "Good then. Why don't the two of you go feed yourselves while we get started on this."

Tawn laughed as she turned to face Harris. "Your first mate is crafty. You see how easily she got rid of us?"

Harris shook his head as he looked toward the exit. "These regular Humans just don't know what good eating is. Look at them. They're skinny. They look malnourished."

Tawn looked down at her belly. "I could use a bit of undernourishment myself."

Harris stopped. "You aren't going?"

Tawn pushed him forward. "Never said that."

Harris pulled his phony badge. "Want to see if we can get it comped?"

Tawn chuckled. "Only if you plan on putting down any deposits."

A feast was had, followed by a visit to see Bannis Morgan. His immediate comms saw four mechanics at the warehouse within two hours of the visit. The disassembly of the Banshee had already begun. Trish and Gandy were meticulous, recording and logging every nut, bolt, and item they removed from the ancient fighter.

Harris sat on a crate next to Tawn. "Look at those two. I'd definitely say this was their calling."

Tawn replied, "Trish said the number of people joining in is about to double. She has five friends and Gandy three. She said they all sounded eager to come by."

Harris looked around the otherwise empty warehouse. "What say you and I go out and find a caterer. We can have a couple tables set up over there with food and beverages for the teams if they get hungry. Which they will."

Tawn stood, placing her right fist on her hip as she pointed towards a corner of the warehouse where a set of bathrooms was located. "They might also be able to make use of a few cots... and maybe a portable shower. Other than buying parts or tools, I don't see either one wanting to leave this warehouse until they have this job done."

In the two days that followed, several trips were made to the local home improvement store. A contractor was contacted and a design request submitted. A handful of extra credits saw to it the job would be expedited.

A caterer was next selected and given the task of providing three meals a day along with a table of readily available snacks and beverages. The pair of Biomarines returned to a warehouse bustling with activity.

Gandy gave direction to a forklift operator as he moved in the hull of a third Banshee. As far as Gandy knew, there was only one other hull remaining on all of Domicile. It was slated for delivery the following day. The first hull had been almost completely stripped.

Harris stood beside Trish. "How's it looking so far?"

None of the hulls have a salvageable drive in them. Electronics are all shot or missing pieces. But this hull and the third one over there are solid. This one has lots of surface marks. I would presume from a fight. The integrity of it looks good though.

"What are you gonna do about a drive?"

Trish pointed at one of Bannis Morgan's mechanics. "Hollis Germ says he thinks he knows of a commercial engine that might fit in that space. It offers more power than the original, but it's not hardened for a war environment. His counterpart, Victoria, she's looking into the nav systems and other electronics. We already found a fusion reactor that will fit nicely where the old unit was."

"Any big holdups?"

Trish glanced back at Hollis. "Only if that drive won't fit. Otherwise we have to modify the hull, and from their estimates that could take three months on its own. They don't make the welders that can handle that thickness of armor anymore."

"What about the plasma inhibitor boxes to go on the outer hull?"

"Mr. Morgan is supposedly sending over two dozen units tomorrow. He says they aren't exactly the same as the military units, but he thinks they can tweak them to get equal, or possibly even better performance. Wouldn't that be cool to just be able to fly right up to one of those warships and blast it?"

Harris chuckled. "Yeah, that would be cool."

Bannis Morgan shuffled through the main door. "Mr. Gruberg, a word with you please."

Harris walked over. "Anything you need?"

Bannis looked over the empty hull. "Yep. I wanted to talk to you about making use of one of those Zwicker hulls you purchased."

"For what purpose?"

Bannis looked around. "Any place we can sit? My sciatica is acting up today."

Harris gestured to their left. "We have crates."

Bannis nodded. "That will do."

The elder industrialist slowly eased himself up onto one of the wooden boxes. "I'd like to take one of those Zwicker hulls, deconstruct it, and add in about 75 percent more room. Put in a modern drive and wormhole generator, and turn it into a raider that can be flown right up to a ship's hull."

Harris laughed. "You planning on storming a ship?"

Bannis shook his head. "I won't be, no. But we may have need of it. I heard about your plan to steal the cargo hauler from Rumford Mine. What if your efforts fail? Taking that ship up in space might be a better option. And what if we decide we want a look at an Earther ship? With a raider and a few dozen of your Biomarines we could take down a destroyer. Would love to know how they are built and what electronics or armaments they have on them.

"During the war, there was an unwritten agreement that neither side would take control of the others ships, nor would we snoop when those ships were destroyed or disabled. Each side was allowed to go in after and collect their dead and their debris. Another of the strange arrangements of that war."

Harris glanced around at the activity in the warehouse. "A raider, huh? I'll have to talk that one over with the colonel, since it would have to be staffed with his people."

Bannis patted Harris on the shoulder. "No need, this was the colonel's idea to begin with. He thought it might be of use should the need of taking a ship arise."

Harris replied, "Then I guess I don't have a problem with it."

"Back on Eden, has the climate-hardened equipment performed as desired?"

"The operators are reporting warmer than normal cabin temperatures. Nothing unlivable, and something we can fix on our own. The equipment itself has done exactly as it was designed to do."

Bannis nodded. "There are always efficiencies to be had. Those will come over time."

Bannis Morgan shifted uncomfortably on his box. "I've been told the Earther colonies are still growing on the other truce worlds. Are there any plans underway to counter those expansions?"

Harris shook his head. "Eden is soaking up most of our time. Once we deliver our first load of titanium plates to Domicile, I'll try to change focus to our own populations there. I've been talking to Fritz about building domes on those planets. If we want settlers to move out there, we need to provide a safe and inviting opportunity."

Bannis returned an unconvinced scowl. "Domes are expensive. While fantastic for a long-term colony solution, we don't have the funds to build them. Any payback from taxes and such would take a century of business from a vibrant settlement. Our pockets are deep, but not on that scale."

"We're building domes here. How is that different?"

"We moved a dome, we're building a second. Unless titanium is sold in quantity we may not be building beyond Fireburg. The members of my consortium are patriots, but they are also capitalists. For them to be willing to commit their time and effort to this project they require that at worst it breaks even. At the moment, I'm peddling patience with the lot of them."

Harris crossed his arms. "Too bad we can't get the military to commit to upgrading the fleet. Titanium would quickly be a sought-after commodity."

Bannis frowned. "There have been three attempts to bring a modernization bill before the Senate. Each time it hasn't made it out for a vote. The pacifists on the defense procurement committee want to see our military budgets cut by half, not expanded. At the moment they outnumber the others seven to four. Did you know we have fewer members of the armed services today than at any time in the last twelve hundred years?"

Harris chuckled. "Don't have to tell me that. I'm one of them."

Tawn sat beside the two men. "Talking about our military?"

Harris nodded. "He was saying the pacies in Congress have managed three times already to stall any attempts to update our fleets. And they want to cut our current budgets in half."

"They do and we won't be able to protect anyone. The Earthers would roll right over the truce colonies. The outer colonies and Domicile would be next. Very short sighted if they think the Earthers are just going to be all fuzzy, friendly, and happy. We might as well be that colony at Dove."

Gandy hustled over to the others. "We found a drive and wormhole generator that will fit in the Banshee. It's a design from a new company though, and they have yet to complete the prototype. The preliminary specs say it will be about 30 percent more powerful than the original. And it has the reactor built into it. We've arranged a meeting to visit with them tomorrow."

Bannis said, "Would you mind if I came along? Would give me a chance to look at this from an investment perspective."

Gandy nodded. "Would love to have you go. I've read where some of these start-ups are scams. Could use your judgment as to whether or not we're wasting our time."

Bannis smiled. "I'd be happy to offer my assistance. I've evaluated hundreds of small companies over the years. The rotten ones are usually easy to sniff out, if you know what to look for."

Trish walked up. "You told them the news, didn't you? I wanted to make it a surprise."

Gandy said, "Mr. Morgan has volunteered to go with us. He can tell us if it's worthwhile or not."

"I hope it's good. It's the only one we've found that will fit in that hull."

Harris' comm chimed. "This is Gruberg."

"Major Divos, sir. From the *Warlift*. I'm coming from shuttling a dozen new recruits out to Eden. The colonel says there's been a new development. A dozen large ships just landed at the Rumford Mine."

"Any other details from the colonel, Major?"

"Sorry, sir. You'll have to get any details from him. I'm heading back to the Retreat."

Harris looked over at Tawn. "You want to come or you staying here?"

Tawn laughed as she pointed at Trish and Gandy. "Depends if you're looking for a partner or a first mate. I assume these two will be staying?"

Harris replied, "They have too much to get done. Don't think we could tear them away from here anyway."

Chapter 11

The *Bangor* set down under the covered docking bay of the main dome at Fireburg. Tawn and Harris made their way to the colonel's office. The colonel was busy ripping through a list of contact messages on a tablet.

Harris asked, "What do you have for us, Colonel?"

"The Earthers just moved in a workforce of a couple thousand people. They're unloading materials and equipment. They're about to build a pipeline, and plan on following that with their own city."

Harris tilted his head. "I didn't think they had the water to expand that much."

The colonel flipped on a device, projecting a map onto a nearby wall. "The big blue dot is the colony. The green is their current well. It's low volume, probably a few hundred liters per hour. The red dot is a well they just completed yesterday. It's approximately the size of ours. The material on those ships is for building a pipeline. They'll be pumping the water thirty-eight kilometers."

Harris rubbed the back of his neck. "So what you're saying is if we can support twenty-five thousand workers here, they can do the same there?"

The colonel nodded. "Exactly. I'd say they will be trying to beat us at our own game. If they get twenty-five thousand settlers on planet before we do, they could take over the government here, or block us from our goal of taking it over."

"So long as the pacies stay in control, I don't see that as a problem."

Robert Thomas shook his head. "Not true. The pacies have the ability to impose taxes. In fact, one of my sources tells me they are drafting up a plan to do that exact thing. A customs fee for any export would be charged. Also in that proposal is a water tax and an environmental impact tax. Looks like they are finally wising up to what being in control means."

"Even if they do that, can't we just pay the tax and keep moving?"

The colonel winced. "What happens if those taxes and fees are exorbitant? We're already beginning to struggle with our finances. They could make titanium so expensive we can't afford to pull it out of the ground."

"Wouldn't that be the same for the Earthers?"

The colonel replied, "They have deep pockets over there, Mr. Gruberg. Our government is not eager to build new ships. As has been said before, we're now on a tight budget. Unless we stick to that, the consortium of industrialists Mr. Morgan has pulled together will collapse. These proposed taxes and fees would certainly push us in that direction."

"So what do we do about the Earthers?"

The colonel pointed at the map. "Sabotage. We need to slow their expansion. We keep that big well from delivering water until we have enough settlers here to throw control of this planet our way. That's four months from now, minimum. Problem is, if we hit them they will retaliate. Might be time we tried to harden this dome."

"How would we do that?"

The colonel changed the image displayed on his wall. "We'll be cranking out titanium plates in volume. One of my men came up with this idea. Instead of storing the plates inside for delivery later, or shipping them back to Domicile, we instead use them to cover the dome's exterior. Those plates are thick and will easily absorb a plasma round from a hand weapon."

"Would it do us any good to throw a few of the ion transducers we use on ship shielding on there?"

The colonel shook his head. "You're asking the wrong person. That might be a question Mr. Morgan could answer for us."

Tawn said, "Seems like we just can't escape the conflict. This war is still being fought."

The colonel leaned back in his chair. "We have three thousand people here at Fireburg. When that second dome is complete, that number will have doubled. That's three thousand more we need to protect and defend. Given the size of the workforce over at the Rumford Mine, we probably have two to three weeks before that water begins to flow. That gives us two to three weeks to fortify this place."

Tawn asked, "When are we expecting the first titanium plates to come out of manufacturing?"

"Today. And our next freight shipment from Domicile will have dozens of welders capable of tacking those plates together. Two spot tacks on each side should hold them in place. We can overlap to get full coverage. Should make for easy tear-down once we're ready to put them to use elsewhere."

Tawn rubbed her chin. "Have you thought any about placing watchtowers around our perimeter?"

"Too much effort to build and maintain. Mr. Morgan has a dozen aerial drones coming our way. If we keep four in the air at all times we can lock this sector down. We would know of any assault force coming our way well ahead of their arrival."

An aide came into the colonel's office. "Sir, you wanted to be informed when the first plate was coming off the production line. That will be happening in the next few minutes."

The colonel stood. "Thank you, Lieutenant."

Robert Thomas gestured toward the door. "Let's go watch. The troops need to see that we're interested."

"Speaking of plates," said Harris. "Anyone had lunch yet?"

Tawn shook her head. "You just don't stop, do you?"

Harris smiled as he walked into the hall, glancing back down at Farker. "Big dog has to eat. Right, boy?"

The robotic dog farked three times.

Harris grinned. "See. He agrees."

Tawn and Harris followed the colonel into the titanium plate production facility. "At the far end, we have the refined ore from the digger machines coming in. That first vat turns the ore into titanium tetrachloride. In the next vat it reacts with magnesium to strip away the chlorine, leaving the pure titanium metal. From there it's formed into ingots, which are rolled into sheets.

"Forty-two of those sheets are bonded together to make a plate that's approximately two meters square. When the bonding is complete, the finished plate should pop out over here. We would normally be stacking twenty to a pallet for storage, but we'll be taking these straight out to the dome.

"When fully up and running we should see as many as ten plates a minute coming off this line. Four lines will be operating at once. Each of the other domes here at Fireburg will be running their own."

Tawn asked, "How many plates to cover the dome?"

"I've been told that number is just under a million. We have two kilometers in diameter by three hundred meters height in the center. Will take three weeks to manufacture those at full output. For comparison, construction of a destroyer requires about fifty thousand of these plates."

Harris studied the operation. "How long before we're at full rate production?"

The colonel smiled. "If we have everything set up right, today. If the output from this line is deemed satisfactory, the other three will begin their own processing."

"We must have quite the stockpile of chlorine and magnesium for those vats. Is that mined here?"

The colonel shook his head. "We've identified the necessary resources. Gathering those from here is still months away. In the meantime we've been ferrying those two materials in from Domicile on a regular basis for the last month. That's been what most of your escort duty was covering. We have enough of that material at the moment to keep these four lines running for about six weeks. We'll continue to ferry it in during that time of course."

The first of the thick, heavy plates rolled off the line and was placed onto the first available pallet. Two minutes later, the full pallet was pulled to the side for a series of short tests. A thumbs-up was given as a result.

The colonel placed his massive hand on Harris' shoulder. "You mentioned lunch? Looks like this might be a good time for it. About two hours from now we should see a pallet coming off those lines every thirty seconds on average."

Harris nodded. "An impressive feat, Colonel. You should all be commended for making this happen."

"You two are the ones who should be commended. You brought this all about, not us."

Harris chuckled. "Might have been our idea, but it's your hard work out here that made it happen."

Tawn said, "You two done fluffing each other's skirts?"

Harris laughed. "You hungry now?"

"I was fine until you mentioned it."

The colonel nodded toward the cafeteria. "Let's go get this over with. I have defenses to plan for."

***

For the three weeks that followed, the *Bangor* ran escort duty for a near continuous stream of freighters ferrying in workers and materials. The second dome was receiving its crown and the first was nearing completion of its titanium outer skin.

The colonel came over the comm. "The Rumford well will be producing come this time tomorrow."

Harris asked, "You have an invasion planned? You mentioned sabotage before. We ready if they hit back?"

The colonel nodded. "As ready as we can be. Hopefully, it won't come to that. We found a way to shut their well down without firing a single plasma round."

Tawn asked, "How are you managing that?"

"We've been busy using our brains. Their well is located in a shallow valley that runs directly toward their mine. We found a spot about a kilometer from the wellhead. We constructed a building—roughly a hundred square meters—and camouflaged it. It's a mini-dome of sorts. We powered it, cooled it, and dug a side well, running at an angle. It intercepts their well at about a kilometer and half depth. We tapped into it yesterday."

Tawn returned a confused look. "You planning to divert the water, or foul it?"

"We're plugging it. We tapped into two spots ten meters apart. Two rubber bladders were inserted and blown up. We then pumped in a limestone cement that matches the substrate of that depth. Plug should be hardened enough to withdraw the bladders in about two hours. When they open that well into their pipe, they'll get a trickle at best."

Harris nodded. "Genius. How long before they have it cleared?"

"Minimum of a day. And it only takes us three hours to plug it again if needed. Best part is our side well offers a bypass. We can bring their production up and down whenever we want. They disassemble the wellhead, insert the laser drill, shove it down the pipe, and just before it reaches our plug we divert full flow through our tap. We can push that laser drill all the way back to the surface."

Tawn asked, "What if they drill another well altogether?"

"We drill a matching well. We need to be within six kilometers of their well to tap in. Unless they place a wellhead out in the middle of flat plain, we should be able to dig our own counter-well. The terrain all around the Rumford claim is uneven. With our wellhead hidden, I think we can keep this game running for some time."

Harris grinned. "That just makes my day, Colonel. Who's our genius that came up with that one?"

"Fritz Romero. He said they used that technique to plug the well at the Jebwa colony so the Earthers couldn't make use of it. It apparently worked, as none of them came back to settle there after the raid. I can only guess they didn't have well drilling equipment of their own."

Tawn cut in: "How long before the next freighter will be coming in?"

"Six hours," replied the colonel.

Tawn looked to Harris. "Sounds like a chance to go check on our first mates."

Harris spoke into the comm. "Colonel, we'll be back before the next freighter comes through. Will check back in then to see how all this is going."

"It's well under control, Mr. Gruberg. Take your time."

***

Harris followed Tawn into the warehouse.

A giddy Gandy rushed over to meet them. "The drive is going in now. I can't believe they got it to us so quick. Mr. Morgan and his group bought their company."

"You saying this could fly soon?" said Tawn.

Gandy nodded. "Real soon. We have the other systems in. It's now just a question of whether or not they all play nice together. The checks we've done so far say they should."

Trish walked up, her arms covered in grease from her hands up to her shoulders. "It's in. They're welding it in place."

Smoke billowed from the back of the fighter as the welding team began its work."

Harris winced. "It supposed to be doing that?"

"Just burning off some of the grease we had to use to force it in there. Won't hurt anything. Whatever is left will burn off and blow out of there as carbon once that drive is in use."

"All the connections made?" asked Gandy.

"They are."

Gandy turned back toward the fighter. "My turn."

Harris began to follow.

Gandy glanced over his shoulder as he walked.

"You need something?"

Harris said, "If it's up and running, I'd be happy to pilot it for you."

Gandy stopped. "You wouldn't dare. Flying one of these has been a lifelong dream. You'd take that away from me?"

Harris laughed. "Wasn't trying to steal your thunder."

"Then don't."

The Biomarine turned back, joining Trish and Tawn at the usual sitting spot on a set of empty crates. "Your brother's getting vicious."

"He's waited his whole life for this."

Harris chuckled. "Whole life? What's that? A couple years?"

"You know what I mean. The Banshee is his dream. Let him enjoy this moment."

Harris raised his hands. "Fine. What are you people so touchy about?"

Trish huffed and stomped off toward the refurbished fighter.

Tawn sighed. "You wanted to fly it, didn't you?"

Harris replied, "I did. It is a cool looking craft."

Tawn smirked. "What are you, like fifteen or something?"

"Didn't you know? Men don't mentally age beyond that point. I thought all you ladies had that in your handbook."

"We do. Was just checking."

Gandy held up a thumb from the cockpit. "Power is on! Systems are reporting in!"

Trish stood on a wing, looking over the console readouts. "It says all green. That can't be right. That was too fast."

"Mr. Morgan did get us the newest model computer system. All the components do a self check and report back the instant power is applied. Now get off the wing. I'm taking her out."

Trish scowled. "That's not safe. We don't even know if this drive works yet. It's the prototype."

Gandy flipped several switches and twisted a knob. The Banshee lifted off the ground, hovering a meter in the air.

Trish said, "You aren't seriously taking this out, are you?"

Gandy pointed toward the floor. "I suggest you hop down. Unless you plan on wing-surfing while I fly."

Trish let out a long breath. "Just be careful, OK? You don't know how she handles yet. I don't want to be having to put up a marker where you came down and dug a pit in the ground with some dumb maneuver."

Gandy grinned. "I promise to be cautious. Don't want to be the first person to die in a Banshee since they were last used."

Trish hopped to the ground. The cockpit quickly closed and sealed.

Gandy pulled on a flight helmet and opened a comm. "Shoot. I can't believe I forgot to come up with a name for her. How can I take her out if she doesn't have a name?"

Trish laughed. "Just call it whatever you want. We can change it later when we register it."

Gandy asked, "Miss Freely, what's a good name for a Banshee?"

"Please don't call it the Boleman," said Harris. "Give it something with class or meaning."

Gandy scowled. "Well, that leaves out the Gruberg too, doesn't it."

Tawn said, "You've wanted to fly one your whole life. How does it make you feel to be sitting there?"

"Like I want to pee my pants I'm so excited, but I'm not using that."

Tawn crossed her arms. "OK, how about something along the lines of 'defiance' or 'boldness' or 'rage.' Feeling any of those?"

Gandy thought for a moment. "*Rage*. I like that. Good name for a Banshee. We'll go with *Rage*."

The warehouse doors were pulled open. The *Rage* began to move slowly forward.

After taking ten seconds to move ten meters, Trish said, "When I said be careful I didn't mean that careful. Come on or we'll all be old before you get out the door."

Gandy replied, "Roger that, ground control. This is the *Rage.* We will be going skyward momentarily."

"Confirmed, *Rage,*" said Trish. "Now get a move on. My hair's turning gray out here."

With a hard rush of air, the *Rage* rocketed out of the warehouse before turning skyward. Trish was nearly blown to the floor.

Gandy came back as he flipped the ancient fighter over, leveling off. "Woo hoo! That was awesome."

"The afterwash almost blew me over," said Trish.

Gandy flipped the control-stick, sending the craft through a series of barrel rolls before making a hard arc back toward the warehouse. "She handles like a dream! Smooth and quiet! I so want to fire this railgun right now."

Harris hopped off his crate. "Not a good idea. We can do testing of that once we're far away from here. Why don't you take her up to space for a minute and then bring her back. I'm sure Morgan's people would like to check over the performance data in the morning."

"Roger that on the space test. Heading up now."

The *Rage* turned hard upward. The gentle blue sky of Domicile quickly turned to the ultra-blackness of space. After several random maneuvers, the Banshee turned for home.

Trish, Tawn, and Harris moved to the door. They watched intently as a small fireball grew to ten meters across. It then extinguished as the fighter slowed before pulling to a perfect stop at a meter off the ground. The smoldering Banshee taxied up. The cockpit canopy opened. Gandy grinned.

Chapter 12

The next few hours saw Harris, Trish, and Tawn taking the *Rage* out for a ride. Each returned with a smile on their face.

Harris said, "Hard to believe you just put that together and it flies like that first time out."

Trish nodded. "Mr. Morgan's mechanics are top notch. And our friends were an unstoppable force. Too bad they'll never know the railgun works. They would absolutely love to see it fire."

Tawn said, "You kept that separate from Morgan's people too, right?"

"I did, as I was told over and over to do. The others don't have a clue. The autofeeder snaps into place. I only dropped it in after they left. I'll pull it before they come in tomorrow."

"It won't be here for them tomorrow," Harris said. "We're pushing it into service today. The *Rage* will be taking over escort duty, leaving us free for whatever else is needed. Have you looked over the second Banshee yet?"

Gandy replied, "Needs just as much work, but nothing we can't do. How cool will it be to have our own little fleet of these flying?"

Harris nodded. "Very cool.

"The colonel is about to make a move against Baxter's mine," said Tawn. "Once that happens, we may be wishing we had a thousand of these."

Gandy looked over the rough hull of the next ship. "We can make more. The Banshee hulls were produced by a hugely expensive welding machine that no longer exists. But Mr. Morgan thinks we may be able to carve a hull out of a solid piece of titanium. If that can be done, we can build your thousand."

Harris shook his head. "For now we'll have to limit our numbers. The Banshee was a warship. It looks like a warship. If people see it they will call it a warship."

Tawn said, "We aren't fighting a war here. At least not an official one. For now let's just keep our focus on getting the hulls we have flying. If we need a thousand later, we'll worry about building them then."

Trish and Gandy got to work on the second hull.

Harris pointed at the *Rage*. "You want to try out the wormhole generator or should I?"

"Where we going?"

"We need to get back to Eden before the freighter comes through. And I'd like to turn this ship over to the colonel to staff. The sooner it's flying, the sooner we're free."

Tawn frowned.

Harris asked, "What's wrong?"

"I just hate the thought of turning this over so soon after we got it. And I know that thought will bother Trish and Gandy as well. It's their sweat and tears in that thing."

Harris nodded. "And they can take solace in the fact that it will be put to good use and well cared for. Which one you want to fly?"

Tawn took a step toward the *Rage*. "The new one, of course."

The *Bangor* lifted from the warehouse district with the *Rage* following close behind. Once in free space, Tawn attempted to use the refurbished Banshee to open a wormhole to Eden.

"Hey, this generator isn't working."

Harris frowned. "Just follow me through then. I want to get it on-station for escort duty. Whoever's flying it won't need a portal anyway. Only has to cover from the incoming jump to the ground. When the next one comes out, we can send this one back to be fixed."

Tawn followed Harris through, staying in orbit as a freighter was due from Domicile. Harris, in the *Bangor*, returned to the dome.

A short walk had him standing in the colonel's office with Farker at his heel.

The colonel chuckled. "That dog go everywhere with you?"

Harris nodded. "He's a lifesaver. What's the latest on the Rumford situation?"

"The well has been repeatedly opened and shut. The outward appearance is the Earthers are confused as to what's happening. We even staged a phony assault on the pipeline just to make them think we think it's fully operational. They have to fly water in from the well at Boxton."

Harris sat forward. "What's the chance we can do the same side-drill on the Boxton well? And for that matter, at Dove? Without water the people at both would have to leave. Could allow us to take over the government with just the people we have here."

The colonel leaned back in his chair. "Interesting thought. I hadn't considered the Dove angle. Boxton is off limits. There aren't any valleys or crevasses nearby where we could start our own wellhead."

"How close did you say you have to be to drill?"

"Six kilometers. Seven at most."

"What's the closest point to Boxton?"

The colonel thought. "Mmm. Maybe twelve kilometers."

"Can we dig tunnels?"

"For what purpose?"

Harris sat forward. "We start at the twelve kilometer location with a long tunnel. When we get it close enough, we make a big underground chamber and start your well drilling."

The colonel slowly scratched the side of his face. "Digging a tunnel that length would take us months. And we'd have nowhere to put the tailings. Managing the tailings coming from a wellhead are troublesome enough. From a tunnel... not going to happen. But keep going. You're on fire this morning."

The colonel rocked back and forth in his chair. "This Dove thing... that could work to our favor in multiple ways. If we manage to control their well, they would either leave, or worst case we provide them with water. Might alleviate some of the pressure they are feeling to impose taxes. Not pressure... more like desire."

Harris said, "Should their water run dry we would of course offer free resettlement back to Domicile... no... wait. What if we re-enable Fritz Romero's colony on Jebwa and offer to move them all there? They'd have farms sitting at the ready, and a climate that is far more friendly than living in this oven we have here.

"With a little work that colony could easily hold all twenty thousand of them. And they'd have room to grow. And with no government there to speak of now, they could again form their own. From what I understand, the Earthers who attacked have all gone."

The colonel looked around Harris on either side. "Who pulled the Gruberg I know and replaced him with you? That is a brilliant plan. Let's call in Mr. Romero and get his opinion as to Jebwa's readiness."

The colonel opened a comm. "Lieutenant, see if Mr. Romero is available. If so, have him come immediately to my office."

Harris crossed his arms. "While we wait, let me fill you in on the Banshee. It flies and performs like a dream—has an issue with the wormhole generator not working at the moment, but is otherwise in good shape. We still need to do some real-world testing, such as firing the railgun. And I'd like to send a low power plasma round or two it's way to see how it handles them."

"Has analysis been done as to how tough she'll be in battle?"

Harris nodded. "Designs say she should be as rugged, if not more-so, than the *Bangor*. She has a single railgun that's equal in power. Her plasma protection should be slightly better. She could use an upgrade to military level sensors, though."

"And she's here now?"

"Tawn wants to fly it for a short bit. After that we turn it over to you for use as a freighter escort. We have two more of those hulls in the works. How's the dome plating coming?"

The colonel smiled. "Finishing up today. That freighter coming in should have a thousand of those shield boxes on it. We get those powered up and running on the dome and we won't have to worry about any ground-based weapon bothering her. Our engineers say another five thousand units and we can take an assault by an Earther warship. I've placed the order. We'll have to see if budgets allow it."

Harris sighed. "I never imagined we'd be building something like this. We had an impressive war-chest to begin with, but things have spiraled out of control. And Mr. Morgan is getting pushback from his friends as well. Our next load of titanium plates will have to be shipped back to Domicile and sold.

"Which brings up a question: With the freighter we have, how many shipments will it take to build a warship?"

The colonel rocked his head slowly back and forth as he worked for an answer. "Mmm, I'd say one for a destroyer and two for a cruiser."

"What about the smaller gunboats that attacked the freighter last time?"

"Maybe a half dozen or so. Why?"

Harris shrugged. "Just curious."

Fritz Romero came into the room. The colonel gestured toward an empty chair and Fritz took a seat.

"You wanted to see me?"

The colonel nodded. "We did. What would it take to get the Jebwa colony in order for a group of twenty thousand settlers?"

Fritz replied, "She was designed for twenty-five. I'd say we could have that up and running in a month—if you can give me the workers."

"How many do you need?" the colonel asked.

Fritz rubbed his chin. "Five hundred to a thousand maybe? Mostly for checking out systems and cleaning it up. It's been empty for six months now. That also relies on the Earthers not having come back and trashed the place since we closed the well."

The colonel sat forward, placing his hands on his desk. "Come up with your list of five hundred, Mr. Romero. We'll want to get started on this immediately."

"Who are you planning to move out there?"

The colonel shook his head. "Would rather not say at this time."

Fritz returned a sly smile. "Only one colony group I know of that numbers twenty thousand, Colonel. My guess is you are planning to convince them they need to move. And Jebwa might be an ideal colony for them. No real strategic value to anyone, decent climate, and only a handful of green valleys to settle in. The pacifists might be much happier there."

The colonel let out a deep breath. "Let's hope so, Mr. Romero. And not a word of this to anyone. If the Earthers find out, they will make every attempt to scuttle our plans."

Fritz stood. "I'll get moving on this straight away."

A comm came in from Tawn. "I'm on my way in with the freighter. And I took the liberty of firing the railgun. Didn't have a real target so I took aim at Eden's sun. First two rounds went out smoothly. On burst mode it got all jammed up after a half dozen rounds went through. Trish has some work to do on this autofeeder."

"Did you try to un-jam it?" asked Harris.

Tawn nodded. "I did. And it worked for a couple rounds before doing the same thing. Maybe the feed alignment is off slightly or something. She'll have to figure that out."

"You have confidence in the manual feed?"

Tawn half frowned. "It seems to have worked OK, but my testing was minimal, so I don't know that I would rely on it."

The colonel cut in: "Bring her in. I'll have one of my pilots take it out to escort the freighter as it leaves. They can follow the freighter through to Domicile for Miss Boleman to check out."

Harris said, "We're in the colonel's office when you get here."

Tawn nodded as she reached to cut off the comm. "Be there in five."

Harris moved over a chair as Tawn came in the door. She said, "Expect a comm from the pilot you had waiting."

After several seconds of thought, the colonel stood. "I didn't have anyone waiting."

Tawn sprinted toward the door, yelling, "Someone just stole it!"

Harris and the colonel were fast behind her. A hard run had them standing in the docking bay looking out into the brightness of the Eden day and the intense heat of the desert.

Tawn growled. "Crap. Can't believe that just happened."

Harris grabbed her shoulder. "Come on, you can be my gunner. They can't jump, so they aren't going anywhere. Let's hope that railgun stays jammed."

Tawn hurried after Harris, hopping up into a waiting *Bangor*. Farker leaped in behind them, skidding to a stop on the deck. Harris slammed himself down in the pilot seat, cinching up his lap belt. Tawn did the same.

"I cleared the jam when I landed. Still set to auto, so maybe it will jam right up again."

Harris powered up the systems. The *Bangor* lifted from the ground, slipping out into the daylight from the overhang before rocketing skyward.

"We have better sensors. And I have more practice flying. Use the nav system to assist with targeting."

Tawn scowled. "I *know* how to use a weapon. You just get me close enough to have a decent shot and I'll take him out. Little rat was all pleasant and chummy when he came up to me as the cockpit opened. I can't believe I just gave it over to him."

Harris shrugged. "You couldn't have known. You just talked to us a couple minutes before. For all you knew the colonel did send him out."

Tawn said, "I have a contact on the nav display. Glad we can match him for speed."

"I never understood why all drives in space top out at the same maximum velocity. Anyone ever explain that to you?"

Tawn shook her head. "No. And can't say I ever cared. It is what it is. Advantage is had by how quickly you can get there. In that, the Banshee has us beat. We should look at updating this ship if we have the chance."

Harris sighed. "Nothing else fits in the drive bay. We'd have to split her hull and reconfigure half her systems. Not worth the effort."

Tawn said, "He's turning back toward us. I'm guessing he just figured out he can't jump."

"Just get that gun ready. First shooter might be the winner in this race."

"I'm ready. Thirty four seconds to firing range. It's been an honor riding with you, Harris. You're like the brother I never had."

Harris chuckled. "Please don't start with the defeatist talk. We're gonna win this little battle. Guy probably doesn't know his port from his starboard."

Tawn gave a sarcastic look. "And right now that matters, why?"

Harris jerked hard port as a half dozen tungsten rounds zipped past their location. "You can fire any time you like now."

Tawn replied, "Five seconds... burst away. Going with a spiral pattern."

Harris turned hard starboard. "He just went past us... heading toward the planet."

Tawn glanced toward her friend and pilot. "You might want to catch him. If he makes it to that dome with that same burst, there won't be anyone left alive inside."

"I'm aware of that fact. Remind me to have Trish and Gandy add a lockout system to any new ships."

Harris opened a general comm. "Listen. I know you can hear me. Give us the ship back and we'll let you walk."

A voice came back with a laugh. "Yeah, when has that ever happened? You people have been meddling in our business out here long enough. I'm either gonna expose you for having a gunship or I'm gonna die taking out your little illegal city down there. Whichever happens is a win for me."

Harris huffed. "Or you're gonna die a horrible death and no one will see it, hear it, or care."

The Banshee performed a hundred-eighty degree spin, firing its railgun in continuous mode. Harris pushed the stick hard down, straightening out seconds later. Tawn unleashed another spiral burst, this time clipping the fuselage of the hardened fighter. A rumble from the impact was heard over the comm.

"More of that coming your way," said Tawn. "As we just said, turn the ship over and we let you walk."

Another blast of pellets came in their direction. Harris maneuvered the *Bangor* out of harm's way. Tawn enabled the second rail.

"Let's see how he does with a double."

Harris said, "We're gonna be getting a bit of buffeting as we head into this atmosphere."

"Won't matter."

She pressed the trigger. The ship vibrated as two streams of pellets left the *Bangor*. The much lighter *Rage* turned hard to port, dodging the tungsten spray pattern before spinning to face the oncoming ship. No rounds left his rails.

Tawn grinned. "We got him. That gun just jammed."

Tawn spoke into the comm. "Sorry, Bob. You just lost your weapon. But I'm still feeling generous. Turn her over and we'll let you go home. We'll even give you a ride over to the Rumford Mine."

The thief replied, "Ever wonder what a small ship like this would do to one of those domes if it hit it while at full throttle?"

"Take him out, Tawn. We've got almost four thousand people down there depending on us."

Tawn took a deep breath. "You've got seconds to put us at an angle. Otherwise our own fire will be raining down on Fireburg."

Harris moved the *Bangor* off a straight line. "Make 'em count. This will be our only shot."

Friction fire raged across the *Bangor*'s surfaces as the boxy ship raced after the Banshee. Tawn Freely made several motions as if to pull the trigger, withholding her shot each time as the small ship in front of them dodged and weaved.

Harris yelled, "Do it!"

Tawn held fast.

Harris glared. "We're coming in too hot to stop ourselves! Pull that trigger!"

The vibrations of the twin railguns could be felt through the buffeting from the atmosphere. As the eighth set of rounds left the rails, the port wing of the Banshee exploded, sending the remainder of the fuselage into a violent spin.

Harris pulled back hard on the controls as the remains of the centuries-old fighter slammed into the rock of the desert a half kilometer away from the dome. Harris gritted his teeth as Tawn tightly gripped the console in front of her. The image on the cockpit display showed the planet's surface rushing up to meet them.

The two Biomarines were rocked in their chairs as a last second maneuver by Harris sent them into the top of an immense dune. Shards of black glass sprayed outward as the Zwicker class hull rapidly came to a rest.

Harris opened an eye, looking around at the still intact cabin as Tawn continued to grimace.

"I think we made it."

Tawn opened her eyes as she let out a breath. "Couldn't cut that any closer?"

The colonel came over the comm. "You two still with us?"

Tawn answered. "Physically yes. Mentally? No."

Robert Thomas's image showed on the cockpit display. "Hang tight. We have a team coming out there."

Harris asked, "How's the dome?"

"Debris missed us. We're still solid."

Chapter 13

The cleanup from the encounter with the Banshee took several hours. The *Bangor* was moved into the open docking bay where it was inspected. Half the ion inhibitor boxes on its underside were damaged. Spares were brought out from the stock at the dome and repairs begun. Harris and Tawn sat in the colonel's office.

Harris said, "We almost killed the lot of you. He could have destroyed this place when he first took off. And we were seconds from losing him and having him slam into the dome with that craft."

The colonel replied, "But you didn't lose him and we're not dead. We lost the Banshee. It can be replaced. As far as I'm concerned you couldn't have done better out there than what you did."

Harris frowned. "Maybe."

Tawn said, "We should think about defenses for this dome. Nothing to stop the Earthers from sending down a handful of suicide missions from above. And we have nothing to stop them."

Harris sat up. "What if we could get Mr. Morgan to build us a half dozen rail cannons to place on or around this building?"

Tawn shook her head. "The pacies won't allow that."

"One more reason we need to get control of this planet."

An officer came over the comm. "Colonel, we have a shuttle coming down through the atmosphere. It's Mr. Morgan's."

The colonel replied, "Have him escorted to my office when he arrives."

The colonel looked up at Tawn and Harris. "You can ask him about your cannons."

Harris said, "Didn't think he was due to come out here. Any idea why?"

The colonel shook his head. "We'll find out in a few minutes. Last time was just for an inspection to satisfy his curiosity as to how things were running."

Several minutes later, Bannis Morgan entered the room. Pleasantries were exchanged. He remained standing.

"Gentleman, Miss Freely, we have a problem. My consortium of associates is disbanding. And it's not because of financials as I feared. It's from political pressure. Most of us have contracts with the military. Certain politicians got wind of our efforts out here and immediately got to work in an attempt to sour the well, so to speak. Veiled threats were made, and as a result the others, as well as myself, have to pull all official support."

"So that's it?" said Harris. "You're done?"

Morgan returned a pursed smile. "I said official. I've set up several shell corporations under my cousin's name and authority. Now, the others haven't agreed to this yet, but I plan on pushing this as a clandestine operation. We will give what stealth support we can, without getting directly involved in any way."

Tawn asked, "What's this mean for our ship production?"

"I've asked my teams at the warehouse if they would be willing to be transferred to the new company. They would. Our funding through that entity will be significantly less, but we'll have to make do. As to the shipyard and freighters we're in the process of building, those efforts will continue. They have civilian uses and are therefore not an issue. As I've said before, the claimed purpose for building them is to increase trade with the Earthers. The politicians are all for that prospect."

Harris said, "We've had some bad news here this morning. The Banshee was stolen right after we landed. We had to go up and destroy it. Thankfully, some key technical problems allowed it."

Bannis replied, "I didn't receive any reports of issues."

"The wormhole generator has problems. That one didn't matter because with that ship on escort duty there's no need to jump. A bigger issue was the railgun feed jammed. Might be something as simple as an alignment issue. Trish can fix that on the next one. I think a bigger issue is that we had no security lockout system in place. Anyone could hop in and fly it away."

Bannis nodded. "I see. An oversight with our design. I'll see to it that is corrected when I return. As well as the other issues. How goes it with the mining operation?"

The colonel replied, "Excellent. All production lines in this facility are fully operational. Stacks of titanium plates are rolling off the lines."

"Has thorough testing been performed on those plates?"

"Yes. And the results say they are high quality."

"Excellent. I could see as I came in... the second dome is nearing completion?"

"Just the dome itself," said Harris. "The environmental systems should be up and cooling it in a couple days. After that, we start on the housing for the workers. We're nearing capacity here, so the timing should be perfect."

Tawn added, "We're already breaking ground for the third and fourth units. The colonel here has been managing a crack team and keeping it all rolling."

Robert Thomas held up a hand. "You can thank Mr. Romero for that. Most of the management and coordination efforts here are coming directly from him and his team. They're tireless workers. And I'd like to add one more item: the recruits he's bringing in from Domicile are highly skilled and motivated. We are paying them well. And the pace doesn't seem to be an issue."

Tawn said, "They're probably excited to be working on a project of this scale. Building this dome city and a mine could easily be replicated on a dozen of the outer colony worlds. We've managed to build something special here."

Harris laughed. "Yeah, well, if we're done congratulating ourselves I'd like to get back to my ship to make sure the repairs are moving forward as planned. We still have freighters to escort."

Tawn asked, "Mr. Morgan, you have any other news for us? Otherwise I'm going with my partner."

Bannis Morgan shook his head. "Other than our political struggles, everything is running as smoothly as it could."

***

Harris slid under the hull to look over one of the ion box repairs. "Looks like a solid job. Welds are smooth."

A tech stood at his feet. "That would be Roger Tillman's work. Everyone is envious of his welds."

Harris slid back out. "I can see why. How many more are we replacing?"

The tech replied, "Just finished the last one. We'll run a few tests to check field strengths. If it all checks out we should be releasing her in about a half hour."

Harris looked up at Tawn.

Tawn shook her head. "You don't even have to ask. I can see it in your face. I'll tell the repair crew chief he can find us in the cafeteria if he has any issues."

The meal ended and the duo were soon finishing up the escort of the freighter. This time it was filled with personnel. The first dome had surpassed its maximum capacity, with a third of the new arrivals having to double bunk as they were assigned to differing shifts. The pay was good, the supervision just, and the work plentiful. Few complaints came in from any of the crews.

Over at the Rumford Mine, they remained confounded as to the difficulties they were having with the new well. Every set of test numbers returned a different value. A dozen theories as to what was happening had been put forth, with no ideas as to a proper solution. Two well placed Domer spies were returning direct information about what was to be tried and when. The colonel's team at the alternate wellhead saw to it that every attempt at a remedy was a failure.

A similar side-well was under construction at the colony of Dove. The engineers hoped to have it up and running in two days. When operational, the offer of the Jebwa colony would be presented.

On Jebwa, Fritz Romero's teams were nearing completion of their refurb efforts. The well was again flowing and power had been restored. The colony would soon only be in need of residents.

Tawn sat back in her chair, propping her feet up on the console.

Harris said, "Trish used to do that."

"You miss her, don't you?"

Harris huffed. "Not that. Please take your feet off. You'll end up wearing off the paint."

Tawn yawned as she looked over at Farker. "The pooch has been awful quiet for the last day or two. I wonder if he took damage in that crash landing."

"It wasn't a crash landing, it was a controlled landing. We came in hot, but damage was minimal."

Tawn laughed. "Controlled, yeah, right. We're lucky we walked away from that. Seriously, though, it might be time to take him back to Midelon. He seems to come out from there all refreshed. Maybe he's in need of a fix."

Harris shook his head. "Or maybe he's just tired of hearing you drone on and on."

Tawn smirked. "No, that's not it. My conversation is stimulating. If it were that boring you'd have fallen asleep already. Speaking of that, what was your longest period without sleep while in the service?"

Harris half frowned. "That would be the Helm Engagement. Only had a handful of cat-naps during that whole affair. Our major ordered us all to take them. For several days we had a fifteen minute nap once every two hours. She set up an alert if there was any Earther activity. How about you?"

"That would be forty-one hours straight. During boot camp."

Harris laughed. "You can't count the rousting they gave us there. We all had to do that."

"Well, that was my longest. I don't think I had any fights that lasted that long. Besides, I'm one of those people who can sleep anywhere. Give me two minutes back in one of those bunks and I could be snoozing. Anyway, about the dog..."

Harris glanced over his shoulder. "Next freighter won't be coming in for eight hours. We can make a jump over once this one's on the ground."

"How many total people does this give us?"

"Fifty-eight hundred. Fritz has another fifteen hundred lined up for transport out here when that second dome is fully operational. He thinks we may have it fully staffed in three weeks' time."

Tawn shook her head. "Crazy how fast this is all moving."

Harris smirked. "What's crazy is that you and I started all this with our gun running. If it hadn't been for the red witch, we might still be struggling to feed ourselves."

Tawn chuckled. "Now, for you at least, you struggle to *not* feed yourself. I bet you've added twenty kilos since we first met."

Harris smiled. "That's been twenty kilos of happy eating. If this keeps going the way it has been, I just might add another twenty just for the fun of it."

Tawn scowled at the thought. "Let's not. I'd rather not get into a firefight with an out-of-breath chubber as my backup."

"Think of it as more of me to fight alongside."

The freighter was soon on the ground. The *Bangor* was turned to the sky. After short ride, a jump was made to Midelon. Farker hopped around the hatch excitedly as the ship settled on the grass outside the bunker door.

Harris said, "You should follow me over. See if it lets you in at the same time."

"That mean I have to run and dive?"

Harris powered down the ship as he stood. "We're about to find out."

Farker sprinted when the hatch opened. Tawn and Harris jumped out behind, rushing to make the door as it opened for the dog. Tawn moved a full step ahead, diving through a closing door as Harris skidded and slammed into it, bouncing off and falling back onto the ground in a daze.

Seconds later, Tawn could be heard yelling through the door. "You OK out there?"

Harris took a moment to clear his head. "I think I might need a few of my ion boxes replaced."

Tawn laughed. "I'll take that as you made it. I see the table and chair you were talking about. Should I have a sit and see what it does?"

Harris replied as he stood, brushing himself off: "Sure. Have at it."

A voice, seemingly from the top of the door, gave a greeting. "Good afternoon, Harris. Welcome back."

The husky Biomarine staggered through as the door opened. "My own access. That would have been nice to know."

Tawn sat in the chair. "So how does this thing work?"

"Turn to face the table and it should come on."

A light shone down on the table. A hologram image of Alexander Gaerten's face appeared just in front of Tawn.

"Hello. I am Doctor Alexander Gaerten. I designed the facility you now occupy. Welcome. I hope your journey here was pleasant."

Tawn chuckled. "Mine was. Harris over there is having a tough time of it though."

"Yes. There is no further need for Mr. Gruberg to rush for the door. If we become friends, it will be the same for you."

Tawn nodded. "Great. I like you already, Doc. Ask me whatever you want."

A series of questions followed, with Tawn becoming increasingly annoyed with each new quiz. "This guy was a smartass."

Harris shook his head. "You know it is listening to everything you say, right? That the way you talk to your friends?"

"That's the way I talk to you."

The hologram asked, "Harris, would you consider Miss Freely a friend?"

Harris crossed his arms. "Well..."

Tawn turned. "Really? This is serious. I might need access to save your ass one day. Tell him I'm your friend."

Harris replied, "Yes, I guess she's my friend. My insecure friend."

"I am about as far from insecure as you can get. All that psychological training saw to that. Now, tell him we're friends before I get up and crack you upside that fat head."

Harris nodded. "OK, she's my friend. My belligerent friend."

The simulation smiled. "Then she is a friend of mine. Tawn, from this moment forward, you have been granted access to this room."

"Welcome to the club," said Harris. "What we have to figure out now is how to get beyond that next door. Seems Farker is a better friend than we are."

"The robotic canine, Archibald, whom you refer to as Farker, is a part of this facility. If and when either of you are deemed trustworthy, you will be granted elevated access as well."

The second door opened. Farker pushed an additional chair into the main room before scampering back as the door closed.

"Harris, if you would care to place the chair in front of the table and have a seat, we can continue."

Harris complied. The questions continued in an alternating fashion for three hours before the hologram closed its eyes.

Harris asked, "Uh, what just happened?"

The voice of the doctor replied, "The answers to the block of questions you have just submitted are under review. When an answer is ready, you will be instructed in how to proceed. If the responses are found to be unacceptable, you will be expelled from the room and granted no further access."

Harris stood.

Tawn asked, "Where you going?"

Harris pointed at the door. "Back out to the *Bangor* for a catnap. Ever since you brought that up I can't get it off my mind. Now I need one."

Tawn smiled. "Wouldn't have anything to do with slamming into that door earlier, would it?"

Harris walked toward the exit, the door opened before him. "It might. I do have a bit of a headache coming on."

"Maybe we'll have to get you checked out when we get back. You make an awful racket when you run into stuff like that. The air being forced from your lungs kind of made this sort of *plegh* sound. Actually, you made quite the thud too. Probably all that extra weight."

"Really? You're going there again? Trying to give me a complex."

Tawn laughed as she stood. "Yeah. If only I could. How many mental slugs and stumps do you know?"

Harris glanced back as he walked. "Where you going?"

"A nap sounds good."

Harris pointed back at the second door. "Yeah, well, how about you wait in here for Farker. I'll lock down the ship before I grab a wink."

Tawn rolled her eyes. "Dog duty. OK, guess I'll hang out here."

Two hours passed before the door opened and the robotic pet again emerged. Tawn followed it out to the *Bangor*, where a snoring Harris was fast asleep.

Tawn shoved her partner. "Hey, Tubby. Wake up."

Harris rubbed his eyes as he slowly sat up. "That was a fast fifteen minutes."

Tawn laughed. "It's been two hours. That was more of a bear-nap than a cat-nap."

"Two hours? Guess I needed the rest. Anything else happen? Any good questions from the hologram?"

Tawn shook her head. "Hologram was silent with its eyes closed the whole time."

"Yeah, it will do that to you. You have to prompt it to start responding again. It can carry on a conversation while it's churning away on those responses."

Tawn looked on in disgust. "Why didn't you mention that before? I just sat in there for two hours picking my nose."

Harris chuckled. "Thanks for the image. Are we ready to head back?"

"I guess. Dog seems happy again. Don't know what they're feeding him in there, but I could use some of it."

Harris shook his head. "Always thinking about food, aren't you."

The *Bangor* turned into a fireball as it rose through the Midelon sky.

Chapter 14

Another two days were spent on escort duty before Tawn and Harris settled in the colonel's office for their daily briefing.

The colonel brought an image up on the wall display.

"The operation at Dove is underway. They saw their first drop in water availability this morning. The complex has a half million liter storage tank buried somewhere in the middle of those buildings. With a total shutoff of the well, we estimate it will take five days to empty it."

"They give any reaction to the loss?" Tawn asked. "Even if it was temporary?"

"Our man said there was two mentions of it in the council chamber. No one cared. We're planning a complete shutdown sometime in the next hour. I expect this time tomorrow the chamber will be all abuzz."

"Fritz have anything to say about Jebwa?"

"He did. It's ready to support the first arrivals. Having the capability to support all twenty thousand of the Dove colonists is expected in the next few days. The timing couldn't be better."

If you need to sweeten the pot, we might offer food support for three months. That would allow the first of their farms and greenhouses to start producing."

The colonel shook his head. "I think the pot is sweet enough. As that water tank dries out, they'll start to see the light."

Harris rubbed the back of his neck. "We're playing dirty on this one. Fair, but dirty. What's the news over at the Rumford Mine?"

"They brought in a specialist from New Earth. So far she's scratching her head. We keep changing the flow. Sometimes going all the way full, but never enough for them to use in the mining process."

Tawn grinned. "Bax has to be going nuts."

The colonel said, "Our spies say she has been quiet throughout all this. I think the Earthers are running things over there. She's just a figurehead."

The briefing continued for an hour before Harris stood. "Since we have a little time to the next escort, we're hopping back to Domicile to check on the new ships. Anything there you need us to expedite?"

"We're expecting a big magnesium shipment. Our stockpile is running low and our suppliers have failed to deliver twice now. If we run out, our titanium processing comes to a screeching halt. You might take a moment to check in with them. Hopefully the politicians haven't gotten wise to our resource purchases. They would shut those down in an instant."

Harris half scowled. "Almost feels like we're working against ourselves sometimes. I'll be glad when this planet has been mined out."

"That won't be for another ten years," said the colonel. "And only if we get full control."

***

Harris followed Tawn into the warehouse on Domicile. "What's your bet on their progress?"

Tawn replied, "I'm guessing two more weeks."

Two shiny Banshees sat on the middle of the warehouse floor. Gandy came over with a grin. "Perfect timing! We're taking them out in about an hour. How's the *Rage* doing?"

Harris winced. "Yeah, we had a few issues."

Trish walked up. "Was the nav system, right? Was giving us fits for a couple days. Kept rebooting."

Harris shook his head. "First it was the wormhole generator. Wouldn't kick in. I had her follow me through behind the *Bangor*."

"Why didn't you just bring it back?"

"I wanted to get it on-station. We don't need to jump for escort duty. Besides, there was more..."

Tawn said, "I tried out the railgun. Fired a few manual rounds and then tried an auto burst. The feeder jammed up."

Trish sighed. "I'm sorry. That must have been my fault. I hurried that through, knowing it needed more time on the test bench. I've had the new feeders available to do that. It shouldn't be a problem with these two."

Harris was silent for several seconds. "Then there was an incident."

Gandy tilted his head. "An incident? Did you crash it?"

Harris chuckled. "No. Tawn let an Earther steal it and we had to shoot it down."

Tawn protested: "Now wait a minute. I didn't *let* anyone steal it."

Harris smirked. "OK, who would you say gave it over to the Earther spy?"

Tawn sighed. "I did. I thought the colonel had sent him to meet me."

Gandy stood with his mouth open. "You let someone steal the *Rage*?"

Harris grinned. "And then she shot it down."

Tawn returned an angry look. "You think this is funny?"

Harris nodded. "Didn't at the time. Seems kind of funny now."

"What happened?" asked Trish.

Harris replied, "The guy was waiting in the docking bay when she arrived. She left the cockpit open for him to hop right in when she landed. He headed for orbit and then figured out he couldn't jump because of the wormhole generator. We pursued him, got in a short firefight.

"He headed back toward Fireburg with the intention of destroying the dome. We followed, his gun jammed, so he decided he was just gonna ram it. I got us close enough and Tawn shot his wing off. The debris landed about a half kilometer from the dome. The colonel's men came out and cleaned it up."

Tawn added. "And *he* crashed us into a dune with his crappy flying."

Harris laughed. "More like I saved our lives with my superior flying and instincts."

Tawn waved him off. "Call it what you want. Long story short is we had to kill the *Rage*. How are these two coming along?"

Gandy crossed his arms. "Can't believe I only got to fly her once."

Trish took a moment to collect her thoughts. "Both are ready for their initial test flights. This closer one is named the *Regal*. The far one is the *Radica*. Both have an improved inertial dampener courtesy of Mr. Morgan. You should be able to take a direct plasma round without it rattling your teeth out. The drives are also the first two off the production line, where the one in the *Rage* was a prototype."

Gandy said, "We'll do a thorough check of the railgun and the wormhole generator this time."

Harris said, "We need some type of lockout mechanism for them too. Either a passcode to fly them or a code we can send over the general comm that will disable a drive and a gun, or something similar. And we'll want this as both a software option and a hardware option.

"Somewhere in that hull you need to hide away a hard switch that we can use to shut things down remotely. For the software side we can ask Mr. Morgan to provide us the expertise for that, since his company builds the computer system. Until at least one of those is in place, we won't be taking these back with us. But we do need this done as soon as possible. Our freighter flights should be picking up soon."

Trish nodded. "We'll make it happen."

The young mechanic grabbed her brother by the arm. "Come on. We've got work to finish."

Tawn and Harris followed the twins with conversation as they saw to their remaining tasks. The *Regal* and the *Radica* were taxied out. Two fireballs raced against the evening sky as the Banshees were put through their paces. The wormhole generators were used to make jumps into empty space. The railguns were tested repeatedly. The Bolemans returned to the ground, taxiing into the warehouse two hours later.

Trish hopped out. "Everything was green. Our issues should be resolved. I'll get to work on a hardware switch."

Gandy laid his cockpit helmet on the seat as he climbed out onto the wing. "I still can't believe you shot down the *Rage*. What a waste of a beautiful machine."

Harris replied, "We had no choice. And what's with all the R names? *Rage*, *Regal*, *Radica*?"

Gandy shrugged. "They're just names. What's it matter?"

Tawn stepped in. "It doesn't. Don't we need to pay a visit to the magnesium guy? They close their offices in an hour."

"You have the coordinates?"

"On the *Bangor* I do."

Harris gestured toward the warehouse door. "After you then, Miss Freely. I'll even let you drive us there if you want."

"You're so magnanimous."

Harris smiled as he followed. "I do what I can."

***

The *Bangor* settled on a concrete landing pad just outside the Grimacle Mines main office. A representative was waiting at the door to take them to a meeting with the principle salesman who had inked the original deal.

Lars Kovensen greeted them as they entered the room. "I hope your trip here was pleasant?"

Harris said, "Let's get right to it. You sold us magnesium. Where is it?"

Lars pursed his lips. "It's coming. We had an equipment malfunction in our processing plant that set our production back. At the same time, another client, a long term and highly valued customer, had an emergency need. We've had to split our production between you while forcing our workers on overtime. We're desperately trying to make up the shortage. I must say that I am deeply sorry about the holdup."

Tawn asked, "How much of the order is available now?"

The salesman winced. "I can't say."

"Well when will our shipment be ready?"

"At the moment it appears as though it may be as many as three weeks."

Harris growled. "This is unacceptable. We have a contract."

Lars nodded. "And the terms state that all will be delivered as scheduled barring production delays. We've had and are having just such a delay. Again, I can't apologize enough. Sometimes these things happen."

"Who is your other customer?"

Lars frowned. "I cannot release that information. Customer privacy is tantamount to us staying in business. We hold your information secure as well."

The back and forth talk continued for most of an hour.

Harris leaned forward onto the table that separated he and Tawn from Lars Kovensen. "I'll need to discuss this with my partner. What is your availability today?"

Lars replied, "We are closed for the evening, but I can stay should you need me. I will be flying out first thing in the morning to meet with other clients."

Harris stood. "We need to discuss our options. Can we meet back here in say... an hour?"

Lars waved his hands at the room surrounding them. "If you'd like you can make use of this room."

Harris shook his head. "Thanks, but I think we'll head outside."

Minutes later they were hopping up into the cabin of the *Bangor*. Harris closed the hatch.

Tawn asked, "What was so urgent?"

"We need to find out who this other customer is. Could be someone has traced our supply line and this is the Earthers' way of disrupting us. Without magnesium we aren't doing any refining."

"Are there any other mines?"

Harris frowned as he shook his head. "Not with any volume. We need this production, even if we have to find out who the mystery client is and try to buy it from them at a premium. And any future contracts need to give us priority production. Anyone else comes along wanting more, that's fine, they can produce all they want once our needs have been fulfilled."

A woman approached the outside of the ship. Harris opened the hatch. The woman smiled.

"Can I help you?"

"Anyone else aboard with you?"

"Just me and my partner."

"The admiral sent me. I've been told to let you know the magnesium supplies you require can be purchased through a third party."

Tawn said, "Let me guess... at an inflated price."

The woman nodded. "Yes. It was purchased by a firm we suspect is collaborating with the Earthers. We purchased it from them under the guise of sending it out to Bella III for use in a new factory. The admiral advises that any future agreement you sign with Grimacle or any other supplier guarantee delivery to you before any other new or updated contracts. And that would be with all suppliers."

"We were just discussing that," said Harris. "We'll make that happen."

The woman added, "The admiral also wanted to send along his congratulations. He's been impressed with your operation. However, he says that you should remain vigilant in your defense. He has word the Earthers have big plans in the works, but he doesn't have any specifics, so watch your backs."

Tawn nodded. "We've been keeping a close eye on them. I do have a question for the admiral while you're here: our funding stream. We haven't received the payment for this week. We need those credits to continue operations. Any slowdown in funds will mean a slowdown in delivery of product. We need those credits."

The woman nodded. "They will be forthcoming. Political pressure is being placed on our military to account for every credit spent. Our previously large black-ops program has been getting squeezed. Ongoing operations have lost a quarter of their budgets. Things will only get tighter as the politicians try to get their controlling fingers on every credit available. We are no longer at war and there are a number of our leaders who question why we have a black-ops program at all."

Harris frowned. "That's not good news. I know love, peace, and harmony between us and the Earthers is the ideal, but they're set on expansion. Our having freedoms are based on them not succeeding at their goals. This is not a 'they do well so everyone does well' situation."

"We are all patriots here, Mr. Gruberg. You will find a message on your system of who to contact about the magnesium. With funds currently held up, I would suggest you attempt a partial purchase now, with the remaining portion later. Our supplier has instructions to hold it for you."

Before Harris could again reply, the woman turned and walked away.

Harris sat in his pilot's chair as he closed the hatch. "Sounds like our support from the admiral is getting thin."

Tawn crossed her arms. "Not good news, that's for sure. If we lose those funds, how long would we be able to keep running?"

"We'd have to stop all expansion and then focus our energies on selling the production we have. That would keep the mine running, but not by much. Rumford and the Earthers are eventually going to figure out how to get water to their mine. When that happens, things are going to explode over there. They won't have any finance issues."

"Maybe it's time we start looking to the outer colonies and truce worlds to expand our supply business?"

Harris scratched the back of his neck. "Only problem I see with that is our credit stream from that would be slow to develop. Will cost us up front to get established, with the payback coming over time."

"What other avenues do we have available to us?"

Harris thought for a moment. "Not sure. Maybe we build colony domes. There are settlement companies on Domicile. And the Earthers are eager to expand. Maybe we get contracts to build domes for them."

"Wouldn't building Earther domes defeat what we're trying to do out there?"

Harris shook his head. "Our priority is to stop them from acquiring titanium. If we can do that, their influence on the other truce worlds won't make a difference. At least not anytime soon."

Tawn gestured toward the door. "Well let's get back in there and ink a new deal."

"What if they want to raise prices on us?"

Tawn shrugged. "Maybe we offer to throw in some titanium plates. I don't know if they'd have use for them or not, but we could use some of that production to help finance this if needed."

Harris stood. "We'll hold that in reserve. Let's go do this."

After a long negotiation, a new deal was signed at the previous price. A ride on the *Bangor* followed with the ship landing outside the warehouse where the Banshees were being tested.

Harris was the first in the door. "How we looking?"

Trish replied, "Both hardware and software lockouts are enabled on the *Regal*. We have the software version done on the *Radica* with the hardware going in now. The pilot will be able to flip a hidden switch to completely disable the ship's systems. There is also a soft passcode they will have to enter when they hop in the cockpit. And we have the broadcast message that will disable the drive and the weapons."

"Who knows about these items?"

"The hard switches? The three of us and Gandy. The passcode and the broadcast message, Mr. Morgan's two engineers came up with those. And for safety's sake, we've already made updates so they can't make use of them."

Gandy walked up. "The switch is in."

"So these two are ready to go?" Tawn asked.

Gandy nodded. "They are. And can I ask that you not shoot them down this time?"

Harris chuckled. "We'll do our best. Can I talk the two of you into taking them out for more flight testing on the way? We can check the wormhole generators, the railguns, and the rest of the systems. When you're satisfied with their performance we'll turn them over to Colonel Thomas for use."

Tawn looked around the warehouse. "You have one more Banshee hull. What comes after that?"

"Next up will be that Zwicker we have over there," said Trish. "Whether or not it flies will depend on getting a new drive and wormhole generator that will fit in her. So far we haven't found anything that we could squeeze in. Nobody makes a drive that shape."

Harris crossed his arms. "I know we were planning to rebuild that one for Tawn, but I have a new proposal. Can it be rebuilt with a drive but no wormhole generator? If so, we can still use it out at Eden for escort duty. Might be a quick addition to having the *Regal* and *Radica*. I'm sure it would be put to use."

Trish pondered the idea for several seconds. "We'll have to talk that one over. If your goal here is to get a third ship on-station as soon as possible, that option might be the way to go."

Harris nodded. "Whatever gets one to us sooner. Make that happen."

The two refurbed Banshees were put through their paces with all systems testing out as green. After a quick delivery to the colonel, Trish and Gandy were flown back to the warehouse, where work began on the newest makeover. A second Zwicker class freight shuttle, this time minus a wormhole generator, was expected to be ready for service in three weeks' time.

Chapter 15

Tawn and Harris sat in the colonel's office.

Harris rubbed his forehead as the colonel talked about charts and tables displayed on his wall. "The pacifists at Dove are being stubborn. Their water reserves are down 60 percent. Our offer to move them to Jebwa has been voted down three times.

"They are convinced they can conserve and get by. Last night we shut the well down completely. With their current reduced needs they will be out of water in less than a week."

Tawn asked, "Why haven't they explored getting a new well drilled?"

The colonel shook his head. "They don't have the funds."

Harris glanced up. "Have we offered them water for concessions? You said the tax they have been looking at was close to being passed. I'm surprised they haven't rammed that through as a bargaining chip. You pay the export tax and we'll buy the water."

"They don't want that co-dependence. To date they have been fully in charge, only yielding to pressure from Domicile. They don't like or trust us or the Earthers."

Harris replied, "Sounds like we need someone from Domicile to convince them."

"Not going to happen. The connections there are the pacifists in the Senate. The senators already don't like what we're doing. Titanium is viewed as a military-use metal.

"The less there is the less likely there is to be war. As far as their allies back on Domicile are concerned, they want us and the Earthers gone from here. They don't have sufficient pull to make that happen, but they can influence the inhabitants of Dove to stay."

"How's managing the well at the Rumford Mine going?"

The colonel nodded. "As good as can be expected. They still have no clue as to what's happening. I'm expecting to see a new wellhead and drilling gear brought in any day now. They'll have to move their flow-pipe, but that would be a minor effort."

"If they drill a new well," Tawn asked, "how long would it take for us to tap into it?"

The colonel frowned. "Four days to be up and running. They have a very large cistern there. Four days of full flow could fill it halfway. That would be enough resource to begin ore processing. They couldn't sustain operations, but it would allow them to flesh out any startup problems they may have, bringing them that much closer to full-rate production."

Harris said, "That sounds like it might be a good opportunity for a clandestine attack on their pipeline. I would think we could stall the flow for a day or two, if not longer."

The colonel sighed. "True, but they would know who was responsible and reciprocate. I'd rather not risk lives over a tit-for-tat with them. They injure or kill a few of our civilian workers and we might have a hard time recruiting. As it stands, we currently have a waiting list."

Tawn asked, "How's the second dome coming?"

"On schedule. We're starting to move workers into the first of the housing. We were expecting to have the first run of a production line in another week. Our budget problems are pushing that back about ten days. Shame too. I think this second unit would have allowed us to turn a profit much sooner. With the single unit, we'll be lucky to break even.

"On a different note, I was able to pass our rail cannon needs off to Mr. Morgan. He said he expects to have a design ready to evaluate in about a week. He's going for a twin cannon design, housed in a turret that will give us three-sixty coverage. First run will install four units that look like radar facilities."

Harris waved his hand over his head in reference to the facility they were currently inside. "This dome have all the inhibitor boxes installed?"

The colonel nodded. "She's as shielded as any warship and then some. Given the thickness of her titanium plating, and the fact we're in an atmosphere, she should be able to take a couple dozen shots to the same spot before things begin to break down. Nothing I'm aware of on the ground will do her harm. And if we get the rail cannons, we can keep plasma weapons at a distance if they attack in warships.

Harris chuckled. "Sounds like we should have named her Fort Fireburg."

A comm came in for the colonel: "Major Rollington, sir, you asked that I report in with results from our Banshee testing."

"Go ahead, Major."

"Sir, the pilots report all systems appear to be functioning normally. Atmospheric as well as spaceborn tests have all gone according to expectations."

The colonel nodded. "Excellent. Move to phase two of the training, Major. And remember, escort duty comes first. All training will be conducted during free time."

The comm closed.

The colonel smiled. "Looks like we have a pair of winners. Congratulations on pulling that off."

"Now if we can just keep them out of the hands of the Earthers," said Tawn.

"This is good timing for us as well. That Rumford ore ship is nearing capacity. We plan to move ahead with commandeering it."

Harris asked, "What's the plan?"

"We have a team of ten who will be dropped in the desert about fifty clicks from their compound. An overnight run will have them in position for a midday raid. We plan to go in when the sun is hottest. Observations have shown that to be the least guarded time. They will hit the expected three guards with sniper shots and should then be able to stroll aboard.

"From best count, we expect four Earthers to be on the ship at that time. They will be taken out quietly. That should leave us with five to eight minutes to power up the ship and to fly it away. They have two spotter ships in orbit. We'll have half an hour of flight minimum to reach a jump point."

Tawn said, "So the Earthers have a thirty minute window available to stop us? Any way for us to stop their spotter ships from reporting?"

The colonel shook his head. "Short of attempting to shoot them down, no. And we attempt that and they will call in reinforcements anyway."

Harris winced. "So how do we get that ship up through the atmosphere and out through a portal? Seems like a suicide mission."

"Unfortunately, at the moment it is."

Harris stood. "I have an alternative. Your team flies that ship out into the desert where we rendezvous with it. They can set waypoints for the ship to take on its own. We'll take the team aboard the *Bangor* and fly along on the hull of that freighter until it's safely away. If the Earthers follow it, we can separate from the hull for a fight. You could even jump the two Banshees through for an assist."

The colonel tapped his fingers on his desk in thought. "Hmm. Not a bad idea. Keeps our people alive. And gives us a better shot at getting that ore away to a safe place."

Tawn said, "You know, we could make use of the skin on the *Bangor* for this. Take a snapshot of the hull of that freighter and upload it as a skin choice. Park right on the hull and enable that. We'd look just like a part of that freighter."

Harris nodded. "Exactly what I was thinking. We flip on our signal stealth and they wouldn't even know we were there."

The colonel leaned back in his chair. "Might be as soon as tomorrow. You gonna be ready?"

Tawn grinned. "We're ready right now. Any way to move this up?"

Harris cut in: "We could even be the ship that drops the team off. With our stealth, we move them in as close as five kilometers instead of fifty. Would leave the team a lot fresher when they arrived for the fight."

The colonel replied, "We've passed midpoint of the day today. Let's plan on tomorrow. And your offer of a ride out is a good alternative."

The colonel stood. "I can give you a full briefing in the morning. Our own freighter should be in and out before noontime, so the escorts will be free. You two up for lunch?"

Tawn chuckled. "He's the last one you have to ask about that, Colonel. Lunch is his game and he plays it to win."

A short walk had the three Biomarines seated in the cafeteria with full plates in front of them.

Just before picking up a bogler rib, Harris asked, "Any good stories from the war, Colonel?"

Robert Thomas took in and let out a deep breath. "You're right, Miss Freely, he plays this lunch game to win. Throws out a wide open question and then digs into his food."

Harris gestured in a swirling motion with his hand. "Please, take a few bites before answering."

The colonel said, "Have you ever been aboard an Earther cruiser?"

Harris shook his head. "A destroyer once. Turned out to be a trap. We barely escaped."

Tawn shook her head. "Same here. Go on."

The colonel took a sip of his beverage. "The main docking bay on the Earther ships is aft. We shot in on a transport. Our mission was to steal the computer core, which was a ruse that would allow the planting of a recorder and tracker. Command hoped to listen in on the bridge crew to get a better understanding of how they operated. They wanted to know the standard tactics used during a battle or an assault.

"Anyway, we stormed this boat, a hundred eighty-six crewmen to our thirty-two. We went right for their contingent of Marines, knocking them out before they had a chance to mount a defense. The remainder of the crew was a turkey shoot. We took out half before the captain and the rest surrendered. One team of four pulled the computer core while the other planted the recorder."

"You got an actual core?" said Tawn. "Why would you need the recorder? The logs in that core should have told you everything you wanted to know."

The colonel nodded. "It would have, but as we suspected, the moment it was pulled it scrubbed itself. After running a few tests to make it look like we were trying to copy the data, we left it sitting on the deck of the bay before leaving. They never knew or suspected the device we had planted."

Harris said, "I thought messing with each other's ships was banned."

"It was, but this was sidestepping that issue. The rules were that we wouldn't take over and capture each other's ships. There was also a direct rule that once a ship had been damaged in battle we wouldn't take parts. That had a seventy-two-hour time restriction. After that it was fair game.

"There was nothing in any agreement about stealing parts from a fully operational ship though. That changed after the raid on the *Chouluta*. Two months later, one of our spy ships shadowed her and retrieved the data using a secure broadcast.

"They never knew it happened. That data changed the way we fought against their fleet for the last three years of the war. Just one of the many reasons we were winning there at the end."

Tawn shoved Harris on his shoulder, causing a rib to slip from his hand and fall on the floor. "I told you we weren't winning just because of you."

Harris scowled. "Now that was uncalled for. You made me lose a perfectly good rib. Apologize."

The colonel laughed. "More concerned with his food than his reputation I see."

Tawn smirked. "He'd steal that ship tomorrow himself if you offered him a side of bogler beef."

The colonel cautioned: "You'll want to keep quiet on our plans in here. These walls have ears. We caught another Earther spy coming in with the latest load of recruits. That's three this month."

Tawn frowned. "Sorry, sir. Got caught up in the moment. Won't happen again."

Harris shook his head. "Knocked a good rib to the floor *and* tried to give away our plans. Which side are you on?"

Tawn sighed, taking a bite from a large roll, consuming half of its size.

"What about you?" the colonel asked. "I'm familiar with the Helm Engagement. You have any other unusual fights?"

Harris thought for a moment. "I was in a team of three—I believe it may have been on Jebwa actually. Anyway, we got dropped in to surveil an Earther outpost. They managed to spot us and then got the drop on us. We held them off, but our time was limited as we had no incoming supplies."

Tawn chuckled, "How'd they spot you? You drop a rib?"

Harris scowled. "No."

"Well, what then?"

Harris hesitated. "Well, just as we all have to do daily, duty called. I selected a rock outcropping about fifty meters from our position and got down to business. Imagine my unease when I was just finishing up and heard footsteps. I managed to slip away, but not before leaving a steaming pile of evidence behind.

"Ordinarily it probably wouldn't have been noticed. We bury it or kick dirt over it as we've been trained to do. This time I didn't have time to. Anyway, the scout who wandered across my position was wearing infrared gear. So my deposit stuck out as a bright spot on an otherwise cool day."

Tawn busted out laughing. "No way! You have to be making that up."

Harris shook his head. "Nope. And they figured it out after the scout called his lieutenant. Jebwa has the super-tall, ultrathin trees. They poked at it with a stick from one of those trees for few minutes before deciding it was definitely human. After that, they flooded the hills around us with soldiers and we ended up in a fierce firefight, a fight that went on for several hours. We were way outnumbered, but with our location they had no way to get to us without fully exposing themselves."

Harris scratched one of his eyebrows. "They had us if they would have just waited us out, but their lieutenant decided he wanted to make sport of it instead. They had a sergeant—the guy was just over two meters in height and weighed in at about a hundred forty kilograms. He was all muscle. His forearms looked almost as big around as my neck.

"Anyway, the Earther lieutenant made us an offer. If any one of us could take Gregor in a fistfight, they would back off and let us walk."

"How'd you know it wasn't a trap?" Tawn asked.

Harris shook his head. "I was certain when Gregor walked out from behind a boulder. He was a monster."

Tawn looked on with interest. "And...?"

Harris sat back, setting the partly eaten rib in his hand carefully on his plate. "I accepted. I was seventeen. Thought I was invincible. What stump would back down from such an offer? Not that I really had a choice."

Tawn chuckled. "So you had this brawl with an Earther on the surface of Jebwa. You're here, so you kicked his ass?"

Harris rubbed his chin with a grimace. "I wouldn't call it that. I first stepped out in the open to face him down. When I got close it turned out he was bigger than I thought. I'd guess he had a thirty-five centimeter height advantage. His reach had me from halfway down his forearm to the end of his fist. Being a stump in this instance wasn't an advantage.

"I nodded, he grinned, then the beating began. I got in the first two blows—did I mention he was quick as well as insanely strong? Those first two punches landed solid. At least they felt solid. I was expecting him to fall back. He hardly moved. Instead he spat a little blood and gave me another grin.

"I got in the next three blows before he caught me with a roundhouse to the jaw. I wobbled to one side before doing a face-plant on the ground. Stars were swirling in my eyes for a few seconds. He was kind enough to wait for me to get up.

"I was bleeding—split lip, couple loose teeth, dirt all over my face. So I got serious. I worked over his ribs and midsection as I bobbed, weaved and dodged, ducking his massive hammer-fists.

"This lasted for a good fifteen minutes before I could tell he was getting tired. I could tell because my energy level was dropping off the charts. But the big mook just kept grinning and kept coming. His face was bloodied with several splits of his own, but he was loving it. Probably the first time in his life he had been challenged, and he still liked his odds."

Tawn asked, "This where you made the comeback?"

Harris shook his head as he chuckled. "Hardly. He nailed me with an uppercut that picked me off my feet. I'm sure my eyes almost popped out of their sockets. I fell back hard on the ground in a daze. I was finished. That's when my partners opened up on the celebrating Earthers. Took out fifteen of their thirty, including their lieutenant. The others retreated, leaving their hero standing there weaponless to defend himself."

Harris went back to eating his rib.

Tawn dropped her jaw. "You can't tell a story and then just leave it like that! That's just not right. What happened? How'd it end?"

Harris took a sip from his beverage, washing down the half-chewed chunk of meat he had just stripped from a rib bone.

"So my teammates had their weapons on him but they didn't fire. I slowly stood, spat out a wad of blood and dirt, gave him a nod and then gestured for him to leave. He returned the nod and walked off into the rock-covered Jebwa landscape. I picked that story to tell because it was a bizarre, somewhat civilized encounter during an otherwise ruthless and brutal war."

Tawn huffed. "Civilized? Your team mowed down half the enemy while they were standing in the open."

"It was civilized up until that point. Anyway, I thought I'd tell that one because you'd find it entertaining."

Tawn chuckled as she shook her head. "You let some Earther beat the crap out of you. That's not entertaining, that's embarrassing."

Harris looked at the colonel. "See what I have to put up with every day?"

The colonel returned a half smile. "Your partner is a slug. Were you expecting sympathy?"

The three Biomarines began to laugh, hardy laughs that lasted all of thirty seconds before they again tore into the food on the plates in front of them.

Chapter 16

The colonel glanced over at Tawn. "Stories from the war?"

Tawn frowned. "Nothing that tops that. Best I got is getting in a brawl back on Domicile at a bar. I was in a platoon of slugs that had been dropped on Pleda II. There were two Earther colonies there with a mountain pass being the way to travel between them. We were dropped in that pass and told to hold it. All the ships and fliers on that planet had been shot down, so our mission was on the ground.

"We set up our perimeters and turned back numerous assaults for a good three months. The Earthers didn't get anyone through that pass while we were there. After a particularly nasty skirmish, a transport landed and took us back to Domicile. We never knew why we were there or if our efforts accomplished anything.

"Once back on Domicile, we were given a week's leave to go unwind. Two of my slug sisters and I picked out this local bar. It had a tropical theme and everyone was walking around in flowery shirts and shorts. The bar was loaded with a bunch of jock regulars.

"My crew found a nice secluded corner where we could watch the locals and get plastered in peace. Two of the regulars decided they were going to arm-wrestle. One of my girls, Mikanda, decided to join the fun. She had just put down her fourth jock when the brawl started.

"For a good ten minutes, bodies flew in the air or were slammed to the ground. It was us three against a crowd of about twenty. We mopped the floor with them of course. Black eyes, busted noses, knocked out teeth, even a couple dislocated jaws. By the time the cops arrived we were sitting at the bar trying to enjoy another beer or two.

"Unfortunately, the locals and the management didn't see the fun in what we had done. They weren't much for sport. Instead we went to jail and then to the brig. Cost us just over a thousand credits each for damages. No charges were filed because we were soldiers and the war was still going on. Even had a couple of the brawlers catch us as we were being transferred from the jail to the brig. They thanked us for our service. Was humbling."

Harris stopped mid-chew. "So three slugs walked into a bar... I think I've heard that one before."

Tawn shrugged. "I told you I didn't have anything to compare."

The meal was finished and preparations were made for the day that would follow. In the morning Tawn and Harris made a quick flight back to the warehouse on Domicile to inform the twins of what was coming. Upon their return, the colonel was standing in the docking bay with ten neatly dressed slugs and stumps.

Harris said, "Couple hours early?"

The colonel nodded. "We moved up the timeline. You two ready to do this?"

Tawn replied, "We are. We have the easy part. You sending them out like that? Looks like they're going to dinner."

The colonel passed Harris a data file over a comm link. "This has the coordinates for the drop and a channel for their comm. Do whatever it takes to not be discovered. Surprise is our key strategy here today.

"Their dress is because we are being watched. You see the trunks the workers are loading on, those are personal trunks. Makes it look like you're transferring them home to Domicile. They'll gear up once you lift off."

Tawn nodded. "Prudent. I guess that's it, then. Will hopefully see you shortly."

The colonel grabbed her forearm. "Thank you both for doing this. Taking that load of ore will keep a half-dozen Earther warships from being built."

Harris laughed. "No need to thank us, Colonel. We'd have done this just for the fun of it. I just wish I could see Baxter

Rumford's face when her first load of ore goes missing. Getting some revenge for all she's done will be sweet."

The gear was stowed and the personnel stepped aboard. As soon as the *Bangor* went into a hover, the trunks were opened and the ten-Biomarine team got to work on gearing-up. A slow ride south through the desert and then west toward the Rumford Mine had the shuttle settling on the sand at the designated location, fifty minutes later.

The squad leader of the slugs and stumps stood ready at the hatch. "Mr. Gruberg, we should be back this way in about thirty-five minutes. We won't be stopping for you, so do what you need to as we pass by."

Harris nodded. "We'll be here and ready. And we'll be listening, so if you need help, don't hesitate to call out."

The squad leader again thanked Harris and Tawn before hopping out onto the brilliant white sand of Eden. His team quickly disappeared into the roiling eddies of heat rising up from the surface. The hatch was closed.

Tawn said, "This is exciting. You excited?"

Harris chuckled. "Just another day at the office for me. I'll get excited when I see that freighter coming this way."

As the team moved within visual range, the three guards given duty on the exterior of the freighter each saw their lives terminated. The ten member squad moved in quickly. The freighter was boarded through an open docking bay hatch, followed by moving through a main hatch into a hallway leading forward.

Another guard was dispatched before the corner was turned into the room where a dozen Earther Marines lounged about. Controlled chaos ensued for the next twelve seconds as the freighter guard was silenced. The team hustled back into the hall, moving their way toward the bridge.

The squad leader whispered, "Marine deck has been cleared. Proceeding on schedule."

Six other crewmen were silenced before the ship was declared clean. The assigned pilot got to work entering the coordinates for the trek across the desert to the *Bangor*'s location. The drives were powered on, brought up to level, and the big freighter began to move. Seconds later, the local controller called in to ask what they were doing. No response was returned.

Tawn said, "Here they come."

"Now we can get excited," said Harris.

The *Bangor* lifted from the sand as the freighter passed overhead. A port docking collar was selected as the landing site and the transfer tube was extended. A hatch on the side of the freighter opened and the Biomarine team came through.

Harris nodded as he congratulated their efforts. "Nice work. No casualties?"

The squad leader replied, "Everything has gone as planned. We should be heading skyward any second. This show now belongs to you."

Tawn said, "We're positioned to take on either of those Earther ships that are in orbit, if needed. Neither has made a move our way."

Tawn glanced at her display. "Heading up now. They don't move in the next two minutes, we may be out of here free and clear."

Harris grinned. "Wish I could see the look on Baxter's face right now. Her first freighter load and we have it."

Tawn winced. "You want to talk to her? She's hailing you on the general comm."

Harris nodded. "Oh, I have to take this."

Turning back toward the Biomarines in the cabin, Harris asked for quiet. The comm camera focused in on his face.

Baxter Rumford's image appeared on the display. "Bad move, goober. Just give it back and I may let this go."

Harris offered his best confused look. "Please tell me what you're referring to. I'd hate to think it was something we've done."

"My ore. Return it or pay the price."

"Are you talking about that freighter we're watching that's moving up through the atmosphere? Looks to be alone. Some criminal element take that from you?"

Baxter leaned into the camera. "You've been warned."

Harris said, "Don't know why you're accusing us. We're just sitting here in the cafeteria about to have lunch."

Baxter shook her head. "You're a moron. I can see you're on your ship. I recognize that bulkhead right behind your chair. Give me my ore."

Harris yawned as he looked intently into the camera. "How many times have you used us? How's it feel to be taken advantage of? All that work and now someone takes away your harvest? That has to smart."

Baxter Rumford faced away from her comm camera. "Do it. I tried."

As the comm closed, four wormholes opened out in free space. The freighter moved into the blackness that surrounded Eden just as four Earther cruisers showed on the nav display.

Tawn said, "We have company."

"They don't know we're here. I doubt they'll destroy her. They want this ore."

"So what do we do if they pull alongside and send over a boarding party?"

Harris smiled. "I don't think they'll have time before we jump. And if they jump after us, and try to dock, we can blast them from point-blank range. We've got this covered."

Repeated general hails to the freighter were ignored as it headed toward free space. Two of the Earther warships closed at an angle as they continued their appeals.

Tawn said, "Calculations say they will intercept us before we can jump."

Harris nodded. "They'll have three and a half minutes to try to board her. I don't see them rushing to do so before completing a few scans."

"Uh, they do that and aren't they gonna see us all gathered right here?"

Harris shook his head. "Not according to the DDI. Scans of this ship should reveal nothing. From the outside it will look like an empty box. Our bigger concern, should they decide to board, is that they retake control of the nav system. They do that and we have no choice but to fight. And I'd really rather not fight in this space. The politicians at home would be calling for our heads."

The two cruisers pulled alongside the fleeing freighter. The *Bangor* remained undetected, its signal emissions inhibited and its exterior skin colored to match the exterior of the ship to which it clung.

Tawn said, "They're moving in for a dock."

The Biomarine squad leader stood. "If you open that hatch, I still have a comm-link to the controls. I could put her in a random zigzag pattern that will make it harder for them to connect."

Harris frowned. "We open that hatch and they know we're here. I'd rather not do that until we have to."

"One minute to jump," said Tawn. "If they attach, that jump wormhole won't open."

Harris scowled. "I need a volunteer to go aboard. If the Earthers manage to dump a team on there, we'll need someone to disable the safeties on that ship reactor. We get that to melt down and we might be able to take the docked cruiser with it. Could be a one-way ticket for whoever accepts."

The squad leader replied, "You open that hatch for one of us and we're all going over. Whoever draws the straw to disable the safeties will need cover if they're going to pull it off."

Tawn said, "Thirty seconds."

Harris rubbed his forehead. "Lieutenant, take your men, prepare to storm aboard. Tawn, when they're across, close that airlock and retract that tube. We'll only have a couple seconds before we have to open up."

As the Biomarines staged for their assault, the airlock was opened. Seven seconds later the opposite airlock closed, followed by that of the *Bangor*. The transfer tube retracted, and the small ship lifted off from the hull.

Tawn said, "Railgun is online!"

"Let's rip 'em open!"

Tawn fired and the hum of tungsten rounds exiting the rails was followed by the starboard side of the cruiser caving in on two decks. The Earther ship quickly dropped back, allowing the *Bangor* to spin up and over the freighter as the second Earther warship withdrew its docking tube. A wormhole opened and the freighter slipped through.

Tawn again squeezed the trigger for the autofeeders of the twin railguns. A steady stream of tungsten ripped into the cruiser's hull as it too powered back, instantly withdrawing from range.

Harris said, "Time for a jump. Wish we hadn't had to do that."

"Seems to have accomplished what we wanted."

Harris shook his head. "We just attacked two Earther warships after stealing a freighter that belongs to them. Both lived to talk, and worst of all, it happened in Eden space. Another fifteen seconds and we'd have gotten away, at least to somewhere that was not here. This will get back to Domicile and the media will have a frenzy with it. We may not be going home after this."

Tawn said, "We could go back and finish them off?"

Harris scowled. "Wish we could. We'd be lucky to get close enough to take a shot now. And I'm sure they've already had comms with those other ships. We may have just flooded Eden space with Earther ships."

"Still, they can't attack our colony. There's no evidence that the people at our colony were responsible."

Harris set the coordinates for a wormhole jump. "No, but they got a good close-up look at us. We've been in and out of all the ports in our territory. Everyone knows what this ship looks like and who it belongs to. I'm thinking this caper may not have been worth the cost."

The *Bangor* slipped through a wormhole, following the freighter's supposed path. The ship they pursued showed on the nav display.

Tawn said, "It's not moving."

Harris opened a comm. The lieutenant yelled, "We could use some help over here. They have us pinned aft. We never got to the reactor and they now have control of the bridge. I expect they'll be turning us back any moment."

Harris replied, "Be there in a sec. Can you get to an airlock?"

"Port side. Deck three. Airlock B."

Harris nodded. "Give us thirty seconds, then make your move. We'll be there."

The lieutenant said, "We have two down. Hurt bad."

Tawn stood. "I'll pull the med-kit."

As Harris pulled the *Bangor* alongside, a wormhole began to form in front of the freighter. Harris moved to weapons control. A quick maneuver saw a tungsten round ripping through the forward decks of the massive ore hauler.

The lieutenant yelled, "We just lost pressure in here! Tell me that was you!"

Harris replied, "Had to, they had a portal opening. Move to the airlock. I'm docking now."

The airlock on the *Bangor* opened to a rush of air and the Biomarines carried their injured through to the open cabin. Tawn opened the med-kit as the lieutenant and his squad got to work on the casualties.

Harris looked over his shoulder. "The Earthers still in control?"

The lieutenant nodded. "Of all decks but the third."

"No chance of taking her back?"

The lieutenant shook his head. "Probably a hundred Marines stormed aboard when they connected. Too many for us to stop without some planning. We took down a dozen or so before they pinned us in."

Harris looked over the image of the damaged freighter on his display. "No way to take control over the comms?"

"They have it blocked out."

Harris opened a general comm. "Talk to me."

A voice came back. "You've violated property of the New Earth Empire. You—"

Harris cut the voice off: "Skip the rhetoric. I'm trying to figure out how we can work this out so you live. You have an issue with that?"

The voice replied, "You can leave us here. Our ships will come looking for us."

Harris scowled. "Not leaving you with that titanium. I may be able to transport you to one of the truce colonies. You'd have to disarm, and it would take a half-dozen trips."

Tawn looked up. "We don't have that kind of time. Earther ships could be coming this way any moment. They know where we jumped to."

"I was hoping to get that one extra hop in before that happened."

The voice came back: "We will not be leaving this cargo. It belongs to us."

Harris frowned. "You aren't leaving me much of a choice."

Five wormholes opened where the freighter had initially jumped through. Harris checked the nav display. All five signatures were Earther warships.

Harris flipped the railgun feed to auto and squeezed the trigger. "I did try."

Hypervelocity tungsten rounds cut through the freighter's superstructure. The ship shattered from stem to stern. White titanium ore spread out in a cloud, illuminated by a nearby star, as the ship to broke apart. Harris maneuvered the *Bangor* around the burning and exploding remains as the railgun continued to do its work.

A diversion toward the incoming ship had Tawn standing. "What are you doing? We can't fight those."

Harris pressed a button on his console. A wormhole opened and the *Bangor* passed through. As it closed behind them, the threat of the New Earth warships was gone.

Tawn asked, "These men need care. That Domicile?"

"Yes. They'll get the best care here. We can swing by to fill Trish and Gandy in on what's happened."

"You think it's safe to go there?"

Harris nodded. "Will take the Earthers a day or two to file a complaint. They'll want to get all the facts in order so they can steer any negotiations in their favor. I just hope we can talk to the admiral while we're here. He might have some suggestions as to how we should proceed."

The Zwicker class freight shuttle moved through Domicile space and down through the atmosphere. The injured were dropped at a medical facility, along with the remainder of the lieutenant's squad.

Chapter 17

Harris sat on a crate, rubbing the back of his neck as Trish and Gandy came over. "We messed up. Not sure we can go back to Eden."

Gandy asked, "What happened?"

"We stole Baxter Rumford's freighter," said Tawn. "We got chased and had to fire on two cruisers. We managed to destroy the freighter and scatter the titanium, but not before revealing ourselves. Bax knows it was us."

"So what do we do now?"

Harris shrugged. "We don't know. Depends if the Earthers protest or not. If they do, Tawn and I would most certainly be placed under arrest pending an investigation. And I'm pretty sure we are guilty. And if I remember, piracy brings a penalty of death if anyone involved is killed. And we had to smoke just over a hundred Earthers when we destroyed the freighter."

Gandy winced. "That is a mess."

Tawn said, "We just wanted to inform the two of you. If we have to disappear, it's because of this. We'd like you to continue your work here and supply the colonel with as many ships as you can. Gandy, I'm transferring half of my wealth to you. Not to keep, but to use as needed for your efforts here. And I guess to pay yourself from. I think I owe you for the last month anyway."

Harris looked at Trish. "I guess I should do the same. And I'd tell you to just keep it if something bad happens to me, but I wouldn't want to give you the incentive to act on that yourself."

Trish returned a sarcastic smile. "Har, har. Not like I'd need credits to want to do that. And don't worry, my friends and I will be careful with it."

Bannis Morgan entered the warehouse. Harris waved him over.

"Well, Mr. Morgan I'm afraid we screwed things up. We stole Rumford's freighter full of titanium and had to shoot two Earther cruisers that tried to stop us. We had to destroy the freighter as a result. Not sure we'll be able to go back to Eden. They'll be looking for the *Bangor*."

Bannis replied, "Can't you just get another ship? Did they see your face?"

Harris shook his head. "Saw it and heard my voice, even though the comm was through a filter, but they knew it was me anyway."

"They think it was you is what you mean. They'll meet with our ambassador, but they won't give your name without proof. They would rather have you come back out there where they can capture you. At least that's what I would do."

Harris rubbed his chin. "Interesting. OK. Hadn't thought about that."

Bannis said, "We just need to find a secure place to store the *Bangor*. I can lease a shuttle for you if you need it."

Tawn replied, "We can have Gandy do that for us. No need to include you further."

Bannis nodded. "That works too. When do you expect to have your first shipment of titanium plates ready?"

Harris sighed. "Not for another week. I know you're waiting on those for your freighter fleet."

"A week is no hardship for us. You expecting trouble getting it off Eden?"

Harris frowned. "I am now. I wish we could have delayed until that time, but the Rumford ship was almost full. We had to make our move or risk missing it altogether."

"Any luck on convincing the pacifists to move to Jebwa?"

"So far they aren't budging. That colony is primed and waiting. It really is a step up for them, but they're being stubborn. They somehow think the rest of us are just gonna go away."

Bannis slowly pulled himself up to sit on a crate. "They need an enticement."

Harris chuckled. "They're almost out of water. We offered to move them. And we offered six months of MREs to supplement their food needs."

Bannis thought for a moment. "Would Mr. Romero be able to open a citizen recruiting center for them here? They are always looking for new blood. Might be something to give them that final kick to get up and move. If they impose taxes like we're expecting them to do, we're sunk as an entity. We can't support a mine that can't break even. My investors will be wanting money back at some point."

Harris let out a long breath. "We can try. If the skies over Eden are filled with warships, as I suspect they are, they might be ready to move anyway."

Tawn said, "What we need is somebody on the inside of the pacifist movement here on Domicile to go out there. You wouldn't happen to know of anyone would you, Mr. Morgan?"

Harris sat up from his crate. "Miss Freely, may I speak with you outside for a moment?"

Tawn followed her partner to the doorway. "What you got rolling around in that hollow space up there?"

"I wonder if the admiral would be able to provide us with a reputable pacifist, someone in our government who he has planted for such an operation, or someone he just owns."

Tawn chuckled. "Why don't you just ask him?"

"How am I supposed to do that?"

Tawn pointed. "The *Bangor* is bugged. Whatever you say, he will hear. I'm sure he knows all about our raid already."

Harris' comm chimed with an incoming request. "Yes?"

The admiral replied, "I can fulfill your request. I can't guarantee results, but I can have a respected government official out to Eden tomorrow. Today if you need him there."

Harris nodded. "Today would be great if that's workable. And how'd you know what we were talking about just now?"

"I know because I'm the DDI. Just remember, if you need anything at all to help complete this mission, just ask. I may not respond, and you may not get what you're asking for, but I will get your message."

Tawn grabbed Harris' arm. "Somebody is on the *Bangor*!"

The admiral said, "Pay him no attention. He works for me. It seems our devices on your ship have several instances where nothing was recorded. Just hours and hours of blank. What can you tell me about that?"

Harris shook his head. "We don't have anything to do with whatever you put on there. We just fly the ship. When did this happen?"

The admiral was quiet for several seconds. "I suspect you know when, and I'll leave it at that."

A second voice could be heard over the admiral's comm.

The admiral said, "Business calls. I'll have to catch up with the two of you later. I look forward to that first shipment of plates coming in next week."

The comm closed.

Tawn took off her comm, laying it on the ground and gesturing for Harris to do the same. The pair walked a short distance from the devices.

"So our comms are tapped."

Harris shrugged. "So? Not like he doesn't know everything already."

Tawn shook her head. "He doesn't know about Midelon. He knows we're going there, but he has no clue as to what's actually there."

"And how would he know we've been going there? He just said the recordings from his bugs were blank."

Tawn frowned. "You are dense, aren't you. He's been listening to our conversations over these comms. You don't think we've mentioned going out there to each other just before going out there? He may not know what's there, but he definitely knows we can go there."

Harris rubbed the back of his neck. "Guess that didn't occur to me. Maybe we need a code word for it instead of just saying Midelon."

Tawn chuckled. "Like he couldn't figure out what we were talking about? No. We have to be super-vigilant about this. No mention of it ever when we're near that ship or a comm. And we need to tell Trish and Gandy the same. We don't talk anything about it unless we have to. Come on."

Tawn walked back into the warehouse, gesturing for Trish and Gandy to remove their comms and to follow her outside. New instructions were given, ensuring the secrets of Midelon would not be further revealed. The group returned to a waiting Bannis Morgan.

Harris said, "Mr. Morgan, I think for your own protection, at least until we know how this Eden thing is gonna shake out, you should stay away from this warehouse and from us. If there are needs, you can contact Colonel Thomas at Fireburg, or we'll have him contact you. There are too many people who know of our efforts out there, and your continued help is critical to our success, so we need to have some separation, for your own protection."

Bannis Morgan waved his hand. "You don't have to worry about me. I still have friends in high places who owe me. And my security team can hold their own. We know someone has been attempting to bug our offices and transports, but they've failed in doing so. My sweep teams are thorough."

Harris said, "I just don't want to see this thing come crashing down on anyone else. We created this problem and we should be the ones responsible for the consequences of what we did."

Bannis nodded. "That attitude is one of the reasons I'm involved. The other, the bigger of the reasons, is that our world is being threatened again by the Earthers. And I won't sit idly by while that happens. So you two go out and do what you gotta do, knowing that I'm here to support you."

Tawn replied, "You're a man of honor, Mr. Morgan. This world is lucky to have you."

"So what's our next move?" Bannis asked.

"Tawn and I will head back to Fireburg. You keep building those freighters. Trish and Gandy will continue to work on refurbing ships. You said you could get us a shuttle to use instead of the *Bangor*? I'd rather not drag Gandy away from what he's doing."

Bannis nodded. "Should be here in the next twenty minutes."

The shuttle arrived and a jump was made to Midelon where the *Bangor* was parked. Tawn, Harris, and Farker continued on to Eden in the borrowed shuttle. Upon arrival, five New Earth destroyers sat in orbit alongside two Domicile cruisers.

Harris shook his head as the shuttle slid down through the atmosphere. "Can't say I like the looks of that."

Tawn replied, "You have to wonder what information the Earthers are giving to our forces. You think they'll give us up and reveal the fact that they lost out to a single small pirate ship? Doesn't seem like something they would want to talk about."

"Maybe that's why we were allowed in here without so much as a hail."

The shuttle parked in the docking bay. Tawn and Harris made their way to the colonel's office.

Robert Thomas waved. "Come in. Sit down."

"Didn't quite go as we'd planned," Harris said.

The colonel sat back in his chair, tapping his fingertips together. We accomplished our goal of keeping that ore out of the hands of the Earthers. As an added bonus, with all the ships up in orbit, we can move about freely. You might have passed by our first freighter loaded with titanium plates heading for home. We should be making that run once a day from here on."

"How goes our efforts with the pacies?" asked Tawn.

"They look to be right on the edge. I have a meeting scheduled with them in about an hour. Water will be running out in two days. Their conservation efforts have failed and we're gaining support among them for a move to Jebwa."

Harris said, "Any way we can convince a delegation to go to Jebwa for a look?"

"We've been pushing for that, but they've had no interest. If they're getting as desperate as they should be, maybe this time we can convince them to go. Mr. Romero has made every effort to make that colony into the Eden they desire. They can move right in and be self sustaining within three to four months. Here, without water, their crops will be dying off at a rapid pace."

Tawn and Harris, with Farker at their heels, followed the colonel to his meeting at the colony of Dove.

Three pacifists had been selected to speak with Robert Thomas. To them he was not a colonel, as they didn't recognize military ranks. They were seated at a table when the team arrived.

The assigned spokesman gestured toward three beanbag style chairs. "Please be seated."

The colonel sat and then said, "We have word that your water situation has become dire. My information says you may only be days away from having used up your reserves. Our offer at Jebwa remains available. And as I've mentioned each time before, should any of you want to visit the colony we have prepared, we would be more than happy to take you there. Our teams have even begun preparing the surrounding fields for planting."

"No doubt your offer is generous, Mr. Thomas. And we do appreciate that you have gone through this effort, but we don't believe it has been done on our behalf. You want control of this planet and its titanium resources. It's war material, and we feel an obligation to prevent it from being used."

The colonel leaned forward. "That is precisely why you need to accept our offer. We only wish to keep the titanium out of the hands of the New Earthers. They will use it to build warships. On Domicile, our politicians are retiring ships, not building more. Each of us has the same goal in mind. We want to prevent war."

The pacifist seated in the center of the three, scowled. "Your position lacks a certain integrity, Mr. Thomas. In the heavens above we have both Domicile and New Earth warships. Each was brought here by the actions of your people. We are fully aware of the rumors that your colony is behind the theft of the Rumford mines' freighter. How can we trust someone who permits or condones such criminal actions?"

Harris said, "The colonists at Fireburg didn't take that ore, that was me. The cargo was destroyed before it could be used by the Earthers to build more ships."

The pacifist asked, "And were any of the crew harmed?"

Harris was quiet for several seconds. "We tried to get them to surrender. They refused. When their warships arrived, we had no choice."

"So you killed them?"

Harris growled. "The taking of their lives was done so that many thousands of others could be saved. Maybe even your own."

The pacifist slowly shook his head. "Again, your violent actions go against everything we stand for."

Harris nodded. "They do, but at least we're honest about our intentions and actions. You know right where we stand and what motivates us. The Earthers offer nothing but lies and deceit. We know they have made repeated offers to sell you water for influence over your votes. You haven't accepted those offers because of your principles. We're of the opinion that was a smart move.

"However, your water is running out and you will have to make a decision as to which side to support. We offer you a complete colony where your self-governance remains intact. It's a fertile planet where agricultural resources abound. As the primary colony, you will still make the rules and laws. You will be in full control.

"And I believe there is one aspect of Jebwa that you and your people are overlooking. You can go outside. You can walk from building to building in the open, with only your robes and sandals. You can stand out in the natural rain and let it wash over you. You can bathe in the streams and rivers as the waters there are completely unpolluted by industry. It's a planet awaiting its symbiotic hosts."

Tawn looked directly at Harris. "Where'd that come from? I'm kind of wanting to move there myself."

The talk went on for most of an hour before the pacifists excused themselves for a private discussion, something that was out of character from their prior actions. Fifteen minutes later they returned.

"Mr. Thomas, we would like to accept your offer for a tour and inspection of the Jebwa colony. This in no way constitutes any agreement between us."

The colonel smiled. "Excellent. We can leave whenever you like."

"We are ready now."

Colonel Robert Thomas, along with Tawn, Harris, and the three pacifists, boarded a shuttle. A run up through the atmosphere was followed by a jump to Jebwa and a descent down to land on a concrete tarmac beside a spaceport building. A driver was sent out with a wheeled vehicle to transport the group into town.

The colonel asked the transport driver to stop atop a hill on the edge of the Haven colony. "There it is, Mr. Marken. We call it Haven. You can call it what you want. You have housing, schools, shops, a hospital, and even a sports complex, which I know you have no interest in, but it's there for whatever use you would want."

Elias Marken, the spokesman for the pacifists replied, "I do like the lush green landscape."

The colonel nodded. "All the land in this region is arable. Good quality soil. Water is plentiful, as you can see from the river running through town. You have a ready-made colony here, Mr. Marken. The current build will support thirty thousand colonists, so it leaves you with room to grow."

"Much will have to be changed to align our symbiotic form of living with that of the surrounding land."

"I'm sure you'll have changes you will want to undertake, if only to make it your own. We've taken care to put in the utilities and other systems so they are sustainable and as environmentally friendly as possible. Driver, please go ahead and take us to the government building."

As the transport began to move, the colonel continued: "You can see this whole valley is organized into farms. We've taken it upon ourselves to prepare the fields for planting. Your growing season here is almost year round. The lands on the southern end open into wide pastures for your ranches if you choose to have them. And we'd be willing to provide you with starter herds of virtually any animals you might want."

"Seems you've thought of almost everything. This colony has to have been expensive to construct and outfit. Who has been bankrolling your operations?"

The colonel replied: "That would be private citizens who are concerned about the titanium falling into the hands of the Earthers, Mr. Marken. We feel our efforts here are worth every credit if it prevents the Great War from returning. With you and your people being about peace, I would think you would be eager to assist in any way you could."

"Ideally the titanium would be left in the ground."

"That would be ideal for both of us, Mr. Marken. Domicile doesn't need titanium. We can build all the ships we want. If we leave the titanium in the ground on Eden, the Earthers will retrieve it and once again build ships and wage war. It's what they do. It's who they are."

The tour of the town and its facilities and accommodations lasted for most of the day. The pacifists seemed impressed and were often stepping aside for quiet discussion. After returning to Eden, the two groups went their separate ways.

Harris plopped himself down in a familiar chair in front of the colonel's desk. "You think they'll move?"

The colonel shrugged. "Hard to say. I was encouraged by all the private discussions they were having. When the three of them stopped in the street, tilting their faces up to feel the

Jebwa sun shining down, I was certain we had closed the deal. But now I don't know."

Chapter 18

The decision came back after only a few short hours. The pacifists at Dove had accepted the Jebwa offer. A series of shuttles and transports were arranged for the move. Over the course of a week all twenty-one-thousand-odd Dove inhabitants and their belongings were taken to Jebwa.

Harris walked into the colonel's office with a huge grin. "The last of them left an hour ago. What are we planning to do with Dove?"

"The water has been restored. I have a contingent of fifty of our fellow Biomarines heading over to watch over it. And for the question you're about to ask... we have a vote scheduled for this afternoon where we will be electing a new President and Senate Council. From there we begin to enact the laws we've had sitting in the planning stages for months."

"How we gonna deal with the Earthers?"

"We'll slow their progress with a series of regulations and inspections. Taxes will follow. They won't be happy with what's coming. We'll be in control from here on out."

"We still set for dome two to be up and running?"

The colonel nodded. "We've moved about five hundred workers in so far. Mr. Romero claims to have another eight hundred coming in the next few weeks, and more after. We should be finishing up on dome three about that same time. That all depends of course on us getting some income from the plates we're shipping back home. Otherwise we'll be having to slow operations to a crawl."

Harris propped his feet up on the corner of the colonel's desk, drawing an unhappy stare. "Sorry... just out of curiosity, how many Bios do we have working here?"

The colonel powered up his wall display, revealing a chart. "Almost twenty-three hundred. Once dome two is up and running, most will begin to transition back to the Retreat on Rabid. They appreciate the opportunities we've given them here, but they'd like to get back and get started on their civilian lives. Personally, I'm right there with them."

Tawn sat forward. "You're leaving us?"

"I'll stay as long as I'm needed, but yes, at some point I want to go home. The management of this colony can be turned over to someone more capable."

"It's not the management we're worried about," said Harris. "It's the security."

Tawn added, "That's my concern as well. How do we protect our assets here?"

"That will have to fall to the regulars. Some of us may be willing to stay on for contract, but most have let it be known they are ready to leave the hot-box. Their Eden is back at the Retreat—which continues to grow, by the way. We now have two-thirds of the Bios committed to living there."

Tawn sighed. "I'd kind of like to get back there myself."

"Each of your properties have become quite valuable. I know you don't need the credits, but your purchases should pay off nicely should you ever want to sell."

Tawn looked over at Harris. "Well, I'm not selling mine."

Harris chuckled. "If you're looking for a commitment, you might as well forget it. I have no idea what the future holds. Maybe I'll sell it, or maybe I'll build my own dome over it."

The colonel scratched the back of his head. "Speaking of that, a number of us have been talking about doing just that. I know the war is at a standstill, but it could reignite at any time should the Earthers get their hands on the titanium they need. I'd like a build a dome similar to this one, shield it, and place a few of these rail cannons around it for defense. We don't have warships of our own, but we can fortify."

In the days that followed, Eden's first President, Fritz Romero, as well as a council of twelve senators, were elected to office. The Earthers were invited to participate, but were not allowed to vote on senators of their own. The fix was in, and the Domers assumed full control.

The second and third domes were completed, and construction of the fourth and fifth was moving along rapidly. The Rumford Mine continued to have water problems, with a decision finally being made to drill a new well. The colonel sent out his men to scout new locations for a counter well.

Sale of the titanium plates back on Domicile had gone better than expected. Bannis Morgan's friends followed through with increased support. The new freighters were well under construction with the first of the titanium plates being fitted to their frames. The first Morgan-produced trade-freighter was expected to begin flight tests within a month.

Trish and Gandy had managed another three escort ships delivered, one a Banshee and two Zwickers. Tawn and Harris headed for Domicile to pick them up.

Harris walked to the warehouse with Tawn. "You think they're ready to get back out there with us?"

Tawn shrugged. "Hard to say. Building ships is what they both like to do."

Gandy greeted them as they walked in. "We found two more Banshee hulls. One is really rough, but the other is in good shape. It was part of a collection in a closed-down museum. The owner had recently shuttered because of a lack of business. With the war over, people no longer have an interest in war machines."

Harris asked, "So you're not ready to come back out with us?"

Gandy shook his head. "No, we are ready. Mr. Morgan's team is willing to do everything that's needed."

Trish added, "Except for the railgun. We'll be doing the refurb on that once they're done with the rest. So we'll have to come back in a few weeks for that. Otherwise, we're ready to fly."

Tawn said, "Well, gather your things, then. We'll be heading out to get the *Bangor*. Now that we're in charge of Eden, there's no issue with us flying it around."

Trish asked, "Any word from Jebwa?"

Harris replied, "As far as we know, they're adapting. Crops have been planted and animals penned or pastured. They're well on their way to their utopia."

Trish said, "We do have one question to ask."

"What's that?"

"We have a friend. I call her my cousin but she's not. She's a computer specialist. Super sharp. Anyway, she helped us with the Banshee systems. We thought she'd be a good addition to our team.

"I know the *Bangor* now has a modern computer, but I think it'd be worth our while to let her look it over. If we have any more issues with bugs and stuff she is really good at sniffing them out. Someone tried to plant some in our last Banshee. Sharvie was able to find and eliminate them."

Tawn asked, "You willing to vouch for her?"

Trish nodded. "With my life. Like I said, she's like my cousin. And she's very patriotic and a big fan of the Biomarines."

Harris puffed up his chest, sporting a grin. "Well, bring her around so we can meet her. If she likes Biomarines she must be smart."

Tawn chuckled. "We'll see if that sentiment holds once she's met you."

Harris winked. "I'm lovable enough. Might be something you need to work on though."

Trish said, "If we're heading back to Eden, can she go along?"

Harris looked at the time on his comm bracelet. "If she can be here in the next fifteen minutes."

Trish turned and yelled, "Sharvie! Come on!"

A short, heavyset girl waddled out to meet them. "This is exciting."

Trish said, "Sharv, this is Tawn Freely and Harris Gruberg. You have your tablet?"

Sharvie Withrow nodded. "In my pack."

"We hear you're some kind of computer genius," said Tawn.

Sharvie half smiled. "I majored in security. Tried to strike out on my own, but contracts have fallen dramatically since the truce. Could barely feed myself. I'm thankful Trisha came around with this job. Couldn't have found anything more fun or exciting to work on. I mean... a real, flying and functional Banshee. That is awesome."

"Well, at least she's enthusiastic," Tawn said.

Harris replied, "Maybe she can take a look at the colonel's cyber team. He's been saying they've been struggling to stay on top of things. Might be she would be good at sniffing out Earther spies for us."

Sharvie nodded. "I appreciate the work. I'll do just about anything you ask."

The five boarded the shuttle, heading back to Eden.

Sharvie looked out a window as the shuttle approached the atmosphere of the desert planet. "That is so cool. I can't believe I'm riding with a slug and a stump to a planet in the truce zone."

The new hire squinted as the ship drew closer to Eden, moving from the dark side into the intense sunlight that baked the desert below.

"Wow. That is bright. I knew it was a desert world, but I didn't think it would look like that."

"Other than microbes," said Gandy, "there's no other life down there. Too hot. Without the proper gear you'd last all of ten minutes outside at high noon."

"Isn't there somewhere better we could get titanium from?"

Gandy shook his head. "It's not us that needs it, it's the Earthers. We're trying to keep it out of their hands. There's enough titanium down there for them to build thousands of new warships. Either we take it, or the Great War restarts."

The shuttle experienced a few moments of minor buffeting before coming to a stop and settling under the edge of the dome in the docking bay.

Harris turned, "You know where the cafeteria is. Give her a tour of the dome and we'll meet you back there for lunch in a couple hours. We're heading out to get the *Bangor*."

Gandy frowned. "If you're worried about her knowing about our hiding place, don't bother. We already told her."

Harris sighed as he put his head down. "Great. One more person who's vulnerable to interrogation. What all did you say? Hold it…"

Harris removed his comm bracelet and signaled for the others to do the same. The five stepped out into the open heat of the bay.

Sharvie winced as the scorching air attacked her body. "Ooh, this is extreme. I feel like I'm standing in front of a giant heat-lamp."

Trish said, "And you won't get used to it either."

After moving a short distance from the shuttle, Harris took control of the conversation. "Just wanted to reiterate, no talk about Midelon when we have comms with us. And no talk of hiding places or anything else. Sharvie, you should know this, the bugs you found planted on the Banshee, those could be from our own DDI or they could be from Earther spies. Either way, we don't talk about where we're about to go."

Harris looked at Gandy. "Does she know about Farker?"

Gandy half frowned. "She knows about everything. But we can trust her."

"It's not about trusting her," said Tawn. "It's about the DDI or the Earther security forces getting a hold of her. They would find out everything she knows. And when they were done, if they let her live, she wouldn't even know what happened. That goes for each of us. We have to keep this information tight. Anyone else finds out that we know something, we all become targets."

"Won't happen again," replied Gandy.

Harris gestured toward the shuttle. "Let's go get our ship."

Just over an hour later, the shuttle settled in the grass field beside the *Bangor*.

Harris opened the hatch, hopping out onto the ground. "Sharvie, before we go anywhere, I'd like to see your computer skills put to use. Scour this shuttle for any bugs or signs of tracking software. When you're done here, you can start on the *Bangor*. Beginning today, we go dark. Let me have everyone's comms."

Harris raised a boot.

Tawn said, "Hold up there, Hoss. Why destroy those now? We may need them while we're here. You can stomp 'em when we're ready to leave."

"I guess that makes sense. Here, take them back."

Tawn looked over at the bunker. "You think it will let us in there?"

Harris shrugged. "Not sure. Farker normally runs for the door when we let him out. Doesn't look like he's going anywhere right now."

Tawn stepped down to the grass and walked to the bunker door. It opened for her.

Harris quickly followed. "That's different."

Tawn walked in, taking a seat at the table.

The image of Alexander Gaerten appeared.

"Hello, Tawn. Welcome back."

"Why was I allowed in this time?"

The image smiled. "You are recognized as a friend. Your actions have shown you to be respectful. As stated before, with time, you may be allowed further into this complex."

Harris patted Tawn on the shoulder. "Keep it up. You may be in for a special award from the cyber-genius."

The AI image asked, "Was that sarcasm, Harris?"

"Ah. It was."

"You enjoy sarcastic speak?"

"I guess I do. What of it?"

"Nothing in particular. That note will be added to your file."

Tawn chuckled. "You've been logged."

Harris asked, "What exactly do we have to do to get further access?"

"Be trustworthy."

"Trustworthy? Don't you have to do or accomplish something to earn that?"

"Yes."

"OK, so what can we do to be deemed more trustworthy?"

"Your ships have recording devices. Those will have to be removed."

"You mean like our log files from traveling?"

"There are sixteen recording devices on the ship you call *Bangor*. The ship you recently arrived on has five."

Tawn reacted. "Sixteen? That's aside from the ship's computer system?"

A slowly rotating image of the ship appeared where the floating head had been. "Since the craft with the moniker of *Bangor* has been residing here, sixteen devices have attempted to connect to an external comm. That places your craft under suspicion. Communications that have no known destination are not to be trusted. Can you explain the purpose of these devices?"

Harris pointed at the image. "Are those flashing red dots the location of the devices?"

"Yes."

"Then no. I can't explain them. I mean I can, but they are not ours."

"Please explain."

"We have an organization called the Domicile Defense Intelligence force, or DDI. They like to keep tabs on people so they can better defend our world. Those were placed on there for them to track our travels. Not by us, by them. We knew there were two such devices. And each time we've returned from here they have been scrubbed of any logs. So we didn't think it mattered."

"I see. But you did allow them to be brought here."

Harris shrugged. "We can't remove them or the DDI will want to know why. So long as they are scrubbed each time, what's it matter?"

The image of Alexander Gaerten returned. "It matters, Harris, because my ability to probe and locate such devices is limited. It is against the policy of this complex, and of my programming, to allow any such logging data to be taken from this facility."

"Well then, help us to take them off. We'd rather the whereabouts of this ship not be known anyway. And that's by the DDI or anyone else."

The image asked, "Would you like to remove the devices now?"

Harris nodded. "Would be happy to."

The image of the *Bangor* returned. "Please use this hologram to identify each of the devices. Point to an individual device for a more complete image of that area of your craft."

Harris held out a finger. "That one looks like a good first candidate. Is that on the doorframe?"

"As you enter the ship from outside, just to your left, a third of the way up the seal, you will find a three centimeter by two centimeter device with an approximate thickness of one millimeter. It appears to be bonded to the interior of the hull."

Harris walked out of the room, returning two minutes later. "I was looking right at it and almost didn't see it. Same color as the wall it was attached to. Tucked nicely behind that seal as well."

The device was set on the table. A second point was made and the area enlarged.

Harris returned several minutes later. "Same device, just on the other side of the hatch door. Would have never guessed it was a bug."

Tawn stood. The image disappeared as the hologram shut down.

Harris said, "Now what'd you do that for?"

"I was gonna go help."

"You can help by sitting your butt back down in the chair. I got this."

Tawn returned to her seat and the image of Alexander Gaerten flashed into view. "Welcome, Tawn."

Harris leaned in. "Can you bring the image of the *Bangor* up? Show us the location of the devices we were just talking about."

The image of the ship returned. The next thirty-four minutes were spent stripping bugging devices from the centuries-old warship.

When the last of the recorders had been removed, Harris dropped it on the table. "There you have it. Sixteen."

An image of the shuttle appeared. "Please remove the five items from the newly-arrived ship."

Harris shook his head. "You're just never satisfied, are you."

"Was that sarcasm?"

Harris chuckled. "Yep."

"Excellent. Then please get your enormous head out to that ship and finish the job."

Tawn burst out laughing. "I am liking this AI. It's already got you figured out."

Harris half frowned. "I'm not complex. Surprised it took this long."

With a scowl, the Biomarine turned and exited the bunker.

Chapter 19

Harris set the last bug on the table.

"Harris? Do you notice anything unusual about the devices?"

"Yeah, these thirteen all look similar. These three are very different."

The image of Alexander Gaerten returned. "Precisely. The three devices you have termed as different have attempted to communicate over a frequency often used by the New Earth Empire."

Tawn asked, "You saying we had New Earth bugs on our ship?"

The image nodded. "It would appear so."

"How do you know the Earthers use that frequency?"

"After you suggested that I open a wormhole to both Domicile and New Earth, I have been listening to each. It took several days to filter the signals and decode the encryption. It seems the New Earth Empire is ahead of you with regards to security. The Domicile frequency encryption was decoded in just over half the time."

Harris cut in: "Wait... are you telling us you can listen in on Earther communications?"

"I can."

"Is there any way for us to be able to do that?"

The image replied, "The partial artificial brain in Archibald has the ability to decode the New Earth encryption. However, if the base frequency is unknown, that effort may take some time to accomplish."

"How long is some time?"

"Perhaps three to four standard days."

"How long if the base frequency is known?"

"Several minutes."

"How do we find this base frequency?"

"The base frequency can be obtained by monitoring a broadcast."

Tawn asked, "So all we need to do is detect a broadcast and a few minutes later we can listen in?"

"That is a correct statement."

Harris said, "This could be huge. We could know what the Earthers are planning before they make a move."

Tawn nodded. "That would offer a huge advantage."

Harris walked out to the *Bangor*. "Sharvie? How's it going?"

"There were four monitoring applications on your computer. And another in your environmental system. And one in your power system. The log files in each of those only go back as far as your last trip to Domicile. They've all been eradicated.

"Never seen anything like these programs. Very well disguised. I only stumbled onto the first one by mistake. That led to the discovery of the others. As far as I can tell, we have them all."

Harris looked down with a chuckle. "Farker? You think the ship is clean of bugs?"

The simulated canine returned a single fark.

Harris replied, "Great... looks like we still have issues. Can you tell us where the bug is, boy?"

The dog trotted two steps to an interior wall, placing his nose onto a conduit that ran the length of the wall. Trish and Gandy pulled the tools needed to open the utility run, revealing a passive recorder inside. Harris, giving orders to his pet, proceeded to find an additional four recorders.

Tawn returned from the bunker. "Looks like I'm still just a friend to the doctor in there. I answered a few dozen more questions. He said I wasn't yet ready for the next step."

"My dog is sniffing out more bugs."

"This is insane," said Tawn. "We were nothing more than a flying recording station. So did we get them all?"

Farker returned three farks.

Harris reached down to rub the simulated fur head of his pet. "I think we have. Now we need to do the same to the shuttle."

Half an hour later, both ships were declared bug free.

Gandy asked, "So what's next? You think the bunker will give us access?"

Harris waved a hand toward the shuttle hatch. "Go see. Just stand in front of it. If it finds you worthy, it will let you in."

Gandy and Trish returned several minutes later. "Nothing. Maybe I need to run in there next time you go in."

Harris winced. "I'd rather not risk it. Tawn and I are on its good side right now and I want to keep it that way."

"Might be time we head back to Eden," said Tawn. "Whenever we're away I get the feeling something big is about to happen."

Harris replied, "How about this: we head back but stop short. If the Earther ships are still in orbit, we sit and listen for that base frequency the AI was talking about. If we catch it, we start decoding their communications."

Tawn nodded. "Sounds like a plan."

The two ships jumped into Eden space. The shuttle continued on to the planet while the *Bangor* held fast. Sharvie remained with Tawn and Harris, overseeing the use of Farker as a decryption tool for the Earther communications. Four comm channels being exchanged between two Earther destroyers were the first to become available.

Sharvie pushed a channel to the comm speaker. "...forty kilos. I can fit it in a standard container if you want. I show a shuttle scheduled to head your way in about an hour."

"Thank you, Mr. Puchkin. That will be adequate."

The conversation continued for several minutes before it was determined to be between maintenance workers on the two destroyers. The trading of supplies was a common occurrence between ships out on-station.

A second and then a third conversation yielded similar results. The fourth was between ship captains.

"...I would not disagree with that, Mamood. They will get what's coming to them in about fifteen minutes. And our Domer friends will do nothing about it."

"Good. That means our efforts here can finally get underway."

A third voice could be heard over the comm channel. "Excuse me, Captain, you asked for the identity of the second ship. The one that remains at its jump point. It is the same ship that attempted to pirate our titanium freighter."

Harris looked down at his console with a scowl. "Gah. Forgot to turn on our stealth. They've been looking right at us this whole time."

Tawn shook her head. "So much for listening in on them."

"Why would you say that?"

Tawn pointed at the name display. "Because they're coming our way. Should we jump, or head for the surface?"

Harris thought for a moment. "Let's head down. They aren't gonna do anything down there while our cruisers are sitting in orbit."

Tawn took control of the stick. "You got it. Should be on the ground in about twenty minutes. And no, they won't make it to us before we make it down. I'll angle us toward those cruisers. That should give them some pause."

Fifteen minutes into the run toward the surface, two wormholes opened in front of the Domicile cruisers. The heavy warships slipped silently through and the portals closed after them.

"Why would they leave?" asked Tawn.

A comm came in from Fireburg. "Harris, we have trouble. It appears the Earthers are on to our shenanigans with their well. They've captured our crews at Rumford and again at Dove. Not sure how they found out, but they did."

"We're on our way down. Be there in five. We recently found a handful of Earther bugs on our ship. I would bet the dome is crawling with them, but don't worry, we have a way to search them out."

The colonel growled. "We've been finding them as well. Caught two of our Domers planting them."

Harris frowned. "Takes all kinds. Do these people not know what's at stake here?"

"Credits talk. They always have. Sadly, I would bet a quarter of our citizens have a price."

"When we arrive, we'll work on getting the spy situation under control. Looks like the Earthers will finally be getting their titanium though."

Harris walked into the colonel's office with Farker at his heel.

The colonel looked around. "Tawn not with you?"

Harris shook his head. "She's showing our newest team member the dome with Trish and Gandy."

The colonel pulled a map up on his wall display. "I'm concerned. Our last report from the Rumford Mines detailed armed soldiers moving about. Since we took over Dove, they've been brazenly displaying as many weapons as they want. They've been conducting mock attacks on their facilities too."

Harris waved his hand. "They won't attack here. Not after last time. They know we have a few thousand Bios here and plenty of arms. I'm sure they know about those railguns out there too. I'm more worried about the destroyers up there. Our cruisers just pulled out."

The colonel stood. "When did that happen?"

Harris scratched his chin. "Ten minutes ago. Why?"

The colonel opened a comm channel. "Major, open the weapons lockers and issue a plasma rifle to every man who can carry one. And place the gunners for those railguns on high alert. Our Domer force has abandoned us."

"Yes, sir!" The major could be heard yelling at his subordinates just before the comm closed.

A comm channel came in to the colonel. "Sir, we have four wormholes opening. New Earth ships are coming through. We count sixteen so far."

Harris asked, "Why would DDF abandon us?"

The colonel took a deep breath and let it out. "They know we stole that freighter. And now they know we're responsible for tampering with the Earther well, as well as convincing the pacifists to move. My guess is they've pulled all support from Eden because they don't want war. We're about to be attacked by the full empire. You might want to think about getting back to your ship."

Harris opened a comm to Tawn. "Get everyone back to the *Bangor* immediately. We're about to be attacked by the Earthers."

Tawn replied, "Our defenses here should be ample for holding them off. They don't have anything that will get through that dome."

Harris shook his head. "Sixteen New Earth warships just jumped into Eden space. We probably only have ten minutes to get out of here."

Tawn nodded. "Will meet you there."

Harris hustled into the hall, heading toward the docking bay. Farker kept pace as Harris' run turned into a full sprint.

Tawn, Trish, Gandy, and Sharvie were waiting at the ship. "Up. In. Go!"

Harris strapped himself in as he powered up the *Bangor*'s drive. As the armored ship taxied toward the open air of Eden, the first of a half-dozen plasma rounds fell from the sky. The Earther ships were beginning to drop through the atmosphere.

"Best you all strap in hard. This could get rough!"

Tawn powered up the railgun circuits. "Guns are online if needed."

Harris turned the ship toward the attackers. The throttle was pushed full. The *Bangor* raced upward as a dozen plasma rounds came from above. A hard left maneuver dodged the incoming. The rounds that followed would not miss.

"Hang on!" Harris yelled.

The hull reverberated and shook violently as four charges impacted and dispersed. Random moves kept the number from the barrage that followed at five.

Three Banshees and another Zwicker popped into view on the nav display.

Gandy held up a fist. "We have help!"

Tawn pressed the trigger for the railgun. A steady hum was followed by forty rounds per minute exiting the end of the rails. Two of the attacking ships took damage. The next volley from the Earthers saw eight simultaneous hits on the *Bangor*.

Tawn said, "Can't take much more! Another hit like that and we're losing inhibitor boxes!"

Harris turned the control stick hard to port, dodging the next set from the destroyers.

A comm was opened: "Colonel, order your fighters off. We have to leave. I'm sending them coordinates for a rendezvous point. If we continue, it's suicide."

The colonel replied: "We're as prepared as we can be. Keep safe. We may need your coordinated help at some point, but that time is not now. The dome is holding and we've yet to fire our rail cannons."

Another volley of plasma rounds struck the hull of the *Bangor* as she sped away. The other fighters followed, with one taking major damage before reaching a safe distance.

"This is Lieutenant Haversham. I'm losing speed. Heading for that plateau."

Harris replied, "Get ready to ditch and run. We're picking you up. Everyone else, proceed to the assigned coordinates."

Harris timed his landing perfectly. A cloud of sand and dust spread outward as the downed pilot dove through an open hatch. As the *Bangor* began to lift away, Tawn unleashed a hail of tungsten rounds, shattering the fighter's hardened hull and pulverizing the remaining pieces.

Harris glanced over his shoulder. "Strap in on one of the benches. We have two of those destroyers heading for us."

The lieutenant parked himself on the closest open seat beside Gandy, latching a belt strap and pulling it tight. "Thanks for the pick-up."

Harris yelled, "Hang on!"

Again the *Bangor*'s hull reverberated and the ship rocked and bounced as the attacking ships sent a continuous stream of plasma their way.

Another pilot's voice came over the comm. "Help is here, Mr. Gruberg. Get the lieutenant out of here. We'll get them off your tail."

Tungsten rounds from the railguns of two Banshees and a Zwicker caved in the forward decks of the nearest destroyer. As the Earther ship headed for the desert floor in smoke and flames, the second ship turned away. Two rounds hit it center-ship, sending streams of debris out the opposite side as the tungsten rounds ripped through the ship's decks. The defending ships turned back toward Harris and the others.

Tawn came over the comm.: "Nice work! Follow us home!"

As the small group of Fireburg escorts made their way into free space, another dozen wormholes opened where the other destroyers had first come through. Twenty-four New Earth warships, including a flagship cruiser, took position in orbit over the Fireburg colony.

Harris shook his head as he let out a long breath. "No way the colonel can hold that off."

Tawn said, "The dome is holding. And they aren't chancing those rail cannons. The other destroyers are keeping their distance."

"Won't matter. They only have food stocks to last about three weeks. All the Earthers have to do is wait them out. The colonel will have to negotiate a surrender, and everyone there will have to be ferried back to Domicile. It's looking like we just spent all that time building the Earthers a premium mine."

Harris clenched his fist in anger.

Tawn asked, "What's creeping around in your head?"

"Baxter Rumford. She just got everything she ever wanted. Once we're gone she'll control the mining on that entire planet."

Tawn winced. "Just as bad, this will do in Mr. Morgan. None of his associates who invested in this will get their money back. And I have no doubt there will be a political penalty to pay as well."

Harris sighed. "They had better not come down too hard. He's a primary military supplier. They're gonna need his help when the Great War returns."

Sharvie asked, "You really think that's coming?"

Harris nodded. "Will take a couple years, but the Earthers, with all this titanium, will be back with a vengeance. Meanwhile our military is being dismantled. We couldn't be in a worse situation."

Tawn crossed her arms as she leaned back in her chair. "We do have a way to prevent it, but we might kill as many people as we save."

"How's that?"

"We shut down that bunker on Midelon. You take away wormholes and nobody will be fighting anybody. Would take the Earthers four hundred years to reach Domicile. Why bother? Problem is, we strand everyone in the truce worlds and outer colonies where they are. A lot of them depend on trade shipments to stay alive. Without the wormholes, life on many of those planets becomes very primitive."

"Even so, if it means we prevent Domicile from being enslaved, we can't take it off the table."

Sharvie looked at Gandy. "What are they talking about?"

"If the bunker on Midelon is attacked or destroyed, we lose the ability to travel by wormhole. That facility and one other generate what's called a boson field. It permeates the space around us and allows the wormhole generators in our ships to work. If the field gets shut down, there won't be any more space travel except on standard drives."

Sharvie frowned. "We don't want that."

Trish said, "It would mean our new home would be wherever we were when that happened. If that's Midelon, be prepared to never see another face besides the ones you're looking at right now."

Harris pointed at his chin. "She'd be lucky to see this face every day for the rest of her life."

"That face?" said Tawn. "Luckier than what? Being trampled by a wild bogler?"

Tawn turned to face the others. "Look, we're alive, we're free. So long as we're able, we'll do whatever it takes to protect our homeworld. If that means sacrificing ourselves, well, I think we've all already signed up for that with just being here.

"Don't worry about it unless that time comes. Like Harris says, we probably have a couple years for the Earthers to build a fleet before they make a move. In the meantime, we'll see if there's any way to slow them down."

Chapter 20

The *Bangor* joined the other three ships at the rendezvous point.

Harris opened a comm: "None of us expected to be here right now and we don't have all the plans. So we're gonna need to have everyone provide input. If you have any ideas about anything, I'd like to hear what they are."

One of the pilots replied, "I could use some food."

Tawn shook her head. "Great. We've got two Harris' in our group."

Harris glanced around the ship. "Has been a while. Not like we're turning back immediately to fight those ships. We might all think better on a full belly."

Tawn scowled. "You're serious?"

Harris asked, "Anyone else hungry?"

Gandy slowly raised his hand. "Sorry, Miss Freely, but we haven't eaten since before leaving Domicile."

Harris pulled up a nav map of the surrounding space. "At six light years we have a planet that's just outside the habitable zone in its system. I say we jump there, park the other ships and take a ride to Midelon."

Tawn shook her head. "I don't think it's a good idea to take anybody else out there."

Harris replied, "Look, they won't know where we are. We have food there. And we can take all the time we need for planning. Might even be able to ask the wizard inside the bunker what he thinks."

Tawn rolled her eyes. "It's an AI. You want an AI planning out our comeback?"

Harris shrugged. "At least it's something. You have a better plan? Spew it out."

Tawn glanced around with a disgusted look on her face before mumbling, "I got nothing."

"What? What'd you say?"

"I got nothing to spew. Let's go and get it over with."

Coordinates were sent to the others. The two Banshees and the Zwicker were parked in what was decided to be a well hidden location on an icy planet. The three pilots joined the others on the *Bangor*. The nav display was hidden from view as the ship jumped to Midelon space. A short run had the team settling on the grassy field just outside the bunker.

Harris stood. "For those of you who are new, this is our private hideaway. You don't need to know where it is and please don't ask because we won't tell. It's better that you don't know. As you exit you'll see a building to your left. That's our supply house. We have it stocked with MREs and other sustainables. You'll find four bunks in there and we have another two here. Make use of any of them, but please respect that others are likely to use them as well.

"We'll head over there to eat, after which you're free to roam about. We're on an island, and you'll want to stay away from the shoreline. We found out the hard way there are sudden tidal surges that will overtake you in seconds if you go down by the water. Other than that, enjoy the sunshine and fresh air.

"Oh, and Tawn and I might be going in and out of a bunker door just outside. Don't try to follow us in, and whatever you do, don't make any attempt to break in or destroy it. What's inside there has important purpose for all of us. I won't say what it is. Just know that it does."

Tawn shook her head as they walked. "Still not sure this was the best of ideas."

Harris huffed. "What would you have had us do, then?"

"Maybe jump back to the Retreat?"

Harris thought for a moment. "Yeah. I guess that wouldn't have been bad either. Why didn't you suggest it?"

"Didn't think of it."

Harris chuckled. "Can't think on an empty stomach?"

Tawn scowled. "More like when I'm frustrated."

Harris stopped. "Sounds like you need a refresher on your psychological training. Not supposed to let stuff get to you enough to cloud your judgment."

Tawn half smiled. "You do that with food."

Harris laughed as he continued to walk. "Yeah, but that's physiological, not psycho. You need to get your logicals straightened out."

"How about I club you on the head with my balled fist?"

"And how would that solve anything?"

Tawn opened the door to the supply house. "Would get rid of my frustration."

Harris hesitated before walking through in front of her. "Yeah, I guess that would."

Twenty minutes was taken for lunch before the group got down to business. Suggestions were made about heading to the Retreat or back to Domicile. An alternate was a trip back to Eden to spy.

After several hours of talk, Harris raised a hand. "Stir the pot with all we've talked about. Tawn and I will be gone for a bit. If you feel the need for a nap or to get out and walk, then do so."

Harris looked down. "Farker? Want to follow us in?"

The robotic pet returned three farks.

Tawn sat at the table. The hologram image of Alexander Gaerten flashed into existence.

"Welcome, Tawn, Harris."

A short discussion ensued, and the current situation was explained.

Harris said, "So we're looking for a way to reverse what's happened."

The image replied, "Time cannot be turned back, Harris. We can only move forward."

"I know that. What we're looking for is suggestions about how to move forward. How do we get the Earthers to leave?"

"Perhaps a compromise is in order? Divide the planet equally and allow each to govern their own half."

Harris shook his head. "Won't work. We can't allow them access to the titanium. That's our whole issue. They get that resource and it leads to the restart of the Great War."

"Perhaps a different compromise is in order? Domicile controls eight outer world colonies. New Earth controls six. The truce worlds comprise sixteen such planetary systems. Cede control of some of those truce worlds in an attempt to placate their expansionist desires. That action may not fully satisfy those desires, but it may buy you time to offer another solution."

Harris frowned. "Problem with that scenario is we—that being Tawn and me—don't control those worlds. The politicians back on Domicile do, and we don't hold any sway with them. If anything, any idea coming from us would be a negative."

Tawn reiterated, "The politicians back home don't care for us. They think our meddling is the cause of the tension out here, which I guess it is, but that's beside the point. We don't have anyone there we can approach."

"You previously said Bannis Morgan has connections. Perhaps those could be made use of?"

"Maybe," said Harris. "Although about now I think he may be toxic to his politician friends as well. Don't you have any suggestions where we could use technology to change the situation? Could the space around Eden be excluded from the boson field? Would be nice if it took them a couple hundred years to get their titanium back to New Earth."

The image frowned. "The boson field is either on or off. We do not control where it permeates other than the distance from this facility. In order to deny boson access to Eden, it would also be denied to Domicile and New Earth."

Tawn crossed her arms. "Too bad we can't just negate the field around an area. Not from here, but from a ship or a building there."

The image was silent for several seconds. "That may be a possibility. When this facility was first constructed, it was found during the testing phase that certain wavelengths of gamma radiation directly interfered with the wormhole generator functionality. The tests proved only temporary and were shown to only have minimal effect once the full strength boson field was online and projecting."

Harris asked, "You saying we may have a way to disrupt a wormhole generator?"

"It may be possible, yes. Tests will have to be performed that are beyond the capability of this facility."

"Well, we're right here and willing to do whatever testing is needed. Just tell us what we need to do and we'll get it done."

Tawn nodded. "Would be great to have an anti-boson generator that we could put on the *Bangor*. That might be just the thing needed to keep them from transporting titanium."

Harris said, "Nice job, Tawn."

Tawn nodded.

The image of Alexander Gaerten frowned. "You may want to temper your enthusiasm until at least the minimum of testing has been conducted. It's possible we may not be able to produce the quantity of radiation required to overcome the strong boson field."

"Don't be so negative," said Harris. "Just tell us what we need to do."

A list of test instruments and devices appeared on the hologram display. "I'm transferring this list to each of your comms. The items requested are not available here on Midelon. You will have to seek them out on Domicile."

Tawn replied, "We can leave right now if it helps. Will we require any special skills to assemble anything?"

"I believe you to be capable of following instructions."

Harris turned toward the door with a wave. "Let's get on this. It'll give us a chance to talk with Mr. Morgan. And we'll stop by Eden on the way to assess the situation."

A short while later, the *Bangor* slowed as it approached the desert planet.

Tawn looked over the console. "Good, you're using the stealth mode."

"I get the feeling we'll be using it a lot. Let's see... the dome looks intact and the Earther ships aren't firing on it anymore."

Tawn said, "Hey, check this out. A zoomed-in image showed the burned-out hulls of two Earther warships. Those are new. The colonel must have opened up with the rail cannons."

"You sure those weren't the ones we tangled with?"

Tawn shook her head as she moved the camera view. "We only took down one and it's over here. Swarming with Earther crewmen. And..."

Tawn shifted the view to a handful of Earther ships sitting in orbit. "Check out this one. That's the hull damage we inflicted. Those two on the ground had to have gotten too close to the dome. Should we try to listen in on their comms?"

Harris turned the *Bangor* away. "We have to pick up the items the AI needs. Would love to know what the Earthers were planning, but whatever that is we can't do anything about it at the moment anyway."

Gandy said, "If we could get their base frequency down to the colonel, maybe they could do the decoding on their own."

Sharvie replied, "Doubt they have the processing power down there to do that. Whatever that dog has in it is much different than even this ship has."

Harris added, "And Farker stays with us. Any decodes will just have to wait."

The *Bangor* was soon settling on the paved lot outside the warehouse on Domicile, having come down to the surface while still in stealth mode. No attempts were made by the Domicile authorities to contact or identify the ship. A comm had Bannis Morgan on his way to meet them.

After entering the warehouse, Gandy circled the remaining Banshee. "They've hardly touched it. And nobody is here. It's too early in the day for everyone to have gone home already."

Bannis walked through the door. "We had a visit from the DDI. They crawled all over it, arrested my mechanics, and shut us down. They were released the following day, but have asked not to have to come back."

Harris held a finger up to his lips, gesturing toward Bannis' comm bracelet. Leaning down, he whispered into Farker's ear. Twenty seconds later the dog farked three times.

Harris said, "Looks like your comm is clear. I guess you've heard about Eden?"

"Only bits and pieces. I'm told our forces are washing their hands of the whole planet, turning it over to the Earthers to control. I heard your well blockers were discovered."

Tawn nodded. "Can't believe our politicians are doing this. Not only will the Earthers be pulling ore from the Rumford Mine, but ours as well. And we know what that ore will be used for."

"I'm told they gave their word it would not be used for warships. Unfortunately, our people accepted that premise without insisting on any sort of verification. I'm beginning to think the entire Senate is made up of fools, my friends included."

Harris frowned. "One of the reasons we came back was to see what you could do about the situation, given your political connections."

Bannis shook his head. "They are all running scared at the moment. The pacifists now control all the key committees. I expect our next budget proposal to slash defense spending by half. It really is the perfect storm."

Harris opened a comm channel. "We have a list of equipment and parts we need for an important project. Any way you could help us get those in an expedited fashion?"

"Depends. Can I pass it on to my people to fulfill or is this a private matter?"

"Don't think there's anything illegal on there, but you might split it up just so anyone snooping around won't have the complete list."

Tawn added, "We found a mountain of bugs on the *Bangor* even though we thought we had swept it thoroughly. The DDI as well as the Earther spies have been following everything we've been doing. Three of the tracking bugs we found were Earther."

Harris walked toward the personal shuttle the industry magnate had come in on.

Tawn asked, "Where you going?"

Harris replied, "Gonna have Farker check his ship for bugs. Mr. Morgan, can we scan your ship's systems?"

Bannis nodded. "Please do."

Fifteen minutes later, Harris stood beside the shuttlecraft. An even dozen, including an Earther device had been found. I'd say you are a popular guy in the intel circles."

Bannis glanced down at the dog. "Would love to borrow your friend for a week."

Harris shook his head. "He stays with me. Can I ask how long you think it will take to get the equipment and parts on that list?"

"One, maybe two days?"

Harris said, "Then you have me and Farker for one or two days. We can search wherever you'd like."

"I'd like to begin with my home and then move to my office. The majority of my time is spent at those two places or on this ship. And I'd like to bring my security team along. Will give them a better idea of what to look for in the future."

Harris returned a half frown. "Might be your own team that's placing them. The arms of the DDI are long. Just know they will be listening with any chance they get. Shall we go?"

Bannis hesitated. "I don't believe our efforts will be worthwhile. If we remove the devices, they will make every effort to install new ones. I would think a better strategy would be to use what's already there to drive the information we want them to have."

"Plant intel?"

"Precisely."

Harris rubbed the back of his neck. "Not sure what we could tell them. And I have to wonder what good it would do anyway. They have to have known about everything we were doing on Eden. I don't see where they made any effort to stop that assault."

Bannis held up a finger. "It does make their motives suspect, but it could also be an inability to act against such a large force without the backing of the government. Small ops they could manage. Something that size... doubtful."

Tawn placed her hands on her hips. "So we can't rely on the DDI to defend us. And we can't rely on our own government. I'd say we're gonna be doing this ourselves."

Harris nodded. "Which is why it's important for us to get that equipment we came for. Any way to expedite that effort?"

Bannis stepped aside, opening a comm. His conversation was short. He lowered his arm as he walked back into the group. "The list is away to my most trusted. She'll divide it up and see to it that it's done as soon as possible."

Gandy asked, "Any chance of us getting that last Banshee operational?"

Harris glanced back at the warehouse. "Take Trish and see what you can do. If you need muscle, I'm sure these three would be happy to assist."

Gandy, Trish, and the three Biomarine pilots headed for the warehouse.

Harris pointed toward the *Bangor*. "Let's go sit in a bug-free environment for a while and chat. You can tell us about your struggles with the DDF budget. Are they seriously cutting it in half?"

Bannis nodded as they walked. "At the moment they are two votes shy of getting that passed. Heavy pressure, as well as generous incentives are being applied. They are basing our needs on our ability to defend against the Earthers with their current resources. With those cuts, it will put us about even with where they are."

Tawn scowled. "Idiots. Don't they realize the Earthers would still be fighting us right now if all things were even? They only stopped because they were losing."

Bannis replied, "Also troubling is the number of New Earth diplomats and business persons we now have on this planet. The New Earth Intelligence Corps knows our exact status. We have our own spies there, but they are closely watched and any information is difficult and risky to come by. Here... we're an open book."

Chapter 21

The last of Bannis Morgan's subordinates returned to the warehouse carrying the requested items. The *Bangor* was loaded and the journey set. Just over an hour later the ship was settling onto the grassy field at Midelon. The items were moved into Trish's amply outfitted shop.

Harris sat in the chair in front of the table in the bunker. The hologram image of Alexander Gaerten came to life.

"Welcome, Harris. Were you able to acquire the equipment I suggested?"

Harris nodded. "We were. We have it in our shop. We have tools there to work with."

The image replied, "Take Archibald and position him where he has a full view of the shop. I will connect with you through him to provide instruction for the device assembly."

Harris returned to the shop, picking up his faithful pet and depositing it on a table with a full view of the shop floor and its benches. A panel near the dog's right hindquarter opened. A smaller hologram image of Alexander Gaerten appeared.

Gandy crossed his arms. "I was wondering what that module back there was."

"Before we begin, in order to simplify our communications, please refer to me as Alex."

"OK, Alex, tell us where to begin."

The team worked through the Midelon night, only stopping for a break as the first light of day began to appear in the sky outside.

Gandy said, "This is supposed to have some effect on the boson field? So far I'm completely lost."

Harris shrugged. "If you're asking me, you're asking the wrong person. Go ask Alex."

Gandy stood in front of Farker. "Alex, how exactly is this contraption supposed to work? What's it do?"

Alex replied, "Are you familiar with the inertial dampener on your ship?"

"Somewhat."

The boson field ties all matter together. When a wormhole is created, two locations within that field can be brought close, allowing direct, instantaneous travel between those points. The inertial dampener divides those same ties along its own field, essentially making two boson fields where one does not interact with the other. This is accomplished in an indirect manner by separating the two, whereas the device you are piecing together, in theory, will negate the field within an area."

Gandy asked, "What happens when the boson field is negated?"

Alex replied, "Theoretically, any wormhole generator within that new area would be unable to spawn a wormhole. However, there may be other side effects the theories do not reveal."

"Such as?"

"Such as all matter within that void being instantly annihilated. Or perhaps it would explode outward, burning like a sun. We won't know until it has been tested."

Gandy stood still for several seconds. "I can't say I like the sound of either of those."

"Theoretically, it could also form a black hole, where all surrounding matter will be pulled in."

"Not liking that option either. So how do we test this without killing ourselves?"

"Remotely. I propose it be flown to a location on the edge of the boson field for a trial run. I would also suggest we do so through a wormhole that is immediately shut down. Once that is done, a second wormhole can be opened at what we would consider a safe viewing distance."

"Well, that doesn't sound so bad. How far away is a safe viewing distance?"

"I believe a quarter light year to be sufficient. You asked earlier what the three devices under construction were. Two are measurement devices. They will record valuable information that will allow us to verify if the main device worked as theorized. The third is the actual boson field negator. We may be producing a small amount of anti-matter in the process of bringing it online. That is where the unknown factors will come into play."

Gandy said, "I thought anti-matter was still theoretical."

"It is. However, with this experiment, we may prove it to be real."

Harris asked, "You understand any of that?"

Gandy half smiled. "Some of it. He's basically saying it will work or we'll all get sucked into a black hole. If it's the latter, we'll be dead in an instant, so I guess it won't matter to us anyway."

Harris chuckled. "Will matter to me."

One of the Biomarine pilots tapped Tawn on the shoulder. "Miss Freely, if it's all the same, while this is going on we'd like to be back at Eden where we can monitor the situation. We still have about sixty-five hundred people down there."

Tawn nodded. "Take a handful of MREs with you. I don't know how long it will be before we make it out there. If you're running out, make a jump back to the Retreat to restock. They should have plenty. When we get you back, I'll have Sharvie scrub your flight logs to have them show the three of you have been doing nothing but observing from Eden space. You never went anywhere else. Got it?"

"Yes, ma'am."

As the others continued work on the anti-boson device, Tawn returned the Biomarines to their ships. Minutes later they were lifting through the cold thin atmosphere of the icy planet on their way back to the space surrounding Eden.

The *Bangor* landed and Tawn walked into the shop. "Don't know what good they'll be able to do there. As much as they were doing here, I suppose. I swung by before my jump back. Status remains the same. A standoff."

Trish said, "We get this one panel cover on and we're finished."

Harris asked, "We'll be ready to test?"

Alex replied, "Low level testing may begin when the panel is applied. Adjustments will have to be made before full deployment and testing can take place."

Gandy stood. "We're good. Light her up."

Power was applied to each of the recorders.

Alex said, "Internal tests reveal no issues. Please apply power to the negation unit."

Trish flipped a toggle switch. A green, bar indicator showed the device was coming to life. As the status bar reached half way, the negation unit began to hum.

Gandy stepped back. "Is it supposed to do that?"

Alex replied, "The theoretical design gave no indication of such a vibration."

As the indicator reached three-quarters, the device began to slowly wobble and the hum became more pronounced.

Harris said, "Should we turn it off?"

Gandy shook his head. "I'm not touching that thing."

The one-meter-cubed box began to walk itself across the floor, backing Trish into a corner. Harris moved to free her, stepping close to the unit as he picked her from the ground behind it. Small violet tentacles of light stretched out from the box, seeming to caress the calf of Harris' left leg.

Harris scowled as he was held in place. "Thing's got a hold of me."

Trish was set on the floor by Harris, where she hurried toward the door as he continued to try to pull away.

Tawn asked, "Alex, what's happening?"

As the indicator reached 100 percent, the negation unit began bouncing off the floor as the frequency of its vibration dropped rapidly. The energy beams holding Harris in place turned from violet to red. Harris let out a howl as a bolt of electricity raced across the beams from the box.

"What the... turn this thing off!"

As a second jolt shot across to Harris' calf, a shockwave emerged from the unit, knocking the others down as it crashed into them and slammed the walls. Items on shelves fell to the floor. The unit shut down.

Alex was the first to speak: "I believe the initial test was a success."

Harris struggled to walk across the room with his now numb leg. "A success? That thing nearly killed us!"

"You were not in danger. The shock you received was mild. Any effect will be temporary."

Tawn grabbed the edge of a table, pulling herself to her feet as she chuckled. "You're walking like you just rode a bull at a bogler rodeo."

Harris stopped, looking down at the biosuit that covered his numb limb. "You think this is funny?"

Tawn laughed. "It's getting funnier."

Alex said, "I have analyzed the initial recordings. The data appears to support the theory behind the device."

Trish said, "I have a question. Why is it we have triple the parts? We building more of these?"

Alex replied, "When the device is fully powered up, its circuits will begin to deteriorate. The duration of the field negation will depend on when the device reaches a condition of critical failure. The data from that live test will tell us how long the effects will last. The device itself will be consumed."

Harris took a seat in a chair as he stomped his numb foot on the floor. "So after this test we have two of these devices to make use of?"

"Assuming the remaining parts are fully functional, yes. Each can be put through a test similar to what we did here. The recording devices can be used again. We only need assemble the negation units themselves."

Trish patted her brother on the back. "That means us. Mr. Gruberg, maybe if you go walk around on it the feeling will come back."

Tawn chuckled. "She's trying to say your whining is disruptive. Come on, I'll take you for a walk."

As Harris stood, Alex spoke: "Trish and Gandy Boleman, you as well as Sharvie Withrow have been added to the friends list for the outer room of the facility. When we are finished here, you will be welcome in the outer room, where the next level of investigation into your trustworthiness can begin."

Gandy replied, "Thanks, I guess."

Sharvie asked, "Could I come over while they are doing the assembly? Or do you need to stay here to communicate through Farker?"

"I am capable of both at once. You are more than welcome in the outer room. Trish, Gandy, I will continue to be available for assembly instruction."

Gandy replied, "Good 'cause I'm sure we'll need it."

Trish picked the first piece off the floor as she turned toward her brother. "Bet you a beverage I can finish mine first."

Gandy dropped to his knees as he pulled the first two parts of the device together. "You're on."

Harris wobbled as he and Tawn walked out onto the grass in front of the shop. "You can let me go now. I can manage."

Tawn chuckled. "I'm thinking of putting on my helmet so I can get a recording of this. The colonel and the other Bios would get a huge kick out of it."

Harris stumbled, catching himself just before hitting the ground. "I just hope they're still alive down there. I feel responsible for getting them into this mess. They could have been out at the Retreat, slowly moving more of us out there to live in peace."

Tawn shook her head. "And the Earthers would have already overrun the pacies and titanium would be flowing freely to their shipyards. We did at least delay that happening."

Harris hopped up and down in place for several seconds. "I think my feeling is coming back. And six months of acceleration might have been a good thing. Who's to say our defenses back home wouldn't have been in better shape? If that budget passes you'll see ships being mothballed so fast it'll make your head spin."

Harris took a short, but awkward, sprint. As he returned he high-stepped with his right leg.

Tawn chuckled. "A recording would have been priceless."

"I think it's good now. Let's go check on Sharvie."

As the two entered the bunker room Harris looked around. "Thought she came in here."

Tawn nodded as she walked toward the usual table and chair. "Alex, did Sharvie not come in here?"

"Yes, Tawn. I invited her into security level two. She is quite adept at computing."

Harris asked, "How she get in there? She couldn't have answered all those questions in the last couple minutes."

Alex replied, "Did you take note of Sharvie's activities while the negation unit was under construction?"

Tawn nodded. "She was messing around on a terminal console. I assumed she was connected to the *Bangor*, running diagnostics or something."

The image of Alex smiled. "She was connected through Archibald to me. Her answers were concise and well matched to the expected answers."

"Well, what's she doing in there?"

"I'm afraid I cannot reveal that to you at this time, Harris. And she is being instructed to remain silent as well. If not, she and whoever she tells will forever lose those privileges, as well as access to this outer room."

"You sure are a struggle to work with," said Tawn.

"Proper answers will allow access. Showing agitation, frustration, or other malevolent responses will only work to slow your acceptance process."

Harris chuckled. "She does get agitated."

Tawn returned an evil eye. "And I can be malevolent when pushed."

Harris smacked her on the back. "Go ahead, swing at me, take another step back. In fact, I'll make a bet with you that I get through that door first."

"Inciting aggression through the use of verbal slights is also cause for concern to the admittance algorithm. Was that an attempt to make fun of Tawn?"

Harris straightened up. "No, of course not. I have the utmost of respect for my partner and fellow Biomarine."

The image of Alex smiled. "Excellent. You are well on your way to achieving level two admittance."

Harris said, "Think I'll go check on the others."

Trish and Gandy hurriedly moved about the floor of the shop as each raced to complete their unit first. Harris sat in a chair next to the table where Farker watched the others as they worked. Harris reached out and stroked the simulated fur on the dog's head.

Gandy looked over. "What happened to Tawn?"

Harris waved. "She's over in front of the hologram."

"What happened to Sharvie?"

"She got invited through the door to the next access level."

Gandy stopped. "She what?"

"She cheated. The whole time you were in here building up that first unit, she was connected with the AI on that console over there. She apparently correctly answered the questions she was asked."

Trish said, "Wow. Can't wait to hear about what's in there."

"She can't talk about it, so don't ask. It seems we each have to make it through on our own."

"You and Tawn made it to the first level together."

Harris smirked. "Or we fouled up by being in there together each time."

"What are you doing right now?" Trish asked.

"Watching you I guess."

"Why not hop on that console and see if you can get through to the next level?"

Harris scrunched up his face, wanting to give a sarcastic reply. "Fine."

The next hour flew past as Trish and Gandy scurried about the shop while Harris made faces at the console in front of him after each question asked. Tawn walked through the door with Sharvie just as the Bolemans were finishing up their work.

"Guess who popped out the second door?"

Harris replied, "Baxter Rumford?"

Tawn returned a half scowl.

Sharvie said, "And before anyone asks, no I can't tell you anything about it other than to say it was interesting... very interesting."

"Did Alex tell you to say that?" Harris asked. "Just to make us all eager to get in there?"

Sharvie shook her head. "It's genuinely interesting."

Trish stood. "Finished!"

Gandy huffed as he attached a final cover plate. "You must have left something out."

Trish defiantly replied, "I don't think so."

Gandy pointed. "Then what is that piece over there?"

Sharvie stepped in. "It was a spare. I did the inventory and we had four of those."

Harris stood from his console. "Let's do the initial test and get this show on the road."

Everyone backed over to the door as a unit was switched on. A repeat of the physical attributes of the first test ensued, culminating in a shockwave that knocked the group down as they attempted to flee from the doorway. A test of the second unit saw a similar result, with the group escaping the final consequence.

Harris said, "Let's get them on the ship and out for a live test."

Gandy asked, "If it works as designed, how do we make use of it?"

Harris shrugged. "I'm guessing Alex will reveal that to us once the test is complete. At the moment I don't have a clue."

Chapter   22

The boson field negation devices were loaded into the cargo hold and the *Bangor* jumped to the preselected target area. The first device was deployed with the two recording devices placed at one-sixteenth light-year intervals moving away. The *Bangor* moved to a location just over a quarter light-year distant. A wormhole was opened close to the unit.

"Let's see what this baby can do."

A start signal was sent and the wormhole closed. As instructed, fifteen minutes later, a second wormhole was opened to the farthest out recorder.

Tawn said, "Still functioning."

The wormhole was closed. An attempt was made to open another beside the closest of the two recorders.

Tawn shook her head. "Won't open."

Trish leaned over Harris' shoulder. "That means it's working, right? And the field it's creating is at least an eighth of a light-year across. On standard engines, it would take us two years to cross that."

Harris nodded. "Sounds like we have a success. The question now is... how long will it stay active?"

Sharvie stepped up. "If we wanted, we could find out exactly how big that field is."

Harris asked, "I'm game. What you want me to do?"

"Open a wormhole halfway between the two recorders. If it gets rejected we know it at least extends out to there. Just keep doing that until we find the edge."

Harris looked over his shoulder with a grin. "Have I ever told you I like you?"

"No."

Harris chuckled. "Good. Wouldn't want you getting a big head over yourself."

Fifteen minutes of testing revealed a negated boson field almost a quarter light-year across.

Harris turned to the others. "I've got just the thing to keep us busy while we wait."

Gandy asked, "That must mean you're hungry."

Harris nodded. "We may be here for a while. Who wants to eat?"

Three meals passed before a check of the negation field showed it was beginning to recede.

Tawn said, "Eighteen hours. The retraction rate is linear. Should be offline in about two hours."

Harris opened a wormhole to the nearest recorder. "Let's go pick them up."

Tawn replied, "We should affix a self-destruct mechanism for when the field has completely dissipated. Don't want the Earthers or anyone else building any of these."

"Not necessary," said Gandy. "Shouldn't be much left of the device when we get to it. Alex said when it goes it should melt into a ball."

The recorders and the now defunct negation unit were collected and the crew jumped back to Midelon. The hologram avatar of Alexander Gaerten uploaded the data from the recorders. Scans of the failed equipment were taken and sent along as well.

Ninety minutes later, an image of Alex appeared. "We have several adjustments to make. Miss Boleman, I'm forwarding the suggestions to your comm as a recording. Listen, make the adjustments, move to the next step."

Harris asked, "It worked. Why are we changing anything?"

"The adjustments will allow one of two modes: the standard mode which you were just witness to, or a timed mode where the field will shut down at a precisely programmed time. This will allow use of the device for more than one occurrence. The timed use is cumulative, with the device failure imminent when the same amount of time has passed."

"Fantastic," said Tawn. "Now we just have to figure out a use for it."

Gandy said, "We could go order enough parts to build hundreds of these. Just keep putting them out and keep the space around Eden at sub-light speeds."

Tawn replied, "It takes you and your sister most of a day to put one together. You prepared to be building these things every day for the next year?"

Gandy shook his head. "The rest of you are capable of doing this too. And maybe we enlist more Biomarines back at the Retreat to help."

Harris rubbed the back of his neck. "No, we can't let anyone else in on this. We lose control of this tech and all the truce worlds and outer colonies would be overrun in a few months. This is our device, our burden. Let's focus our brainpower on how we might use it to liberate the colonel and everyone else on Eden."

Sharvie turned toward the hologram. "Alex, we can capture and decode the Earthers' comms. That would mean we can get through their security. Is there any way we could hack into their ships' systems and take control? Even if only temporarily?"

"That would depend on how they organize their security. If they isolate systems, the answer is no. In that instance, for example, access gained to their comms would be limited to their comm system."

"How are the systems arranged on the *Bangor*?" asked Harris.

"They are connected, although each system maintains a separate firewall against intrusion."

Harris nodded. "So a hack might be worthwhile."

Gandy asked, "Could you analyze an Earther ship for security purposes if we brought one here?"

"I could."

Harris held up a hand. "Hold on, I don't know that I like the sound of that."

"Not suggesting we bring a full ship here," said Gandy. "If we could steal an empty one, Alex could help us crack their systems."

Harris chuckled. "Sure, there's hundreds of empty Earther warships lying about out there. All ripe for the taking."

Tawn crossed her arms. "What if we could get them to evacuate one? If we managed to hack their control systems we could then fly it out remotely."

Harris laughed. "You people need to come back to reality. The only way we got control of an Earther ship in the centuries we were fighting them was with a highly-trained boarding crew and a vessel that allowed us to get alongside them. We don't have either. Why are you wasting time on this?"

Tawn scowled. "It's called brainstorming. And if you had a brain maybe you could join in."

"I thought we were looking for ways to make use of the negation unit?"

"We are. Doesn't mean we can't mix in other ideas at the same time."

Harris shook his head. "Other than preventing the Earthers from moving titanium ore, what advantage can we gain by not having wormhole generators? Solving that is where our efforts should be. Alex gave us this great tech. How do we make use of it?"

Gandy said, "What we need is a way to better shield us from the plasma strikes, or a way to hold the Earther ships in place. The inertial dampener field lets us accelerate and turn like we do. Any way to negate that?"

Harris looked over at the hologram. "Alex?"

"I will have to study both of those suggestions. Should either receive priority?"

Harris glanced around the room. "You're the genius here. Take a pick. Solutions to either of those would allow us to take that planet back. Maybe an even more powerful weapon would work too."

"I'm sorry, Harris, my programming was written so as not to allow the development of weapons. The dampener negation or the enhanced defensive shield are both acceptable courses of research."

"Fine then. Do those. How long will this research take?"

The image of Alex pursed its lips. "I'm afraid I don't have enough information on either subject to provide an accurate answer. Each must be evaluated and weighed against known criteria, after which—"

Harris held up a hand. "Save the explanation. Just get started on them. You can tell us when you have something to discuss."

Harris looked directly at Farker. "Come on, boy, let's go for a walk."

The image of Alexander Gaerten shut off as the robotic pet hopped down to the floor.

Tawn said, "Hey, what are we supposed to do in the meantime? You're taking our interface."

Harris gestured toward the bunker. "You all have access over there. Go sit around the table and chat it up if that's what you want. My dog and I are going for a walk so we can think. That a problem?"

Tawn shook her head. "Nope. Probably better for all of us."

Harris came to a stop. "Why you say that?"

"Because you're like this giant idea disruptor. We get onto something and you cut in to kill it."

Harris laughed. "You mean like the idea to steal an Earther ship? Yeah, good luck with that one. We couldn't even steal an unmanned freighter. Anyway, I'll be back in an hour. We'll see where we are by then."

Sharvie said, "I'm going to the inner chamber to see if there's anything I can do there."

Tawn turned to Trish and Gandy. "OK, you two bozos are with me then."

Trish asked, "Bozos, what does that even mean?"

Tawn walked for the door. "Come on. I'll tell you as we go. You see, back in the days when Humans were on Earth, for whatever reason, they had what they called clowns, people who dressed up in funny outfits and caked on makeup and such with the goal of being cute and funny. Was mostly intended as entertainment for kids.

"Of course, just like with just about everything else, it eventually morphed into adult entertainment where it was scary and sick and twisted. Anyway, one of the early clowns that made it popular was named Bozo. So calling someone a bozo was associated with being a clown, or clowning around."

Gandy shook his head. "What's a clown again exactly?"

Tawn sighed. "Skip it. Doesn't matter. Just another dead reference."

"How'd you know about it?" Trish asked.

Tawn held up a finger. "As part of our training we had to study Earth history for three years. Was supposed to give us insight into why things are the way they are. Since the New Earthers had that same history, it was supposed to help us to evaluate our enemies, who are really just us with a different philosophy."

"What other Earth history things did they teach?"

Tawn stopped at the table, taking a seat as she looked back at her two pupils. "Well, from what I understand, the Earth was divided into what they called countries. The people of each country were sovereign over the land they controlled. Space travel was limited to exploring their own star system back then.

"Anyway, when it was determined that the great apocalypse was coming, those countries aligned themselves into two camps. At the same time, a wormhole leading to our space out here opened. Probes were sent through and Domicile and New Earth were discovered. Right there, within reach, were two habitable planets where none had ever been available before.

"The two teams each built a massive colony ship and each was launched and made their way through the wormhole.

Afterward it closed, so we don't know the fate of Earth. Our history accounts aren't clear either. Some say it was an asteroid that was projected to wipe out everything. Others say it was from resources being used up. And still others because the star of that system was showing signs of becoming unstable.

"Whatever the reason, the two colony ships left. Our ship was made up of fully elected governments. Those were governments where the politicians were supposed to serve the people. I think we all could agree that from time to time ours has gotten out of control in that respect. And the Earthers, theirs were dictators, emperors, kings, and tightly controlled ruling parties or families. That's why New Earth is an empire today.

Gandy asked, "Is there a point to all this?"

Tawn chuckled. "Just that it's better to know where you came from if you're trying to figure out where to go. The Earthers want us either dead or as slaves. Or best case, as subjects of their emperor. I'd much rather be free."

An image of Alex popped into view as Tawn sat. "Your historical synopsis is reasonably accurate. The governing laws on Domicile have always had an emphasis on individual freedom while those of New Earth have been about the collective, as you said, usually to the benefit of a ruling party or family. The current emperor is one such person, having had the empire passed down to him from his father."

Harris walked into the now open bunker door. "I'm taking a ride to Eden. Just to check on the situation. Probably best that you all stay here and focus on your current efforts. I'd also like to check on our Banshee pilots. Should be back in a couple hours."

"So you're trapping us here," Tawn said.

Harris pointed out the door. "You still have the shuttle."

"And you have Farker. We can't go anywhere without him."

Harris thought for a moment. "Alex, is that true? Are they limited without Farker?"

"My programming can allow passage out of this system, but not back in. Should you desire to leave, the only way back is with Archibald. That will change for anyone who achieves level four of acceptance."

Tawn said, "How many levels of acceptance are there?"

"I am not at liberty to release that information."

Harris walked to the *Bangor*, boarded, and was soon slowing as he came into the Eden System, this time with the ship's stealth mode enabled. After a half hour ride, closing on Eden, it became apparent that nothing had changed. The Earther ships sat in high orbit. The domes remained intact.

Several jumps and scans identified one of the Banshees. A short run had Harris parked beside the ship with a low power comm enabled.

The pilot said, "I had a moment of panic when you first appeared on my nav display. You were only three minutes from this location."

Harris nodded. "Good to know. How has everything been going? You and the others OK on food?"

"We're good for a few more days. The Earthers attempted an assault about twelve hours ago. They couldn't get close enough to do any damage with those rail cannons running. That dome has turned out to be tougher than we thought. Might be something to consider if we want to build ground-based forts anywhere in our colonies. I would suggest the colonel try to build us one at the Retreat, once he's freed up from down there."

"Any other ships coming or going?"

"Four new destroyers came through. Three damaged ships went home."

"Anything smaller?"

"There's been no other movement that I'm aware of. Lieutenant Himes will be here in about two hours. We've been taking twelve hour shifts, parking back on that ice planet during off times."

Harris said, "I'm going in closer to have a look at the Rumford Mine. Just keep doing what you're doing. I'll make a trip out in a couple days to bring you more food supplies."

The comm closed and the *Bangor* accelerated toward the planet. Twenty minutes later, she slowed, coming to a stop in high orbit.

Harris shook his head as he glanced down at Farker. "Even looks hot from up here. Too bad you don't speak."

The dog replied, "I can if that's the preferred form of communication."

Harris stared. "How long have you been able to do that?"

"Nineteen hundred seventy-four years."

Harris chuckled to himself. "Great. Now I feel like an idiot for not having asked before."

"My speaking or not would have no effect on your intelligence level."

"So now you're a smartass dog, huh?"

"A recent update from the main facility programming provided an understanding of what you term sarcasm. If you would like, I can suppress those response patterns."

Harris shook his head. "No. I like the thought of having a pet who can put people down. In fact, I can't wait to hear you throw a few comments at Tawn."

"Would that qualify as entertainment?"

Harris laughed. "Yes. Yes it would."

"I'm sorry, Harris, my entertainment programming is limited to pet-like reactions."

"If you take orders, then I want you to not talk to or around anyone but me. This will be our secret."

"If you feel that is beneficial to the situation, I will comply."

Harris nodded. "It's beneficial. You're now on silent mode unless we're alone. Got it?"

"Got it."

Chapter 23

"Harris."

Harris chuckled to himself. "A talking dog. All this time. I feel like an idiot."

"Harris."

"You think I'm an idiot?"

"Harris."

"What?"

"There is a vessel approaching on the nav display. It's not an exact trajectory. They may not have seen us."

Harris grinned as a ship ID showed on the screen. "It's Baxter Rumford. And she's gonna be in range of our railguns in thirty seconds."

"Harris, I would advise against destroying that ship while we are this close. It would not only give away our position, but would also inform the New Earthers that we have some level of stealth capability."

Harris turned the *Bangor* toward the *Fargo* as it passed their location. A slow acceleration had him closing on the slightly slower ship.

Harris grinned. "Finally I get some revenge for the trouble she's caused. In five minutes she'll be out of their sensor range and it will be *Goodbye, Baxter Rumford*."

Farker said, "Would it not be better to overtake and then question her about the Earthers and their plans?"

"Probably, but it wouldn't be as satisfying."

Farker tilted his head. "Is vengeful satisfaction more important than the rescue of your people?"

Harris frowned as he looked down at the dog. "Well, no, but it would be more satisfying."

"Is that standard Human reasoning?"

Harris sighed. "Fine. I'll try to make her stop so I can beat some information out of her. Come to think of it, that might be more satisfying than ending it with a tungsten pellet. Of course, I'll have to listen to her voice again. That's a big negative."

The dog tilted its head in the other direction.

Harris growled. "Whose side are you on anyway?"

The dog stared.

"Great. I'm being guilted by a mechanical pet. Fine. I'll see what she has to say."

As the ships passed safely to a distance that was beyond sensor range of the Earthers, Harris opened a low power general comm.

"Hello, Red."

"Goober? Is that you? Where are you? We need to talk."

Harris chuckled. "Good. I was just about to suggest that. Why don't you bring the *Fargo* to a stop. We'll dock and you can come on over."

"Good, your timing couldn't be better. I'll see you in a minute."

The ships came to a stop and a docking tube extended. As the airlock on the *Bangor* opened, Baxter Rumford strolled through.

Harris met her with a Fox-40 in his hand. "I've been waiting a long time for this meeting."

Bax scowled as she waved. "Put the gun away. What I have to say, you're gonna want to hear."

Harris chuckled. "That you're sorry? That you didn't mean it?"

Bax sighed. "No. That we're on the same side."

Harris laughed. "Yeah, like I'm buying that one. You've repeatedly tried to have us killed. You left us out to dry more than a couple times, and to top it off... you're annoying. You're all perfect until you open your lying mouth."

Bax sat on one of the bench chairs in the cabin. "So you like me. Never would have guessed."

Harris returned a disgusted look. "Like you? I'd like to see you spaced, or vaporized maybe. Or maybe staked out on the desert down there at high noon. I'd like you in any of those three circumstances."

"Are you done?"

"Well, not yet. You're gonna tell me what you know about the Earthers' plans."

Baxter scowled. "You already know what their plans are, you moron. They want the titanium. And thanks to you it looks like they're gonna get it."

Harris waved his Fox-40 back and forth. "Wait a minute, who's the one that opened a mine for them? Who already tried to deliver a shipload of refined ore to new Earth?"

"I delayed that shipment as long as I could. The Earthers are persistent and don't take no for an answer. Had you not stolen that ship it would have been destroyed through sabotage. Thanks to you though, I didn't have to reveal myself."

Harris laughed as he sat on the other bench. "This is rich. You expect me to believe you were about to blow that ship?"

"I was. And I would have paid the ultimate price for it."

"And I suppose you were heading back to Domicile to tell everyone you were sorry for possibly bringing the Great War back?"

Bax shook her head. "I was being called to New Earth for a direct discussion with the emperor. I don't think it was planned for me to make a return trip. I'm being blamed for your people keeping that new well offline. As I should be. I did everything I could to keep them going in the wrong direction on that."

Harris sat back, rolling his eyes. "And you expect me to believe you were voluntarily heading to New Earth, even though you suspect they would off you? Come on, that's a long stretch you're expecting me to buy into. You have to have something better than that."

Baxter nervously tapped her fingers on her leg. "OK. How about this? I know you're working for the DDI. For Admiral Warmouth."

"And how did you come to have that bit of information? From your Earther spies? They have moles inside the DDI?"

"No. I got that word from the admiral himself."

"Warmouth told you I worked for him?"

"Yes."

"Oh. This tale just keeps getting better."

Baxter Rumford let out a long sigh. "During the war I did contract jobs for the admiral. When the truce came, he brought me into the DDI fold as an operative. He wanted to know what the Earthers were up to on Eden, and we set up a sting with you to get them to show their hand. Only you kept interceding and fouling things up."

"You expect me to believe you work for the admiral?"

"That's called being good at what I do. You and Tawn, I actually like you both. You're patriots, you're courageous, and best of all, you get things done. Not sure how sometimes, but you do.

"Anyway, I think I've had enough of the admiral. I don't trust his motives. He says he's setting up things with the promise of a big surprise coming for the Earthers, and then nothing happens, or things change so much that it no longer matters."

Harris shook his head. "So you feel like the admiral has been working you, huh? That all this you've been doing is somehow for the good of Domicile and her citizens? You really disgust me. I wish I had gone ahead and wasted you with my railguns."

Baxter shrugged. "If you want, I'll get back in there and you can do just that. I'm dead anyway. If not by the Earthers, then by the admiral."

"And why would he do that?"

Bax leaned forward. "Remember I said I was planning to destroy that first freighter of titanium that was leaving my mine? Well, a second one launched yesterday."

"Funny. My people said there hasn't been any ship movement coming off that planet."

Bax nodded. "That's because it never made it off the planet. If you take a scan about fifty kilometers east of the mine, you'll see the remains of a freighter. I blew it up. Scattered a full load of ore to the winds. That was against the wishes of the admiral. And that's why I'm being called to New Earth.

"I had a couple patsies who were gonna take the fall for me, but one of them somehow walked away from that freighter. The forward section stayed intact after the explosion and he managed to live as it crashed down from two kilometers up. Unbelievable, really, but he somehow survived. Anyway, I'm already dead."

"Now why would the admiral be against blowing that up?"

Baxter smirked. "This is the one that will get you riled up. He wants the war restarted. They've been threatening to cut the DDF budget in half, which includes monies for the DDI. The admiral was gonna be out of a job. He has some crazy notion that the war is somehow better than peace. And you know what? With the mistakes some of those politicians are making, he might be right."

"How could the war possibly be better?"

"Think about it. If our military has half its resources and power stripped away, and at the same time the Earthers go through a massive buildup, we would have no way of stopping them. They would roll through our reduced fleet and come all the way to Domicile before we had a chance to rebuild. It's a doomsday scenario, and the admiral thought he could head it off by bringing the war back before it was too late."

Harris sat back. "You know, my brain is screaming to listen to your message, but my gut is telling me to undock and shove you out that airlock."

"You want to know what the Earthers are planning?"

Harris gave his best fake smile. "Here we go. Give me your wisdom."

Bax stood. "In the next few days, you're gonna see several ships dragging a fat asteroid into high orbit. It will be positioned directly above Fireburg. Once they're ready, that asteroid will be directed at your dome.

"Now, of course this will cause panic and elicit a response from those rail cannons you have positioned around it. And they will likely do a good job of pulverizing that rock into small enough pieces that your precious dome will survive. At the same time, they will attack with ships, but not enough to do any real damage and not close enough to take any damage.

"What your people won't see coming is the team who will be raiding your pumphouse and destroying the wellhead. If I'm not mistaken, you already used your spare. So your entire compound will be without water, probably in a matter of hours. It will be a forced surrender."

Harris thought for several seconds. "What do you think, Farker? Any of that make sense."

"It sounds like a reasonable scenario."

"The dog talks?"

Harris held up his hands. "I just told you to never speak around anyone else!"

Farker replied, "You asked me a question, which implied you desired a response."

"Seriously, the mutt talks?"

"Long story. Which you don't deserve to hear."

Harris took two steps, pushing Baxter back onto the bench as he began to pace back and forth. "This is not what I was expecting to come out here and find."

Harris walked over to the command console, pressing a button that disconnected the docking collar and retracted the tube.

Bax asked, "What are you doing?"

"I'm verifying your freighter story. Just sit back and enjoy the ride. And keep in mind if you're having thoughts of trying anything, my reflexes are insanely fast and I won't hesitate to splatter your innards all over this cabin."

Bax smiled. "Not a problem. I'm just fun and friendly Bax now."

Harris scowled. "Like I would believe that."

Ten minutes later the *Bangor* was again docking with the *Fargo*.

Bax laid her arm across the back of the bench. "I hate to burst your little time bubble, but we probably only have about a half hour before the Earthers will be sending out ships to track me down. Their emperor doesn't take kindly to being stood up. You got a plan here or what?"

"I'm thinking. Let's say I cut you loose. Why not run back to Domicile?"

Bax laughed. "And do what, blend in? In case you haven't noticed, I don't blend in well anywhere. This face, this body, this hair... it's as much of a curse as it is a blessing. They will open doors, but they don't let me hide anywhere."

Harris gave a sarcastic frown. "Yeah, well, you see these tears of mine rolling down my cheeks for you, right? You're really a piece of work, you know that?"

"I've been told."

Harris said, "OK, I know I'm going to regret this, but you're coming with me. I haven't figured out why yet, but I'll have a use for you somehow."

"And telling me this is gonna help you how?"

Harris smiled. "It allows me to irritate you. So it helps to relieve frustration."

"I thought you Biomarines were heavily trained in psychology. You aren't supposed to get frustrated."

Harris glanced over his shoulder. "Just shut up. I'm trying to think."

After a jump to a far planet in the Eden System, the *Fargo* was parked on the surface of a small rocky moon. Harris covered the nav display while making Baxter look away as he made another jump back to Midelon. Forty minutes later they were settling on the grass outside the bunker.

Harris said, "We'll determine what to do with you as a group."

Bax smiled. "I look forward to your decision."

Harris opened a comm: "Tawn, bring the others out here. We have something to discuss."

The hatch opened and seconds later Tawn Freely and the Boleman twins stepped up into the cabin.

"Can't get Sharvie. She's—"

Tawn stopped and stared. "What the... you caught her?"

Harris nodded. "I did."

Tawn took a step forward with a grin. "Let the beatings begin."

Harris cut her off. "Not so fast. She has a story to tell. Listen to it first. If you still want to give her a beating, she'll be right here after."

Tawn stepped back. "This is gonna have to be one whopping tale."

"Have a seat," said Harris. "Will take more than a minute. Same for you two."

Tawn, Trish, and Gandy all sat on the bench across from their nemesis. Baxter Rumford began to tell her story, to scowls and headshakes. She told of getting captured by the Earthers, of reporting it to the DDI and being made a double agent. She told of setting up Harris and how it was out of her control, and why the gunrunning operation had been conducted and why it had been such a success.

Her story finished with her capture by Harris just off Eden. "I had nowhere to run. And now I'm here. And I won't say sorry because it wouldn't be genuine and you wouldn't believe it anyway. All I've done was for Domicile. My days of kissing up to the Earthers to further my cover are finally over."

Tawn huffed. "And you expect us to believe the admiral wants the war back on?"

Bax leaned forward. "He hasn't said as much, but the evidence all points that way. Look, I stuck my neck out when I destroyed that last freighter. My cover was about to be blown.

And with that went my ability to blame slowdowns and delays on Domer sabotage. I can't believe the only thing you people did to stop us, aside from that hijacking, was tampering with that well. While effective, there was so much more you could have done. But you weren't doing anything, so I had to coordinate those actions myself."

Tawn crossed her arms and asked. "So tell us how you sabotaged your own efforts."

Bax sat back, throwing her arm up on the back of the bench. "My team detonated sixteen bombs, destroying vital equipment. Twelve Earthers with key skills mysteriously disappeared. Their bodies are out there buried in the desert somewhere. There were a multitude of accidents and spills that slowed progress. Each time we were successful at pinning the blame on incompetent Earthers.

"Look, you have no idea what a tightrope I've been walking over there. Every move I made had to have a solid, believable alibi for my people. Since we've been there, they've only captured one of us, Davo Kostov. He was as true a patriot as I've ever known.

"He was chased into a medical lab, where he barricaded himself in, and instead of giving up and allowing himself to be interrogated, he turned on a scanning machine and irradiated his brain for two hours before they gave up negotiations and broke in. He was drooling on himself when they grabbed him. They saw they wouldn't get anything and instead shoved him out into the sunlight."

"And of course we have no way to verify any of this," said Tawn.

Harris replied, "We do have a crashed freighter with a load of titanium scattered over a hundred square kilometers."

Tawn turned. "And who's to say that wasn't done by our people, despite her? She could be using that effort as another cover. And why would you bring her here of all places?"

Harris shook his head. "She doesn't know where we are."

Bax laughed. "Midelon? Everyone knows you're here. They just don't know how you get here. Both sides have been trying to get to this planet for centuries. How you knuckleheads figured it out is beyond me, but here we are."

Harris said, "There's more. Tell them about the Earther plans."

Bax propped her hands on her knees as she leaned forward. "At this moment they are pushing an asteroid toward Eden. Sometime soon that asteroid will be dropping like a big foot to stomp down on Fireburg. Your rail cannons will likely stop it, but they won't stop the sabotage against your lone wellhead.

"When that water source stops to deliver, your people will be ready to surrender within hours. Transports back to Domicile will even be offered. The Earthers will take over a fully functioning mine that will be up and running in a few day's time. Then they'll be producing enough titanium plates to build one new ship a day. I tell you, for them it's a dream come true."

Tawn spat on the deck. "All this time I thought it was our greed that brought this situation about. Turns out it was your stupidity for trusting in the likes of Warmouth. Well, now we're all sitting in the same pot and the fire underneath is starting to get hot."

Bax replied, "The way I see it, we probably only have a day to figure out how to stop this. Maybe we ask your talking dog?"

Chapter 24

Harris scowled. "We have five smart people sitting here. We have knowledge of the situation. So come on people, let's kick around some ideas. How do we stop the coming assault on the domes?"

"Seems easy to me," said Trish. "Get notice to the colonel that they are planning an attack on the wellhead. They stop that and it sounds like this whole thing fails. And if done right they might even be able to round up a bunch of Earther spies."

Tawn looked up. "I agree. We fly in and signal the colonel. All we have to do is get inside comm range. Leave the message and run before they can get close enough to shoot."

Gandy nodded. "I like that plan."

Harris said, "Well then, strap yourselves in. We're going for a ride."

"What about Sharvie?" asked Trish.

Harris turned. "Farker, get a message to Sharvie that we should be back in a few hours. Tell her to keep doing whatever it is she's doing."

Harris sat in the pilot's chair. The *Bangor* lifted and shot up through the atmosphere. After a jump, the stealth ship slowed as they approached Eden.

"They're all parked in high orbit above Fireburg," said Tawn. "All we have to do is come in at an angle, blast out our message, and turn away. Simple."

Harris shook his head. "Look at the comm console. They're broadcasting interference. We'll have to go almost to the ground to get a message off."

Bax stood over their shoulder. "You've got a bigger problem. They have the asteroid and it's already on its way down. See those three blips? That third reflection doesn't have a signature because it's just a big rock. Unless you can get that message to the colonel in the next five minutes, you're too late."

Harris pushed the throttle full.

Tawn asked, "What are you doing?"

"We can't get to the surface, but we can get to that capital ship. Sensors show it as the origin of the comm interference."

Tawn powered up the railgun circuits.

Bax shook her head. "This is suicide."

Harris glanced over his shoulder. "Unless you want to get tossed around this cabin like a ragdoll, I suggest you strap yourself to one of those benches."

Tawn said, "We'll be in range in thirty seconds. They still haven't see us."

"Hold your fire until we're within three. I don't want to give them time to react. If we can make it in close, unload with both barrels."

Tawn nodded. "They'll get everything we can give. What's our exit plan?"

"Our plan is that you make those first rounds count. I plan on jumping through a wormhole before we smack into them."

Tawn frowned. "This close to the planet? You sure it will even open?"

"Harris shook his head. We're about to find out. I'd suggest everyone check your straps. This will get nasty in a hurry if the wormhole doesn't form."

"Ten seconds... five... here we go."

The vibration of the railguns firing reverberated through the ship. As feared, a wormhole wouldn't form. A multitude of plasma rounds came their way as Harris pulled hard left on the control stick.

The first of the quarter-light-speed tungsten rounds found their mark. The guts of the Earther flagship blasted out through its back side, sending debris in every direction. A message was blasted out to the colonel as the first of the plasma charges struck the *Bangor*'s hull.

The minor rumbles and shakes of those first hits were soon replaced with violent jolts and concussion waves bouncing around the inside of the small freight shuttle. Harris fought with the control stick as the rest of the Earther fleet unloaded. Systems sparked, smoke beginning to pour from several panels as a hull breach indicator sounded on the pilot's console.

In an instant the pounding of plasma shots came to an end as the crippled ship gained distance from the fleet.

Harris looked at the nav display. "What's happening?"

Tawn replied, "The Banshees and our other Zwicker is what's happening. And I have a comm coming up from the colonel."

"Gruberg. We got 'em. Stopped just short of the pumphouse. We're in good shape down here. Get yourself safe."

Tawn winced. "We just lost a Banshee. And there's the other. Plasma rounds are coming our way."

The wormhole generator whirred as a portal to another place in space formed just in front of them. As the portal closed, they opened a second to Midelon, jumping before any Earther ships could pursue.

Harris let out a long sigh. "Everyone OK?"

Tawn powered off the rail circuits. "They sacrificed themselves for us."

Harris gave a somber reply. "We'd have done the same for them."

Baxter Rumford unfastened her lap belt. "That's what I like about you slugs and stumps. You're hardcore. You can be counted upon to commit and to see that commitment through."

Harris said, "Let's get this ship on the ground and get after any needed repairs. The Earthers aren't gonna just sit still. I'd bet they have a backup plan that's being put in motion right now."

The heavily-hammered ship landed. Systems were checked and repairs effected. The worst of the damage was a crack in the hull running halfway across the back of the ship. The *Bangor* would remain airtight until and unless a major strike by a plasma round swelled and rocked the joints around it. A third of the cabin air had been lost to space during such hits.

Gandy looked it over. "You can barely see it, but it's there plain as day on the scans. And we don't have the welders out here to seal that up. We have them at the warehouse, but not here."

"Sounds like we have a visit to Domicile coming," said Harris. "Finish up the rest of the fixes and we'll make a jump."

Tawn said, "You think they'll allow us back? That was a capital ship we just took out. Word of that is probably already there. The politicians will be lining up to call for us to be hanged."

"You have a better way to weld up that crack?"

Tawn shook her head. "Not saying we don't go, just that we'll have to watch ourselves while we're there. Won't be any registering that we're visiting this time. Just a sneak in and a sneak out."

Baxter cut into the conversation. "There's another option available."

"And what would that be?" asked Tawn.

"I take your shuttle out there and go get you a welder. I still have a free pass to get on the planet. You... they'll be looking for."

Harris said, "I thought you said the DDI would be looking for you now."

Bax nodded. "They are, or will be. But they gave me the tools I need to move around without being detected. Unless someone physically sees me, they'll never know Baxter Rumford was there. And I won't be going to your warehouse. I'm certain it's being watched. I'll be going to purchase a welder from a distributor. They won't ask questions, if only to make a sale."

Harris chuckled. "And we're supposed to trust that you will do this without disappearing?"

Bax crossed her arms. "Well, believe it or not I have the best interests of my home at heart. I made a commitment to see this through and I won't be out-shined by a couple of genetically enhanced nitwits who are stumbling through this whole fight. So yeah, you'll have to trust that I won't disappear. Besides... where would I go?"

Harris rubbed the back of his neck in thought. "OK. We'll do as you suggest. We'll escort you to Domicile space. You go in, get a welder, and come back. We'll be waiting where we released you. And if you fail to come back or if anyone else approaches us, know this... Tawn Freely and I will stop at nothing to make sure that bright red head of yours gets separated from that tall thin body."

Bax smiled. "See. I knew you liked me."

Tawn stepped forward. "I tried to be your friend once. You treated me like dirt and stabbed me in the back repeatedly."

Bax laughed. "Stabbed you? Who's the one who stole my cargo? Did you know the admiral almost had me offed because of that one episode? That's right. And I had to talk him out of killing you two as well. So don't be trying to school me on being almost friends. I've protected your butts on several occasions. And why'd I do that you ask? Because I... like... you."

Bax turned away for dramatic effect.

Harris chuckled. "Well, your acting hasn't improved any. That was worse than some of your prior attempts."

Bax smiled. "Honest, I'll get your welder. You two are the only thing keeping me alive and in this fight right now. So if I can help you accomplish your goal of preventing the Great War from returning... use me as you will."

Half a day later the *Bangor* and the shuttle were landing at Midelon with the equipment needed for repairs. Trish and Gandy got to immediate work.

Bax sat in the open hatch of the *Bangor*. "You two gonna tell me the deal on that door into the ground over there?"

Harris shook his head. "Nope. Just forget it exists."

Bax asked, "So what's our plan? What do we do from here? How do we stop this?"

"Our current goal is to keep the colonel and the others at Fireburg safe."

Bax winced. "As long as the Earthers control the space around Eden, whoever is down on that planet will be in danger. Maybe a better plan would be to get the people out, trash those mines, and keep trashing any mines the Earthers try to build. I don't see any other avenues for us to pursue."

Tawn walked from behind the ship where the welding was taking place. "Trish says another hour. What are we talking about here?"

"Our options," replied Bax.

"What'd you come up with?"

"I came up with attacking and destroying the mines. He came up with nothing."

Harris protested: "You just asked that question thirty seconds ago."

"Well, tell us what you got."

Harris stood silently.

"Well?"

"Well... give me a chance to think on it. I'm not some memory bank of solutions always at the ready to spit them out. I need time to evaluate the situation. Mull over possibilities. Think about actions."

Tawn chuckled. "You got nothing."

Harris shook his head. "I got nothing. But we don't need an instant answer. The colonel managed to thwart the asteroid attack. We have time. And we lost three good men back there because we weren't prepared. I'd rather not do that again."

The discussion ran on for ninety minutes until Trish and Gandy walked from behind the ship. "Weld's complete."

Gandy said, "And it looks good. I don't think we'll have any problems. But we did lose our skin color changing abilities over that section. We now have a shiny bright area on the back of the ship."

Tawn asked, "Can we just spray it flat black?"

Trish nodded. "I have the paint in the shop. Can't say how long it will last on there though. We do go into some harsh environments."

"We can only do what we can do. Maybe investigate something more permanent when we get back home."

Gandy sighed. "Home. It seems like a distant memory now."

Tawn laughed. "We've only been gone a couple days."

Gandy shook his head. "Not from that. From where we grew up. That life seems like an eternity ago."

"Well," said Bax, "if you want to protect it we need ideas. How do we take and secure Eden?"

Farker trotted up, taking a seat on his haunches in front of Bax.

"Maybe the dog has an idea. Tell us what you think, boy."

Everyone was quiet for several seconds as the mechanical canine looked up with his unusual grin.

Bax said, "Now that's just creepy. At least say something."

"It's a dog," said Gandy. "It can't talk."

Bax scowled at the young mechanic. "Yes it can. I heard it only a short time ago. When Goober first found me."

"It's Gruberg," said Harris "And you must have been hallucinating or something. It's a simulated dog. Dogs can't talk."

Bax crossed her arms, "Oh, I see. Make the newbie sound insane. I heard the dog talk. You heard the dog talk."

Gandy said, "Farker can take and understand orders, but talking back? That's ludicrous. We've had him for ages now and he doesn't talk."

The dog looked up at Harris to shaking head. Permission would not be granted.

"OK, back to the subject at hand. How do we secure Eden?"

"Bax," Tawn said, "how heavily defended is your mine?"

"Maybe five hundred Marines with plasma rifles. Why?"

"No air defenses?"

Bax shook her head. "None were needed. Who was going to attack with a ship? That would bring the Earthers. There is a destroyer parked over it right now."

Tawn said, "The Earthers think you went to New Earth. They would have no issue with you coming back, right?"

"I don't think they expect it, but I suppose not."

"I think we can all agree that we aren't getting anywhere near Fireburg, but maybe we can take out the Rumford Mine."

"They call it the Tallis Mine, after the emperor," said Bax. "How you planning to get past the destroyer? They will be watching for an attack."

Tawn held up her arms, placing one hand behind the other. "The *Bangor* is slightly smaller than the *Fargo*. They won't have issue with the *Fargo* coming in. We need to get close to that destroyer to make use of our railguns, so we'll follow you through a wormhole and all the way down through the atmosphere.

"If we come in at a distance from those other ships in stealth mode, they won't be able to detect us. We can fly straight in right behind the *Fargo* and blast that destroyer before it has a chance to return fire. After that, we'll do whatever damage we can to the mine and its facilities."

"I still have people down there."

"You think you could land and pick them up?" asked Harris. "You'll only have a couple minutes before those other ships head our way. Designate a landing spot, and when we start with our destruction, we'll avoid it."

Tawn added, "Look, stopping that production is a priority. Your people knew sacrifices would have to be made. You pick any up that you can and we'll try to give cover while you run. Just know that it won't be much and it may only last for a few seconds."

"Give me a few minutes to mull this over. It's not a bad plan. I just want to have a good chance to rescue our agents."

The idea was kicked around for another hour before Harris put it to a vote. The vote was unanimous.

Harris looked at Farker. "Send Sharvie a note that we'll be back. Trish, you and Gandy remain here. No sense in us putting you in jeopardy. If we don't come back and you need to leave, you only have to convince the hologram to allow it."

The twins nodded. The message to Sharvie was delivered. A jump was made to retrieve the *Fargo*.

Chapter 25

Harris stood at the airlock as Bax walked through the docking tube. "I can't believe I'm saying this, but good luck down there. I think you're gonna need it."

Bax looked back with a genuine pursed smile. "Thanks, Goober. And best of luck to you as well. Make every one of those pellets count. And when the Earthers come, get yourselves out. Don't worry about me."

The base frequency of the Earther comms was loaded into Farker. Several tests of Bax's comm encryption had a decode scheme up and running. Whatever comms would happen between Bax and the Earthers would be heard on the *Bangor*.

A jump was made to Eden space with the *Bangor* snuggled up to the aft of the *Fargo*.

"Hope this works," said Tawn.

Harris nodded. "As long as they don't try to stop her, it will."

A comm came in to the approaching craft. "*Fargo*, state your return business."

Bax replied, "I have new orders from the emperor. He wants increased production at the mine and I'm being sent back to oversee it."

The comm was silent for several seconds before a new voice came online. "Miss Rumford, we were told you wouldn't be returning."

Bax laughed. "Yeah, well, go tell that to Tallis. He decided my skills would be put to better use here on the ground than rotting in some torture prison. I wholeheartedly agreed with him. It's time we ramped up our production and our security. No more mishaps and no more acts of sabotage. I'll be calling in my most trusted staff to get this all rolling."

"We'll have to confirm these plans."

Bax nodded. "Go ahead. But know they are an unhappy lot back on New Earth. We're behind schedule. So comm if you must, but be prepared for the unpleasantries. And I'm sure they'll want to know more about your recent failed assault of the Domer colony. Makes me think you have some double agents down there in the ranks. How else would they have known about that raid?"

The voice was again quiet for several seconds. "Let us know if you need any assistance with meeting your new quotas."

Bax smiled. "Thanks. Will do."

The comm closed.

Harris looked at Tawn. "She's too good at making that stuff up."

"Yeah, we already knew that. Question is, will they comm back to New Earth to check?"

Harris gave a half smile. "They have about seven minutes to decide that. If you detect a wormhole opening, we'll know what's coming."

The *Fargo* pushed out flames as it plummeted through the hot atmosphere of the planet Eden. Tawn powered up the railgun circuits.

"Fifteen seconds," Harris warned. "Ten... five... breaking off. Open up."

As the *Bangor* slowed dramatically, the autofeeders of the twin railguns whirred to life. The unsuspecting destroyer began exploding debris as the tungsten pellets ripped into its hull and out the other side. Seconds after the first shots, the massive ship began to drop from its position at two kilometers altitude.

Tawn said, "That was easy. Wish they would all just sit still like that."

Harris looked at the nav display as he turned the *Bangor* toward the mine. "I've been wanting to do this since we found out Bax weaseled her way into that claim. Not much of a revenge since we're now doing this *for* her."

Tawn chuckled as she worked the targeting grid. "Yeah, I have to admit I was looking forward to getting even too. This isn't quite as satisfying now that she's on our side."

Harris shook his head. "About that, I still think we have to be careful around her. The old Bax, DDI agent or not, was all about herself. Her acting isn't so good that she could hide her selfish side. Bryce Porter and Cletus Dodger can testify to that. She had no problem leading them to their deaths at the hand of New Earthers."

Tawn half scowled. "Yeah, I still think about that a lot. I'm sure she'd say she had no choice, but I have to think otherwise. Of course, we're no angels either. How many Earthers have we killed since this all started?"

"You can't make that same comparison. We killed soldiers who were out to kill our people."

Tawn shrugged. "In the grand scheme of things we're just a couple thugs for the other side."

"For the right side. We have no problem leaving them alone if they leave us alone. That's not the world we live in. Baxter made her choices. Good or bad, they were hers. She owns the outcome."

The last of the Rumford Mine buildings were scattered across the landscape. Hundreds of survivors scurried back and forth in the intense heat. The *Fargo* remained on the ground as half a dozen new Earth warships raced their way.

"We have to go," said Harris.

"Ten seconds and they're gonna be all over her."

A general comm went out over the Earther channels. "Get down here! We have injured!"

Tawn slowly shook her head as the *Bangor* angled away from the chaos. "She's not leaving."

Harris winced. "She feed us a load of crap? Did we just let her go for no good reason?"

Tawn clenched her hand in a fist. "I told you we had no way to verify anything she said. Now I'm pissed."

Harris replied, "Worse, she knows about our stealth and our base at Midelon."

"She's still there. Not running. You said she was headed to New Earth when you caught her?"

"That's what she said."

Tawn pulled back her head. "Was she flying in that direction at least?"

Harris thought. "Well, no. But you don't have to be when you're going through a wormhole. You can be headed anywhere."

"That's true, but nobody does that. If you're heading to Domicile, you head toward Domicile before opening a wormhole. Doesn't make any difference travel-wise other than you might have to turn back that way once you go through. So which way was she heading?"

Harris rubbed the back of his neck. "Now that you mention it... Domicile."

Tawn smacked her forehead. "You know, sometimes you're a mental midget. She just played us back there."

"Explain why she volunteered us taking out her mine then. That doesn't make any sense."

"Doesn't make sense unless you're trying to keep yourself from taking a beating. She couldn't care less about that mine or those people. She probably just strengthened her ties with the Earthers by staying there and claiming to help."

Harris said, "Then explain the broadcast she made about following orders of the emperor. How's she gonna get away with that if they go check?"

Tawn shrugged. "Maybe she had those orders before you caught her? Who knows. What I do know is she's definitely a double agent. And probably working both sides."

Harris shook his head. "So just that quick we're back in the 'we hate Bax' club. She does know how to get under your skin."

A wormhole opened and the *Bangor* slipped through to Midelon space. A forty minute ride had the small freight-shuttle landing just outside the bunker.

Sharvie was sitting out on the grass with the others.

Harris was the first to hop out. "I see the AI released you. Learn anything new?"

"I did, but I can't talk about it. What happened at the mine?"

Tawn said, "We destroyed it, but Bax turned herself over to the Earthers. We think she was serving us all a load while she was here in an attempt to save her own skin."

Gandy shook his head. "That girl knows how to lie. Everything she said made sense to me."

"She's good at what she does," said Harris. "At least that mine is done for."

"They can't rebuild it?"

Harris stared. "Of course they can rebuild, but it's not functional right now. Which is the part of all this we don't get. She must have her own purpose for letting it be destroyed."

Gandy asked, "So what's our next move?"

Harris looked over at Tawn. "I think we go back to Domicile and see if we can get a meeting with the admiral. If restarting the war is what he's interested in, we should be able to sniff that out."

"Or get our throats cut," Tawn said. "Tell me how we test his motives? I don't think we'll be using any of the interrogation techniques we're used to using. Might not go over well with a DDI admiral."

Harris turned to face Sharvie. "Alex have any more suggestions for tech updates we can do? Our stealth might be compromised with the Earthers now. Anything to make us less visible? And wasn't he... or it... working on an evaluation of our shielding? Anything come of that?"

Sharvie faced the dog. "Farker, can you show us Alex?"

A hologram image floated above the dog.

Tawn frowned. "Almost can't see him in the daylight."

Alex said, "Archibald's projectors are working at maximum. I'm sorry, Tawn. The hologram equipment was not made for outdoors."

Harris asked, "Any research breakthroughs for us?"

"Yes. Improvements can be made to both your inertial dampeners and external plasma shielding with minor adjustments. Both technologies rely on a set of frequency tables that are largely linear in scale. Calculations reveal a number of frequencies that will allow improved fields for each.

"The inertial dampener should benefit from a 2.2 percent reduction in field reaction time. That should mean a less bumpy ride when moving through the atmosphere and a slightly improved turning radius when at speed. Tests reveal a 3.4 percent improvement to the plasma inhibitor field of your shields. Both solutions may be implemented with a minor update to your system software."

Harris nodded. "Can you make that happen?"

Alex replied, "The new frequency values have been incorporated."

"Just like that?"

Alex smiled. "Just like that, Harris."

"Do you have any other improvements in the testing phases?"

"Many."

"Can you say what they are?"

"I'd rather not until I have sufficient resultant data. Do you have any further requests?"

Gandy said, "How about our speed? Any way we can go faster on standard drives? And our stealthiness. Any way we could improve that?"

Tawn nodded. "Good thoughts. Which reminds me, if we manage to see the admiral, we should ask about getting the skin coating on the back of the ship fixed. I'd like us to have just as small a signature when we're running away from someone as when we're approaching."

Harris huffed. "What we need to ask the admiral is how we drive the Earthers away from Eden. Every day the colonel and the others are there is one day closer to them being out of food. Time is running out."

Tawn pointed at the *Bangor*. "Let's go, then. Trish, Gandy, and Sharvie, follow us out in the shuttle. You can take it to the warehouse and see if any work has been done on the last Banshee."

Before they piled into the ship, Trish asked, "The admiral... you've never told us who he is or what your connection is."

Tawn sighed. "I guess we're all far enough into this it doesn't matter anymore. Harris and I were approached by the DDI to come out here to the truce worlds to spy. At first we were just supposed to set up trade routes with truce world colonies, on both sides. That quickly morphed in building Fireburg."

Gandy said, "Wait... we're working for the DDI?"

Harris replied, "Sort of... they made the updates to the *Bangor* and funded all our early purchases. That all kind of came to an end when we built the first dome—the financial support, that is. Anyway, we really haven't had any direction or help since we first went out to Eden. We were definitely expecting some direction. I have a hard time believing what we did was what they wanted us to do."

Gandy frowned. "If what Baxter Rumford said was true, it makes sense. Everything we did out there would only enrage the Earthers. Maybe that's what the admiral wanted all along. And he put Miss Rumford out there so we had that physical enemy we could see and plot against."

Harris said, "When you get back to the warehouse I want you to be careful. If the admiral has decided to pull the plug on our operations, that could include you. Watch your backs."

The *Bangor* was soon rocketing upward.

Tawn asked, "So how do you propose we get in touch with the admiral?"

Harris smiled. "We go right to their complex and ask for him."

"And what if the politicos are looking for us? Before we land we should check for any outstanding warrants."

Harris nodded. "Not a bad idea. We should look for the same on Trish and Gandy."

"And if we find any warrants on them?"

"We open a comm and send them back here. They aren't deserving of jail. Us... probably. But not them."

As the *Bangor* neared Chicago Port Station, they conducted a check for warrants. All records showed as clear.

Harris looked longingly at the station as they slipped past her toward the planet of Domicile. "I tell you, I could use a week in the hotel and some binge-ing at those buffets."

Tawn nodded, glancing down at her credit store. Several presses later a scowl appeared on her face. "Check your store. Mine's been drained."

Harris looked. "Two hundred forty-six credits? Great. Now how do you suppose that happened?"

"You think the admiral did this?"

"He's the one with the means. I doubt the Earthers would be so brazen as to do that to accounts here."

Harris pulled the *Bangor* to a stop. A comm wormhole was opened to the Retreat. A quick check verified the resettlement fund account to be intact.

A separate comm was opened. "Trish? You and Gandy check your credit stores. Ours have been drained."

Gandy looked. "Fifteen credits! I've been robbed!"

"Mine's the same," said Trish. "Almost empty. What do we do?"

Harris said, "Were you planning on buying anything?"

"We have to eat!" Trish snapped back. "This won't even get us one meal."

"I can transfer you a hundred credits, but not much more."

Sharvie could be heard in the background. "I have some saved. I can share."

Gandy looked at his credit store in disgust. "How'd they do this?"

Harris asked, "When was the last time you checked?"

"Mmm. Probably before you picked us up last. Haven't had the need to look since then."

Sharvie said, "If someone hacked your accounts I might be able to figure out who. Cyber tracking is... was... kind of what I was into."

Gandy asked, "You were a hacker?"

Sharvie tilted her head one way and then the other. "Yes and no. Was more of a hobby. I never did it for money, but I made plenty of contacts who did. Some owe me some favors. I'll see if I can cash those in. I just can't mention that the DDI might be involved. They'd probably all go running."

Half an hour later the *Bangor* was landing on the tarmac outside the massive underground DDI facility.

Tawn looked over the nav display. "This doesn't look right."

Harris replied, "Where are all the ships? There were a couple dozen parked here last time."

Tawn nodded. "And no security. Not so much as a comm to ask for our identity. Nobody rushing out to meet us."

The ship settled and the hatch opened. Harris stepped out onto the concrete.

"There's nobody here. At all."

Chapter 26

"**U**h, look at those signs out toward the roadway," said Tawn. "For lease. This whole place is empty."

A short walk had the Biomarines staring at a large sign that hung next to the main building entrance.

Tawn raised her comm bracelet.

Harris asked, "What you doing?"

"I'm contacting that channel."

A voice responded. "Lightus Corporation leasing. How may I be of assistance today?"

Tawn said, "I'm looking at a property with a reference number of L257. What can you tell me about it?"

"Oh, that's an excellent property. It's available at a very affordable price due to its unique underground architecture. It was originally constructed as an operations center for part of our military. We had a temporary tenant in there for about six months. It was empty for several decades before that, but has always been well maintained."

"Who was this tenant?"

"I'm sorry, I'm not at liberty to say. We keep our clients' information in the strictest of confidence. I had hopes they would be a long-term tenant, but they up and closed up shop over a weekend. That was about two months ago."

Harris tapped into the comm. "Look, this is a matter of vital importance to the security of this planet and all her citizens. We need to know who was in there."

"My apologies that I cannot assist you with this. However, most of that information should be readily available from your district government office. They would have to register and pay taxes and fees just like everyone else. That office would be the best place for you to begin. Can I show you the property?"

"Did they leave it clean?"

"Impeccably so," the voice replied. "Our normal crew was disappointed we didn't have work for them. Most tenants leave at least a modest amount of cleaning to be done. This tenant was on the ideal end of that cleaning spectrum. I believe it's the first time the security deposit was returned in full. Are you sure you're not interested. As I said, it's in marvelous condition. And it's ready to move in."

Tawn said, "Thanks. We'll be in further touch if we have any interest."

Before the leasing agent could respond, she closed the comm.

"I do not like the looks of this at all. That was not a DDI facility they were marching us around in.

Tawn glanced over at her partner. "You thinking what I'm thinking?"

Harris hesitated to answer.

Tawn rolled her eyes. "You were thinking about food, weren't you."

Harris chuckled. "I can't help it. Has been eating away at me ever since we talked about the buffet while coming in. Anyway, I think better on a full stomach."

Tawn waved toward the *Bangor* as she turned and walked. "Let's get you filled up so you're able to brainstorm for us. You're no use to me if you're walking around like a hungry two-year-old."

Harris smiled. "Good. After this I say we check the district office and then sic Sharvie on tracking them down. They were here. There has to be records of some kind that can be traced back to somewhere."

Tawn raised a finger. "Hey, I have a thought. We landed the *Bangor* out here at least once. The logs would show any active transponders that were in close proximity. We might be able to draw out a clue from there. Ships don't just disappear."

Harris gestured at their Zwicker. "Ours does."

"OK, most ships. There were a couple dozen parked out here. They have to be somewhere."

Harris frowned. "This gonna slow down getting dinner?"

"Maybe."

Harris sighed. "Thought so."

"Can you live with that?"

"I can. Prefer not to though."

Tawn shook her head. "You sure you were in the Biomarines? I'm starting to think the Earthers could have lured you away with a couple bogler steaks."

Harris half smiled as he thought about the juicy, rare, marinated steaks from the Grand Emporium Buffet on Chicago Port Station. Tawn scowled in disbelief at his expression.

After a short flight, the ship set down beside the district records office.

Before they got up from their chairs, Tawn said, "Every one of those ships in the log is coming back as leased. And all from Mytallis Industries. Using the emperor's name like that is just a slap in the face. I think we were recruited by Earthers, not the DDI."

"Then we go to the real DDI and tell them what's going on."

Tawn planted the palm of her hand on her forehead. "First we go get you some food."

"What about the records? We're already here."

Tawn shook her head. "You're too dumb to be looking over records. Besides, sign on the door says they aren't open for a couple hours yet. You think you can eat sufficiently in that amount of time?"

Harris nodded. "I'll do my best."

A run was made to the warehouse to collect the others.

Gandy was the first aboard. "They haven't touched the Banshee. Oh, and Sharvie already has a lead on our accounts."

"I know where the credits were moved," said Sharvie. "And moved again from there almost immediately after. That account is being difficult to break into, but I'll get there. This will be the first favor I have to call in."

Tawn asked, "Any of your hacker friends patriots?"

Sharvie thought for a moment. "I think so. Although usually for the people and not so much the government."

Harris said, "What about against Earthers?"

Sharvie smirked. "Definitely against Earthers. Why?"

"I think that may be who did this to us. The facility we were originally taken to is completely empty. I think it might have been an Earther operation to recruit us. Pretty elaborate if that's the case."

Sharvie tilted her head to one side. "There has been some chatter about what appear to be accounts that originated from New Earth. They do have a flood of diplomats here from there.

"Some of my friends have made it their life's mission to get into the Earther banking system. Tough to do from such a distance. All comms to and from New Earth go through one portal that's kept open constantly. Traffic through there is highly restricted, so I don't know if anyone has made it through yet."

Harris waved, "Let's go eat. Tawn's treat. When we get back we can dig into all this further."

Tawn shook her head. "I never said it would be my treat."

"There, you just said 'my treat' in that sentence. Everyone heard you."

Tawn rubbed her forehead. "Fine. Just get in the ship. Your intelligence level has dropped to that of about a twelve-year-old."

Harris grinned. "Excellent. Must be getting my second wind. That's up from being a two-year-old about twenty minutes ago."

An eating establishment was located and a feast had. The team of five were transported to the district government's record office, where it was discovered that all records pertaining to Mytallis Industries had vanished. Management was called in and the proper complaint forms filled out.

Harris was the first aboard the *Bangor*. "Other than the registered name, they cleaned that place out."

"You have a console I can connect through?" asked Sharvie.

Tawn pointed. "In the bunkroom. It's tucked in the corner. Just try to keep us anonymous if you can."

"Always." Sharvie headed to the back of the ship.

Trish asked, "Where to now, boss?"

"Any work you can do on the Banshee?" asked Harris.

"Some."

"We'll take you back there while we wait for Sharvie to work her magic."

A run was made back to the warehouse. Trish and Gandy hopped out to get to work. Harris and Tawn waited in the ship.

A comm opened from the back room. "Check your console up there. I have a few things to show."

Harris said, "You've only been in there a few minutes."

"I have friends. They've been busy. Anyway, your credits made three hops before they landed in an account registered to Gnaway Corp. Lots of small-to-medium transactions going through there. Might be a clearinghouse for daily activities. Definitely looks like an expense account. You have a few dozen people working for you and they have to eat, sleep, and travel around. We have transports, lodging, clothing, even groceries."

"Can you get us our credits back?"

"Not without signaling that we have access. It might be better to see what other accounts branch from this one. It shows hundreds of larger transactions that are between accounts and not merchants."

Tawn said, "Seventy-two million credits. More than enough to refill our accounts. Any idea when you might be in the position to bring our credits back?"

"I could do that now, but I think it best we let them sit for a while. My friends are tracking down the other accounts. Might take us an hour to spider through all that are connected. We get that and we might be able to track down anyone using the account network to do business just by their merchant purchases. Merchants, hotels, transports... they all have recorders. Give us a little time and we might be able to build a portfolio of users, including locations, shopping patterns, and images."

Harris asked, "You telling us this might give us the goods on the whole Earther spy network?"

"That wouldn't be very smart on their part, would it? My guess would be this is the network for one mission project or organization. If this is the people you were dealing with and they stole from you, we might have all the people working toward getting Eden under the control of New Earth."

"That would be huge," said Tawn. "If we could uncover that, the politicians might just see the light and demand the Earthers leave Eden alone. That would solve all our problems."

Sharvie shook her head. "Exposure would not be good for my people. You can be ultra-quiet and hard to find if all you're doing is looking. You expose this and the real DDI would be working to find out who made it happen. If my people thought for a moment you'd do that to them, they would all pull out."

Tawn looked at Harris. "This is a possible gold mine. We can't just let this go away."

Harris pointed at the display. "Hey, what's happening? The credits are dropping hard."

"Don't worry," said Sharvie. "We have the account they are moving to. Could just be part of their security protocol. That account was only created two days ago."

Harris sat back in his chair. "An entire world out there that's accessible from a console. Scary when you think about it."

Tawn nodded. "Scary enough that they sucked our accounts dry without us knowing about it."

Sharvie said, "Uh oh. We have a problem. Someone is trying to get into this console."

Tawn replied, "Should we disconnect?"

"Not yet. Don't know where you got this computer, but it's loaded with firewalls."

Harris yelled. "Shut it down! Close that connection!"

Sharvie flipped a switch. "We're offline."

Harris said, "We got these systems from the Earthers."

Sharvie nodded. "That explains it. That's why I was so easily accepted into their network. This system configuration was probably recognized as one of their own."

"Can you send whatever this configuration is off to your friends?"

Sharvie asked, "Have you done this before?"

Harris shook his head. "No."

"That's actually a good suggestion. It's something we typically do once we're in a system. As I said, makes it easier to move around."

The console display in the cockpit lit up with account information. "You back in?"

Sharvie replied, "I am. This time we're routing through the connection of a friend, so we're secure."

For the next hour, links were traced, hotel and transport footage retrieved, and a database of users and their profiles established. Harris stood to get the circulation in his legs moving. When he moved into the cabin, a man was waiting there with a Fox-40 in his hand.

"Mr. Gruberg, please come outside with me."

Harris walked toward the hatch.

The man held up a hand as he backed up and hopped out onto the ground. "No sudden moves please. I know who and what you are and what you're capable of. I'm only here to talk."

Harris gestured at the man's hand. "Not the most friendly of invitations I've ever had."

The Biomarine stepped back across the concrete parking lot. "Miss Freely, please remain in your seat. I can see you from here. As I said, I'm only here to talk."

Harris asked, "What is it? Who are you."

The man flipped out a badge. "Mantor Boswick. I work for the DDI."

"We've heard that before."

"Yes, you appear to have stumbled onto a network that we've been investigating for months. I'm here to assess your connection to them."

"Our connection to them is they ripped us off, drained our credit stores, and took about fifteen million credits from my partner and I. We'd like those credits back."

"Interesting. The transaction logs show the transfers originating from your stores. Care to explain that?"

"The logs are wrong. Anyway, let me see that badge again. I've seen too many fakes."

"If you are referring to your use of the Sheriff's Cleaners badge in an attempt to get comped for food, I can assure you this one is real."

"You know about my badge?"

"We have a long file on most of your operations. At the moment we're trying to determine which side you are on. You've accepted millions of credits to move illicit weapons. You've attempted to mine millions of tons of titanium ore, something New Earth desperately wants, and most troubling of all has been your travels to a planet called Midelon. Would you care to tell me about that?"

Harris drew in a deep breath. "How do I know I'm talking to the real DDI?"

Mantor replied, "We were first contacted by an associate of yours, Mr. Bannis Morgan. A name that is very well respected in our circles."

"Mr. Morgan will vouch for me."

"As I said, Mr. Morgan was who called you to our attention. Now back to my question. What can you tell me about Midelon?"

Farker moved into the hatchway, sitting on his haunches as he observed the situation.

Harris repeated himself: "I can't tell you anything about Midelon, other than to say I won't be telling you anything about Midelon."

"You do realize the DDI has methods for extracting that information. Some of those I'm told are quite unpleasant. Are you certain you want to maintain that response?"

"I am. Now it's my turn to ask a question. Why is it our fleet pulled back from Eden when you know the Earthers are after the titanium there? We still have the upper hand, although maybe not for long. Anyway, we could go in and force them to leave. We have five or six thousand of our citizens trapped out there. The DDI just gonna sit on their butts while they get slaughtered by the Earthers?"

"Our intel says the personnel there are currently in a superior position."

"Until they run out of food. Probably another week. Two, tops."

"Negotiations for the safe removal of our citizens are underway. Once that is accomplished, the titanium problem will be dealt with. This situation is under control."

Harris shook his head. "Hardly. The Earthers tried an assault a couple days ago and they would have been successful had it not been for us."

"Yes. Your stunt was determined to be a provocation, causing the new Earth fleet to go ahead with their attack."

"That's not how it happened. When we came up, that assault was well underway. We happened to get word to the colonel that prevented its success. Who said we started it?"

"The New Earth diplomats who are part of the negotiations. And I can tell you, regardless of what actually occurred, their accounts were believed. Your unprovoked assault on the Rumford Mine has only added to their demands for a complete withdrawal from that system. All of that is of course irrelevant. You have no evidence to support your account of what happened."

"I have my ship's logs."

Mantor shook his head. "Which can be altered."

Harris said, "Look, the way I see it, you need us. I have a database of their complete network in there. You can take that, arrest those people, and use it in your negotiations to level the table of discussions with the Earthers. Show them their spy network has been captured and demand they withdraw from Eden because they are in violation of the truce."

Chapter 27

Mantor shook his head. "That option is already off the table. Our politicians don't see that as a suitable resolution because it brings with it the possibility of war. If we declare them to be in violation of the truce, the truce has effectively ended. That creates a tremendous political problem for the current administration."

Harris crossed his arms. "Look, give me a dozen destroyers and a budget, and in six months I can run that whole fleet out of there. I even have the people willing to take on that fight."

"We both know that isn't going to happen, Mr. Gruberg. Your only concern at the moment should be about you and your friends here. The DDI has the Eden situation under control."

"So I guess we'll just be leaving then."

Mantor shook his head. "Sorry, I've been instructed to either get your cooperation on Midelon or to bring you in for interrogation. The choice is yours. Tell me what I want to know, come in peacefully, or we can do this the hard way."

Tawn stepped into the hatchway. "Now that sounds like a direct threat. The DDI must be getting desperate. Frankly, I'm a bit surprised you still have funding. And I'd say this conversation is over."

Mantor said, "I have a dozen agents waiting on the other side of this building. Please step out of the ship and we'll get this taken care of as quickly as possible."

Tawn shook her head. "Not going anywhere with you."

The DDI agent began to raise his Fox-40 toward the hundred kilogram Biomarine slug in the doorway. Farker's mouth opened and a concussion wave emerged, knocking Harris from his feet and lifting Mantor Boswick into the air. The regular Human agent tumbled backward, slamming into the concrete with his head, where he was knocked unconscious.

Tawn jumped to the ground, hurrying to Harris' side, helping the groggy stump to his feet. "You OK?"

Harris looked at Tawn. "What? I can't hear you."

Tawn turned him toward the hatchway and gave him a shove. As she sprinted for the warehouse door, Trish and Gandy came into view.

Gandy said, "What happened?"

"Don't have time to explain! Just run!"

The team was quickly aboard and the hatch closed. "Strap him in. He's deaf at the moment."

Tawn powered on the drive and the *Bangor* lifted toward the sky as small weapons fire pinged off her hull from the grounds around the warehouse.

Gandy again asked, "What happened? Who was that guy?"

"That was the real DDI. They wanted to know about Midelon. Farker took him down. I think he was about to shoot me."

Sharvie came from the back with a grin. "I did it! Check your stores!"

Tawn shook her head. "Won't matter now. We can't spend them here anymore."

"What happened? Are we moving?"

Gandy replied, "We got a visit from the DDI. The real DDI. They wanted to know about Midelon. Farker shot him. At least that's what she said."

Tawn growled. "Great. If you aren't strapped in, you'll want to be. We have two Domicile cruisers moving to intercept us."

Sharvie sat, pulling a belt across her lap and fastening it on the other side. "That was the real DDI?"

Tawn nodded. "They know all about us. Bannis Morgan has been working with them. What they don't know is anything about Midelon. And they aren't getting that from us."

Trish said, "That where we're headed now?"

Tawn nodded. "Yep. I think it just became our new home."

Harris wiggled a finger in his ear. "Was there an explosion or something? All I can hear is ringing."

As the cruisers approached, Tawn turned the *Bangor* back toward the surface. "They had the angle on us. We'll have to stay low and near populated areas until we can get a little distance between us."

Trish rushed up, jumping into the copilot's seat and strapping herself in. "You need the railgun. I'll run it."

Tawn shook her head. "No. Those are our people out there. Our military. They're only trying to protect Domicile. We don't use weapons against them."

"So we just run?"

"Yep. Just run."

The *Bangor* flew at supersonic speeds over neighborhoods and small towns. "Good afternoon, Denver Flats."

A hard turn was made toward a mountain range named after a similar range on Earth, the Adirondacks.

Tawn watched on her nav display. "Come on. Drop another kilometer. Come down to me."

As the modified Zwicker Class freight-shuttle shot across the plains outside the city of Denver Flats, the Domicile Defense Force cruiser captains did what Tawn was wanting. As their altitudes evened, Tawn took the ship vertical.

"This is our one shot of breaking out of here. Expect it to get bumpy."

Repeated plasma rounds came their way now that the threat of peripheral damage was no longer an issue. The hull of the *Bangor* clanged, rocked, bounced and reverberated as repeated rounds struck her aft. As she broke free of the atmosphere, still accelerating, the plasma strikes become more pronounced.

"They're starting to gain on us," said Trish.

Tawn winced. "Three minutes and we should be able to jump."

The hull boomed and shook as each round impacted, the plasma charges spreading out before dissipating. Minor jogs to the right or left kept half the rounds from striking home.

Sharvie cringed with each hit and Gandy covered his ears.

Harris asked with a loud voice. "What's happening? Who's shooting at us?"

With his ears still ringing, he could not hear the response.

"She can't take much more of this," said Trish.

Tawn opened a comm. "We want to negotiate."

A voice replied as the plasma rounds ceased to come. "Bring your craft to an immediate stop and prepare to be boarded."

Tawn replied, "OK, hold on. I have to get back to the controls. I got knocked out of my chair."

Trish asked, "What are you doing?"

Tawn turned. "I'm buying us time. When that yellow jump bar goes green we can go. Need another ninety seconds or so for that to happen. Expect our last minute to be the roughest. They aren't gonna want to let us go. How do our systems look?"

Trish scanned the console. "Everything is good still."

"Bring your ship to an immediate stop!"

Tawn replied, "Still trying to get back in the cockpit! There's debris scattered all about in here! One sec!"

Tawn let out a long breath. "They won't buy any more. Grab your ass and hold on. The rounds are about to start, and they will be coming in from two ships now. Twenty-five seconds."

"OK. I'm almost to my chair! I can almost reach the controls!"

The jump bar went green. Tawn Freely slapped the generator button on the console. A wormhole opened and the *Bangor* slipped through, taking an immediate hard turn to port once through.

"Not sure why they didn't fire."

Trish said, "I have wormholes opening to starboard."

Tawn checked the distance. "Excellent. They took the bait."

As the Domicile cruisers came through, they were heading in a direction away from the *Bangor*. Tawn opened a new portal, slipping away into Midelon space. The Domicile cruisers were too far away to follow.

Harris stood from the bench and walked to the cockpit. "What are we doing?"

Tawn said, "Can you hear me?"

"Barely. What happened?"

"Farker sensed Mantor was about to pull the trigger on his Fox, so he blasted him with a concussion wave. You took it in the back. We dragged you aboard and ran. Two Domicile cruisers chased us. We got away. Heading back to Midelon now. Will be on the ground in forty minutes or so."

Harris fiddled with his ears in frustration. So that's it, then. We can't go home."

Tawn nodded. "We can't go home."

Trish asked, "So what do we do with ourselves now?"

Tawn turned. "Same as before. We have to stop the Earthers at Eden. Only now we're completely on our own."

Harris said, "We have food. We have fuel—at least for a while. We'll just have to put our heads together to figure out how we keep ourselves in the game."

Gandy stepped up behind the others. "Wish we could have finished that Banshee. All the systems were in, they just needed hooking up. Any chance we can sneak back and grab it?"

Tawn shook her head. "That warehouse has to be crawling with DDI. Give them fifteen minutes and that ship probably won't even be there anymore. I don't think we'll be going back to Domicile unless Alex figures out how to make us invisible. Even then, we won't be able to set foot on the ground without some camera ID'ing us. Unless something dramatic happens, we're now officially outlaws."

Trish flopped back in her chair with a frown. "My whole life ahead of me and I'm an outcast."

Gandy said, "We can always bounce around on the truce colonies. There are no extradition treaties from out there."

Sharvie said, "Well, we might not be able to go home, but at least we have the credits to live decent lives. I did manage to get your money back. And then some."

Tawn asked, "And then some?"

"Yeah. My friends decided the Earthers weren't in need of their funds, so they kind of moved them all. Turns out it was about four hundred twenty million credits. Of course they are all scrambling to cover their tracks now, but that whole operation should be bankrupt."

Tawn returned a half smile. "Well, at least that's something positive."

She glanced down at her credit store. "So when will those credits show in my account?"

Sharvie shook her head. "We'll have to get you a new account. That goes for all of us. If that was the DDI back there, they've already locked down everything about us."

"Well, where's the money right now?"

"It's probably spread out over hundreds of thousands of dark accounts. My friends have moved monies before with a few hundred accounts, but nothing like this. The government monitors all moves of a thousand credits or more. So that's... wow. That's over four hundred thousand accounts. That's insane."

The *Bangor* landed on Midelon in its usual spot.

Sharvie was the first out the door. "Alex can get me a comm connection back to Domicile. I'm going to check on my friends. Be back in a bit."

Harris squiggled his ear with his finger. "I almost heard all of that. Trish, thanks for bringing her aboard. She's been a real asset."

"I've known her for years. Learning new things about her every day. She was into all that cyber stuff back in school, but I never knew how much."

Gandy stepped out into the warm sun of Midelon. "Well, at least if we're gonna be stranded somewhere where it's like paradise. The temperature here is always perfect."

Tawn followed Harris out, with Farker and Trish just behind.

Harris knelt to show his dog affection. "So my pup saved me again. And now we know he has some kind of concussion weapon. That's a heckuva bark you got there, boy."

Three farks were returned.

Trish said, "And now the million credit question... what do we do with ourselves?"

Harris sat back, resting on his elbows, basking in the Midelon sun. "The way I see it, we have two missions now. One is our continued survival here. We might have to plant crops and get practiced at fishing. Alex might be a good source to ask about both of those.

"The second is still our Eden problem. We need to get the colonel and the others out of there and drive off the Earthers. We've got a good stockpile of food and fuel, so I'd still put Eden as our higher priority effort right now."

Tawn said, "Definitely Eden as priority."

Harris glanced around. "Crap. We lost the shuttle. Left it back there at the warehouse."

Tawn shrugged. "We'll have to pick up another."

"Where are we gonna get another out here?"

Tawn thought for a moment. "We could always jump to Earther space and steal one. Sharvie could probably hack in and fly one away to us. A little shuttle like that isn't gonna have all the security of a warship, and we can already get into the comm system of one of those."

Gandy sat. "Pirates around New Earth. Now that sounds exciting. And, you know, if we were able to steal an Earther warship, we could always bring it back here and park it. They'd never get it back."

Trish said, "Maybe if we can't stop the titanium, we can swipe enough ships so they still can't conduct war."

Tawn laughed. "I'll give it to you two, you sure are dreamers. Even if we managed to steal one New Earth destroyer, it would be highly unlikely we would ever get another. They would change all their security systems and protocols. And they'd be looking for us next time around. So while that sounds great, I don't think it's possible."

Harris chuckled. "There you go again, just being Debbie Downer, squashing everyone's dreams."

Tawn returned a stare. "How about I squash your big round pumpkin head?"

Harris sighed. "Now see what you've done? You've gone and made me hungry."

~~~~~

What's Next?

(Preview)
ARMS
(Vol. 3)
Jebwa Atrocity

This Human is asking for your help! In return for that help I have a free science fiction eBook short story, titled "THE SQUAD", waiting for anyone who joins my email list. Also, find out when the next exciting release is available by joining the email list at comments@arsenex.com. If you enjoyed this book, please leave a review on the site where it was purchased. Visit the author's website at www.arsenex.com for links to this series and other works.

The following preview is the first chapter of the next book in the series and is provided for your reading pleasure.

Stephen

Chapter 3.1

Several days were spent kicking around ideas about Eden. No solutions were put forth that showed promise. After another long session with Alex, Sharvie returned to the group, resting on the grass in front of the bunker.

"You all have new accounts with your prior amounts in them. I have the account codes we can enter into your stores whenever you're ready. As a backup, we're still sitting on over four hundred million credits. And my friends say the accounts and other information we collected might lead to what they believe are other well-funded Earther operations. If they determine that's true, that four hundred million might grow."

Trish said, "Fat good it does us out here. Wealthy beyond our wildest dreams and nowhere to spend it."

Sharvie replied, "That may not be entirely true. Alex was reviewing what we have done to date. I entered what I knew into his databanks. Anyway, he thinks we should set up trade with Jebwa. We can trade them credits for food. Those credits they can spend back on Domicile on whatever they need. And our food situation is taken care of. Alex projects Jebwa may be producing almost double the food they need within only a few months."

Gandy added, "Maybe we could get them to buy fuel to resell to us as well. We could certainly make it worth their while."

Harris nodded. "That would solve two of our biggest problems here. Nice work, Sharvie. I think we should make a jump to Jebwa right now. And, you know, we might even be able to get them to purchase a shuttle to resell to us. Would save us from getting involved in any pirating mess with New Earth."

Gandy frowned. "I was looking forward to being a pirate."

Harris stood. "Sorry to burst your adventure bubble, but if we can get what we need through Jebwa, I'd rather not risk putting us in Earther territory."

Tawn asked, "You going somewhere?"

Harris pointed at the ship. "Jebwa. Might as well get out there and see what we can trade for. Lying around here might be relaxing but it doesn't accomplish anything. We've been here for days. It's time we finally started getting stuff done. Our friends are still running out of food on Eden."

The group piled into the *Bangor's* cabin. Two hours later they were settling on the tarmac at the Haven spaceport. A Jebwa citizen came out to meet them with a transport.

"Welcome to Haven. Can I ask what business you might have with us today?"

Harris said, "You can take us to your main meeting hall. We're interested in discussing trade with your council."

The man nodded. "Very well. Have you been here before?"

Harris smiled. "We built this place. Hope things have been working out for you."

The man replied, "Oh, they couldn't be better. Everyone is busy, busy, busy. This setting is idyllic compared to Eden. Our lives have changed so much for the better. We can enjoy the outdoors, nature... our whole environment is now centered around living and not survival. Survival here comes easy."

"Glad to hear you're doing well."

"Better than well. We have a waiting list of applicants who wish to move here. That hasn't happened since our colony at Dove was first made available. It is an exciting time for all of us. Life couldn't get any better."

"Sounds like you've found your utopia," said Tawn. "Driving this transport your job?"

"I volunteer for this on Tildays."

"What's a Tilday?"

"On Jebwa, our rotation spans nineteen standard hours, and we traverse once around the sun every two hundred days, so we created our own timebase with new names for our months and weekdays. For instance, one hundred crons makes up a bellet. There are one hundred bellets in a meg, and one hundred megs in a talla. A talla is a Jebwa day. Tilday is the fifth day in the Jebwa week, of which there are ten days."

Harris chuckled. "Sounds like a lot of work to memorize. Why not stick with the standards that everyone else uses?"

"Because this is our colony and our planet. We want our customs and traditions to be our own. The new system makes sense for this planet. What the rest of the galaxy does with regards to time is their business. Here, it's ours."

The transport pulled to a stop in front of a domed building. As they walked through the doors they entered a great hall. Red velvet drapes adorned the walls, while the ceiling of the dome had been covered in murals and frescoes. Large beanbag style seating circled a center stage.

Harris nodded. "I like what you've done to the place."

The man replied, "All decisions are made here by the council. If you have a request, take it to the center and let those in attendance know what you desire."

Harris looked at Tawn. "You want to do this or should I?"

Tawn chuckled. "Neither of us are salesmen, but I think our ideas might just sell themselves here."

Tawn walked to the center stage, climbing the three steps to the main platform. Twenty townies were lying about in their robes and sandals.

"Ladies and gentleman of Haven, we've come here today looking for trade. We would like to purchase food and possibly other items from you. Our current needs are meager as we only have five mouths to feed, but we are willing to pay a premium."

A voice came from a townie. "What are you looking to trade?"

"Standard credits. I know you might prefer to barter instead, but I also know you have to purchase goods from Domicile from time to time. We offer credits, and as I said, we are more than willing to pay a premium to ensure we have sustenance for our small colony."

Another voice said, "Why not join this one? As you can see, we are well fed, clothed, housed, and worked."

Tawn replied, "Just as you enjoy your colony, we enjoy ours."

The awkward negotiations took two additional hours before the group was directed into another building to meet with a trade minister. After repeating much of her pitch, a deal was finalized and signed.

The Jebwa colony would provide twenty-five hundred prepackaged meals per standard month for a tidy sum of sixty thousand credits per delivery. The meals would be made available for collection on the tarmac at the preapproved dates and times. The group returned to the meeting hall for a second negotiation.

Tawn gestured toward the platform. "This one's yours."

Harris winced, "I'm not the best person for negotiating the price for a ship. I can propose it, but one of these two needs to finalize it."

Trish said, "You want a shuttle like what we just had?"

Harris nodded. "I think that one worked well."

Trish shoved him as she walked past. "Get out of my way. I'll do it."

Gandy quickly followed. Wait, let me set the stage for your tougher deal-making."

Three hours later, the group emerged from the trade minister's office. "Will be here in three weeks at most. He has the model number and where to purchase it. We offered a 25 percent premium for them to manage the effort on Domicile. As a colony purchase for Jebwa, there won't be any scrutiny. And with them being a collective, nobody back home knows their finances either."

Sharvie said, "You transferred credits to an account, right?"

Trish nodded. "A down payment."

Sharvie smiled. "Give me the account number and I can tell you exactly how much they have. That includes what's in that account and any related accounts they've moved credits to or from."

Harris held up a hand. "No need to hack their accounts. We need to keep them happy and our business here under wraps. Unless we have further business here, I suggest we get back and figure out a way to save Eden."

The trip back saw discussion about how promising the colony of Haven looked. People were out walking about with smiles on their faces. Cats, the preferred pet of the pacifists, roamed about freely. Haven would likely never have a vermin problem.

More than a thousand species of birds filled the skies and the trees with song, to the cat's delight. Other docile animals moved about the colony as all predator species had been wiped out by the prior colonists. By all accounts, it was a happy and friendly place. Even the attitudes of the pacifists had changed for the better. They were living in their nirvana.

Harris paced back and forth in the grass. "We should make a run to check on the colonel."

Sharvie said, "We can open a comm to him if we want."

Harris stopped. "What? When did this happen?"

Sharvie shrugged. "Has always been. Just ask Alex to open a wormhole comm to there and you can connect. No different than what the AI has been doing to gather intel on Domicile and New Earth."

Tawn rolled her eyes. "How long have we been here and we're just now thinking of that?"

Harris said, "Sharvie, go see if you can make that happen. Have it connect to us through Farker."

Sharvie nodded and headed for the bunker door.

Harris crossed his arms. "People, this is the thing we have these brainstorming sessions for, the easy answers. Now why didn't we come up with this before?"

Tawn said, "'Cause we're slow like you?"

Harris nodded. "Exactly. No... wait. Yeah, I guess that sums it up. Anyway, what other low hanging fruit have we neglected to pick?"

"If we need to talk to Mr. Morgan we could do the same," said Trish.

Tawn huffed. "Why would we talk to him? He's a DDI collaborator."

Harris said, "Because we are both still on the same side. OK, if we need anything technical for repairs or whatnot, Bannis might be our man. What else?"

The chime of a comm came through.

Harris answered. "Colonel?"

The colonel replied, "Where are you?"

Harris asked Farker to initiate his hologram display and to feed the colonel's video image to it. A barely visible face floated just above the dog.

Harris said, "We're safe, although we're no longer welcome on Domicile. It appears our prior connections to the DDI were phony. Those agents were actually from New Earth. The real DDI showed up with some demands and we kind of messed things up and had to run. What's your status there?"

"Six days of food left. That's with rationing. Don't suppose you could get any to us?"

Harris shook his head. "We don't have any way of getting around the Earthers."

"How is it you're getting this comm here?"

"It's just a wormhole comm."

The colonel shook his head. "That means they are listening to us. Otherwise they would be jamming all comms. Especially our frequencies. Also probably means they know where you are."

The comm shut down.

Sharvie emerged from the bunker only seconds later. "They almost had us. Broke through three firewalls before I realized they were even trying. Had they made it through the fourth, I wouldn't have been able to close the comm. They could have snooped their way around every system in there, and maybe even triggered an automatic shutdown of the boson field."

Harris asked, "Is there a way we can open that comm securely? We could use the colonel's help with ideas."

"I can't do it from here, but my friends could. That would mean giving them full access to everything in there though."

Tawn said, "We can't risk that."

Harris rubbed the back of his neck. "I agree. Any way to get their help without compromising the whole place?"

Sharvie shrugged. "I'll have to ask Alex. I do know a few things I could do to help with security, but those are only on the alert end. Blocking is a whole different beast. On a high note, it looks like we have about forty seconds of talk before they get through the third firewall. We could talk for that length of time and then disconnect before they get inside. Cracking those firewalls should take just as long a second time as it did the first."

Harris said, "Set up your alerts and punch us back through to the colonel. I'll tell him the situation, then we'll cut the comm and do it all over again."

Sharvie said, "Well, I did say it should take just as long. I might limit our time to half that just to be safe. I am only a handful of years into all this cyber stuff. Would feel better if I had my people available to discuss it with."

"Then let's go back in and open a comm to Domicile. Talk to your people. If they give a green light, we comm the colonel back."

Sharvie headed into the bunker.

Tawn stood and stretched.

"I think I'll go for a run. Might clear my brain. And I could sure use the exercise."

"Enjoy yourself. I'll be stretching out here on the lawn."

Ten minutes passed before Sharvie emerged. "They said don't do it. Second time in they would blast through those firewalls.

We might have all of five seconds. For a reset of those times you would want a different system altogether."

"Can you add more layers of security?"

"Alex is exploring that right now. He's not sure when he will have an answer. As part of his investigation he's contacting Domicile to scan document libraries for modern cyber-security methods and practices. I asked him to also look for any hardware upgrades we could make to his system that he might benefit from. The stuff that system is built on is almost two thousand years old. Perfectly maintained, but ancient."

Tawn returned from her run.

Harris asked, "So what's your breakthrough?"

"What?"

"You said a run was gonna clear your mind. Anything shake out from that?"

"Other than I'm probably in the worst shape of my life... no."

Alex opened a comm to Sharvie through Farker. "I believe I have a temporary solution, although I will have to cease all other operations to maintain vigil on access firewalls. I can construct software firewalls where each must be broken through before the next will be accessed.

"Unfortunately the monitoring necessary for this approach will consume large amounts of my processing power. In turn, speech conversion over the comm may experience delays of as much as three seconds. Conversations at times may sound broken."

Sharvie asked, "How long can you maintain that connection before we have to cut away?"

"Potentially several minutes, but as few as fifteen seconds. It depends on the skill and the speed of the New Earth technology we have to deal with. I would suggest making a list of requests so no time is spent on coming up with things to ask."

The group pushed questions back and forth for several minutes before a list of five emerged. Harris gave the go-ahead for Sharvie to initiate the comm.

Gandy said, "Hope this works and the colonel has something for us to try."

Tawn replied, "If we get a chance, we should go back and see if the Earthers are trying to rebuild the Rumford Mine."

Harris crossed his arms as he shook his head. "We won't have a ship to follow behind this time if we do."

"No, but it's a stationary target. We can shoot at it from farther away."

Trish said, "Not that far away. Anything we shoot from orbit will burn up before it makes it to the ground."

"Well, maybe we follow the lead of the Earthers and push an asteroid at it. Just need one big enough to make it to the surface."

Harris nodded. "Might not be a bad idea. Maybe Alex can run the numbers for us for that."

The comm chirped to life. "Colonel, Harris again. Sorry we got cut short. I have five questions to ask. With good answers we might be on our way to a solution to some of your problems."

"Not gonna happen right now, Harris. The Earthers are attacking in force on the ground. Been sniping our lookouts for a week. Managed to come in force with little notice. Don't know if we'll be able to hold them off this time. We're looking at thousands of hardcore regulars. I'll have to catch you up later."

The comm closed.

Harris looked around at the others in disbelief before turning toward the *Bangor* in a run.

"We have to get out there now! Call Sharvie in! We have to get moving!"

"Tawn followed, hustling past and into the copilot's chair. "Not what I was expecting to hear."

Harris sat as the ship's systems came to life one by one. Sharvie ran from the bunker, breathing heavily as she jumped up into the cabin. Gandy closed the hatch and the *Bangor* rocketed skyward, friction flames bursting from its forward surfaces as it accelerated.

The ride to free space, followed by a jump and then the run toward the planet, would take most of ninety minutes.

~~~~~

Once again, this Human is asking for your help! If you enjoyed the book, please leave a review on the site where it was purchased. And by all means, please tell your friends! Any help with spreading the word is highly appreciated!

Also, I have a free science fiction eBook short story, titled "THE SQUAD", waiting for anyone who joins my email list! By joining, also find out when the next exciting release is available. Join at comments@arsenex.com. Visit the author's website at www.arsenex.com for links to this series and other works!

Take care and have a great day!

Stephen

Printed in Great Britain
by Amazon